PREJUDICIAL
ERROR

BILL BLUM

PREJUDICIAL ERROR

A DUTTON BOOK

DUTTON
Published by the Penguin Group
Penguin Books USA Inc., 375 Hudson Street,
New York, New York 10014, U.S.A.
Penguin Books Ltd, 27 Wrights Lane,
London W8 5TZ, England
Penguin Books Australia Ltd, Ringwood,
Victoria, Australia
Penguin Books Canada Ltd, 10 Alcorn Avenue,
Toronto, Ontario, Canada M4V 3B2
Penguin Books (N.Z.) Ltd, 182-190 Wairau Road,
Auckland 10, New Zealand

Penguin Books Ltd, Registered Offices:
Harmondsworth, Middlesex, England

First published by Dutton, an imprint of Dutton Signet,
a division of Penguin Books USA Inc.
Distributed in Canada by McClelland & Stewart Inc.

First Printing, April 1995
10 9 8 7 6 5 4 3 2 1

 REGISTERED TRADEMARK—MARCA REGISTRADA

LIBRARY OF CONGRESS CATALOGING-IN-PUBLICATION DATA:

Blum, Bill.
    Prejudicial error / Bill Blum.
    p. cm.
    ISBN 0-525-93905-9
    I. Title.
PS3552.L834P74   1995
813'.54--dc20   94-32362
                                                  CIP

Printed in the United States of America
Set in Sabon
Designed by Leonard Telesca

PUBLISHER'S NOTE
This is a work of fiction. Names, characters, places, and incidents either are the products of the author's imagination or are used fictitiously, and any resemblance to actual persons, living or dead, events, or locales is entirely coincidental.

This book is printed on acid-free paper

For Gina

ACKNOWLEDGMENTS

This book might never have come about had it not been for the encouragement, advice and assistance of a great many kind-hearted and talented people.

At the top of the list, special thanks are due to my friend and colleague John Caire III, who collaborated with me in developing the characters and story behind the book and in writing a screenplay from which the novel ultimately evolved.

No less a contribution was made by my wife, former writing partner, soulmate and fellow-traveler, Gina Lobaco, who read, reread and improved draft after draft of the book and performed innumerable other tasks, far beyond the call of any concept of matrimonial duty.

Thanks also to my agent Mike Hamilburg and his associate Joanie Socola, for finding a wonderful publisher for the book, and to my editor at Dutton, Ed Stackler, for his deft editing and careful mentoring of the novel.

Acknowledgments

A profound debt of gratitude is also due to a number of people who provided me with invaluable feedback, criticism and insight regarding both the book and various legal aspects of the story—attorneys Mark Rosenbaum, Verna Wefald, Jim Bisnow, television producer Glenn Silber, veteran journalist Allan Parachini, my brother Eric Blum, my friend of more than thirty years Mitchell Weintraub, and my father-in-law, Fred Holt, the world's most voracious reader.

Thanks to Karen Miyahara for keeping my home computer running and to all the guys who have helped me to keep my middle-aged body and mediocre basketball game alive and well.

In the final analysis, this book is the product of a love for writing, which I learned as a child from my parents, Stan and Eleanor Blum, and which I hope to pass on to my own children, Max and Sam.

PREJUDICIAL
ERROR

CHAPTER 1

Swanson's Bar and Grille was a Los Angeles rarity—a New York–style watering hole, with sawdust on the floor, oak and leather booths, celebrity photos hanging on the walls, and a team of red-cheeked Irish bartenders who looked as if they'd just stepped off a commuter train at Grand Central Station. Located less than three blocks from the Criminal Courts Building and the *Los Angeles Times,* it was a mecca for self-absorbed trial attorneys bent on trading the latest war stories from the justice system and the beer-swilling crew of reporters from the city desk who always seemed eager to listen.

For John Phillip Solomon, former chief trial deputy of the Los Angeles district attorney's office, Swanson's had become a second home or, as he was inclined to admit in his more candid moments, a safe harbor in a sea of personal failure. In the four years since a sexual indiscretion forced his resignation, he'd managed to eke out a living on small-time court appointments— drunk driving, second-degree burglaries, simple assaults—the kinds of cases first-year lawyers handle and routinely screw up on behalf of indigent clients from Central America, the Philippines, and Asia, a bewildered series of fungible miscreants who spoke little or no English and couldn't tell the difference between Clarence Darrow and a stumble-bum in a discount suit.

Now even the court appointments had dried up. He'd roll into Swanson's each day for something he still called "lunch" after it was clear there would be no calls from the court clerk and no paying clients beating down the doors of his two-room downtown office. He'd order a pitcher of Bud or, if he felt lucky, Löwenbräu, tossing out a now very stale joke to Linda, the dark-haired waitress with the concerned look, that he was on a liquid diet.

Today promised to be much the same as yesterday or the day before that or last Wednesday, for that matter. "The usual," he shouted to Linda as he settled into a corner booth that should have had a plaque with his name inscribed on it. The first swallow was the only one that really mattered, he thought, as his attention was diverted by a chorus of cheers from the bar area. A rookie shortstop had just parked a homer in a rare afternoon Dodgers game broadcast live on the bar's large-screen TV. There were high fives all around as the well-dressed lunch crowd whooped and hollered like a gang of high school jocks.

Above the din the words of one gravel-voiced patron stood out as if they were spoken into a megaphone: "That kid's got a great future ahead of him."

To Solomon, the words evoked a distant memory, a prelude to a dream from his own past. As if on cue, he was back in 1960. He was eight years old again and in Philadelphia, sitting on the sunporch playing canasta with his sixty-five-year-old grandmother, his Bubbie, a nervous gray-haired old woman with a heart condition and an uncommon sense of foreboding nurtured during a childhood spent in the Ukraine waiting for the Cossacks to sweep down in the middle of the night.

But even his Bubbie's terminal anxiety couldn't spoil this golden October afternoon, not in the dream and not in real life. Not when his beloved New York Yankees were about to dispatch the Pittsburgh Pirates, those upstarts with the ugly black-sleeved uniforms, into World Series oblivion in the decisive seventh game. His idol—the clear-eyed, clean-cut Oklahoma superhero Mickey Mantle (Mickey Mendel, his Bubbie called him)—would see to that.

But when the dust settled that day in Pittsburgh's Forbes Field, it was the light-hitting little second baseman, Bill Mazeroski, who stood triumphant, sending a ninth-inning homer over the left-field wall. It was a shot heard around the world, a shot that killed the age of heroes forever.

It would be three or four months before the mob found its way to his childhood home. A succession of tough guys named Vinnie, Frankie, and Sal, straight out of an episode of *The Untouchables,* replete with five o'clock shadows, double-breasted suits, and faces that never cracked a smile, came looking for his old man. They came to collect the ten grand his father had placed on the seventh game, a debt he could pay only by selling the house, declaring bankruptcy, and moving the family to a run-down apartment house not unlike the inner-city tenements that East Coast Jews once populated by the thousands.

Life after that was different for John Solomon. There were no more new shoes at the beginning of the school year, no more new baseball gloves in the spring, and no more summers at the Jersey Shore. He watched his mother yield to a state of permanent depression, and he learned to live with, and resent, the silent judgment of his more affluent classmates.

It would be another twenty-five years before he learned the truth about Maz's moon shot and what it had meant for his family. He was still married and with two recent first-degree murder convictions under his belt, newly appointed to the chief trial deputy post, a golden boy with his own great future in a profession dominated by jaded old men. As he sat at the side of his father's hospital bed, the old man terminally ill with cancer, it was a time for setting the record straight. He had known about his father's gambling habits but had always attributed the loss of the house to a long-past recession that drove his father out of business.

Hearing the truth caused him a mixture of wonder and pain. A series of careworn clichés came to mind. You never really know the people you love. Nothing is exactly what it appears to be. Life stinks.

The funniest thing was that his father had no regrets. "I'd take the 1960 Yankees any day over the Pirates," he said in a barely audible rasp. "It was a good bet."

"I think you've had enough," Linda told him, tugging at his sleeve. "A nice-looking guy like you, it ain't right." She chided him quietly.

"Just one more," he said, brushing a mop of unruly brown hair off his forehead. For a ruminating forty-year-old inebriate in a rumpled suit, Solomon was still a presentable specimen, standing nearly six feet tall, with soft brown eyes, a broad, straight nose, and a square chin. Except for a burgeoning beer belly and a self-inflicted hangdog expression, he had an almost youthful appearance.

Present conditions notwithstanding, he had also lost none of his former mental agility. Given a clear head and a fair chance, he knew he could still charm the pants off a jury. Shit, in the old days hardly a defense attorney could be found with the balls to take a case to trial against him. They'd slink back to his office during recesses or the early evening and beg for plea bargains. For the most part he'd just lean back in his desk chair, shake his head, and tell his disappointed adversaries that their cases would have to be decided by the twelve registered voters "in the box."

On rare occasions, though, when the facts and circumstances warranted leniency, Solomon was known to drop a murder charge to manslaughter or recommend probation for crimes of economic hardship. Unlike most other prosecutors, he was able to see the shades of gray and moral ambiguity in the law. He took seriously the old shibboleth that a prosecutor's first duty was not to secure convictions but to do justice. These were qualities that made him a superior attorney but also something of an oddity—a prosecutor with a soul, to paraphrase Fiorello La Guardia—in the tight-knit fraternity of true believers that was the district attorney's office.

But all that was over now. As he sat there at Swanson's, looking at the bottom of a glass of beer, Solomon entertained the notion that somehow his dismissal from the office was part of an inexorable intergenerational losing streak that began with his father's gambling and was destined to hex his life, too, sooner or later.

Once more in the present, he looked up and noticed that both the Dodger game and the lunch crowd were history. Another afternoon shot to hell. Why he had flashed back to the '60 Series was a mystery, but on a certain level he knew that his father was right. You get nothing by mourning the past. It was a lesson he had yet to master.

He chased down another beer, stood up to leave, and staggered out the door.

CHAPTER 2

There are dreams and there are dreams. If John Solomon longed for paradise lost, the multiracial crowd of Japanese businessmen, development girls from the movie studios, and diehard party animals who assembled for the curtain call at the Mustang Club was convinced it had found the promised land.

There were other tits and ass joints in L.A., but the west side's Mustang Club had one thing that set it apart from the competition and kept it packed until the lights went out at 2:00 A.M.: its lead dancer, Sally Sutton. With a thick mane of highlighted blond hair spilling over her tanned shoulders, wide green eyes, and a body straight out of a *Penthouse* photo spread, she was a male fantasy come to life. Her special trademark, the one that sent the Japanese contingent into a virtual frenzy, was the nightly closer—a solo prance and shake along the club's narrow stage in black panties, fishnets, and spiked heels to the beat of Buddy Guy's rendition of "Mustang Sally."

Word on the street was that she was the former mistress of a New York–based Cuban crime kingpin—a rumor the club's Cuban owner, Joey Hidalgo, originated himself, thinking it would be good for business. It was. Sally had become Hidalgo's meal ticket, and he took a measure of personal pride in the mystique that surrounded her. Anything to keep the customers paying and the cops happy: that was Hidalgo's motto and the club's credo.

In fact, Sally was a twenty-six-year-old transplant from a small Nebraska farm town, a onetime cheerleader and homecoming queen who thought there was more to life than county fairs and Cornhusker football games. Los Angeles, with its film and modeling industries, was like a magnet to such women. But for Sally, the hostess gigs at car shows and convention hospitality suites paid like shit, and the only movie moguls who showed any interest were "independent" producers with small-time checkbooks, permanent hard-ons, and no connections to the major studios. She tried her hand as an aerobics instructor, a waitress, a secretary, and even a rent-a-babe at a high-price escort service, before Joe discovered her at a rival strip bar.

It was one of the hottest Junes on record, and the smoke that had collected from a long night of debauchery mingled with the perfume, aftershave, and sweat of the crowd to produce an otherworldly haze as the houselights dimmed. Trussed up in a white tux like a dissipated Ricky Ricardo, Joey took up the microphone at the far end of the stage.

"Ladies and gentlemen," he announced with a heavy accent, struggling to be heard over the restless onlookers, "the number you've so patiently waited for. Our very own Mustang Sally!"

A single spotlight snapped on. Sally, resting against a chrome disco pole, one arm raised above her head, assumed the accustomed pose of sexual tension and anticipation. As the sound system clicked in, she turned to face the pole, grabbing it suggestively in her right hand and nuzzling her firm naked breasts, round pink nipples erect, against it.

The crowd's approval was immediate and loud. Most of the men, and even some of the women, began to offer up dollar bills, depositing them in small heart-shaped containers positioned strategically along the outer edge of the stage. This was, after all, what they came for. In their wildest imaginations, it would never be this good.

As Sally turned again to begin her first stroll along the stage, she was greeted by a drunken middle-aged salaryman who, having left his inhibitions and common sense in Tokyo, had clambered over the footlights, much to the delight of his equally pickled comrades. He stood in front of her, arms outstretched, blocking her path. Urged on by the crowd, he began to swivel his hips and sing in broken English. As the salaryman lunged clumsily for Sally's waist, a large hairy hand wrapped itself around his left ankle and with a swift tug yanked him back into the first row.

The salaryman fell into the laps of his laughing countrymen and shouted something that sounded like "your mother sucks ducklings" in Japanese. He quieted down immediately, however, when the owner of the hairy hand, the club's head bouncer, George Ortiz, a former boxer from the Lincoln Heights barrio, walked up to him and calmly offered to send him back to the Toyota factory in a gift-wrapped box.

Sally remained unfazed by the excitement. Even the sight of the good-looking black vice cop flashing his badge at the front entrance failed to distract her. The cop's name was Joe

Richards. Dressed in a well-tailored sports coat and slacks, he seemed to be looking for someone, craning his neck in the direction of the bar, where another, younger black man seemed to be making a hasty retreat. "At least it's not me he's after," she thought, with some relief.

Sally made a few more quick turns, and suddenly both the song and the show were over. The houselights came on, and it was time to go home. George and his crew of beef-cake *carnales* formed a protective corridor for Sally as she slipped into a silk kimono, gathered up the tip money, and skipped quickly down the rear steps of the stage.

"A little toot, baby?" Jim Rowinski asked as she stepped inside her dressing room. Big, rugged, brash, and dumb, Rowinski acted as if he owned the place, lifting a small vial of powdered cocaine to his nostrils and taking two sharp snorts.

"You do too much of that, you know," she replied, offering her cheek for a kiss and sliding into the seat in front of her makeup table.

"Two hundred lousy bucks," she complained, pulling a thin wad of bills, mostly fives and tens, from her panties. "This recession sucks."

"The President says there is no recession," Rowinski countered, removing a roll of twenties from his shirt pocket with a shit-eating grin. He moved closer to her. "I believe him."

"Only a fucking cop would say that," Sally said, turning around and planting a kiss on his smiling lips.

"Speaking of cops," she continued, "I saw Richards."
"When?"
"During the close. He's probably still here."

She knew that the mere mention of Richards would send Rowinski, a SWAT team specialist with aspirations to become a homicide dick, into a predictable rage. He was a hothead with a big mouth, but in some perverse way she enjoyed setting him off.

"Fuck it," he bellowed, "I'm gonna end it right now."

"No, Jim, don't," she cautioned, realizing just what he might do with a brainful of powder. "Leave Richards to me."

She stood up, unbuttoned his shirt, and began stroking his chest. She planted another kiss on his mouth, this time offering her tongue. "Meet me at my place in a half hour."

He released her and turned to leave, another savage beast calmed and contented.

Sally watched Rowinski close the door behind him. He had the key to her apartment, and she knew he'd be waiting for her, hot and bothered and ready to get naked, when she arrived. As much as Rowinski hated Richards, his sex drive was even stronger, especially when he was coked out. Richards, however, was another problem. With any luck, she thought as she sat down to remove her makeup, he would be gone by the time she was ready to leave. She pondered the odds for another ten minutes and slipped out the rear entrance.

Richards was waiting for her in the parking lot. As a fifteen-year veteran of the vice squad he knew all the games. He and Sally were also well acquainted, although not in the carnal way he might have preferred.

"What now, Richards? I'm on my way home," she complained in a tired voice.

Richards strolled over to her with a macho swagger. "I thought we had an understanding," he said, putting his arm around her waist.

"I'm not some piece of meat you guys can pass around," she protested, pulling away.

"I know he was here," Richards said, suddenly all business.

"Look, I told you, I don't know anything about this shit," she said.

As she spoke, a late-model Camaro slowly approached them from the rear of the parking lot.

The Camaro pulled up alongside them and came to a stop. The tinted driver-side window rolled down, and the driver, a black man with a fade hairstyle, called, "Hey, bro, know where I can pick up some rock?"

Richards recognized the driver immediately, and the adrenaline surged through his body. In one smooth motion he pushed Sally aside and reached for his service revolver. It was too late. Three slugs from a .357 magnum ripped holes the size of golf balls in his chest, dropping him with an audible thud.

The Camaro burned rubber out of the parking lot as Sally's screams broke the silence of the early morning. The blood spurting from Richards' coronary artery collected in a pastel pool under the fluorescent sign of the Mustang Club.

CHAPTER 3

Los Angeles in the early 1990s had become the gang capital of the world. There were gangs in virtually every section of the city, from the South Bay to the San Fernando Valley—black gangs, Chicano gangs, Asian as well as white. Their *placas* and tags defaced buildings, public and private, in both commercial and residential neighborhoods, turning an already seedy landscape into one where tensions rose at every intersection.

No one knew exactly how many gangbangers were out there on the streets. Depending on who was doing the counting and the hysteria of the moment, estimates ranged from 70,000 to 150,000. There was no real disagreement, however, that the biggest, baddest gangs of all were those that terrorized the poor black sections of South Central L.A.—the Crips and the Bloods. Together they controlled a large part of the lucrative street trade in crack cocaine and were responsible for an alarming share of the city's ever-growing homicide rate. Equipped with the latest automatic weapons and assisted by gun control laws so weak that even the cops were turning in their NRA memberships, they had perfected the drive-by shooting into a macabre Southern California art form.

But unlike the old-line Italian mobs, the South Central gangs lacked a truly organized command structure and enjoyed few, if any, direct connections to corrupt politicians. Like grass-roots agitators, they exercised their power in local groups called sets, committed to defending the honor and the turf of their neighborhoods. To the gangbanger, the set was a surrogate family, providing supportive relationships, a sense of brotherhood, rules of conduct, and structure for young people who otherwise lacked any semblance of cohesive family life. Even kids who didn't come from completely dysfunctional homes were often drawn to the gangs by the pressures of conformity, the need for personal protection, and the glitz, glamour, and hard cash they promised. To acquire a "rep" for "bangin' in the 'hood" was the most coveted prize many young men with no discernible futures could attain.

To Juan Javahn Thomas, gangbanging was a way of life. His father had abandoned him when Thomas was seven, leaving him and his older brother to be raised by an alcoholic mother who supplemented her county welfare checks with cash raised turning occasional tricks for neighborhood johns at twenty bucks a throw. On the streets the inevitable happened, and Thomas learned the closest thing to male role models were the OGs, or "original gangstas," who controlled the 65th Street Mainline Crips, one of South Central's most notorious sets.

Thomas became a tiny G, taking on the tag, or nickname, of Stone, for his hard-edged demeanor. He served his set faithfully in every way he was asked, first as a lookout, then as a runner, a street-fighting "warrior," and finally as a dealer. Now, with a three-year stint at the California Youth Authority and a two-year term at state prison to his credit, both for possession of crack with intent to sell, he was an OG himself, an accomplished all-purpose hustler well accustomed to the perks and privileges that came with his elevated stature.

One of the perks was pussy on demand. This morning's entrée was Shanique Travis, an eighteen-year-old senior from Manual Arts High School, a track star with long braided hair, small breasts, and a tight, well-muscled ass that drove Thomas crazy. So crazy that, as he entered her for the fourth time in an hour, he didn't hear the thick, angry voices at the front of his small wood-frame house.

Six black-and-white squad cars had blocked off the street outside Thomas' home, following a script that was played out on a daily basis in the counterinsurgency war waged by the Los Angeles Police Department against the city's gangs. Two officers were dispatched to the rear of the house, and two more to each of the sides. Another group of four crushed open the front door with a hand-held battering ram and stormed inside. The rest was a piece of cake.

The first to reach Thomas was the officer in charge, Homicide Lieutenant Tom Gallagher, a big rawboned Irishman with hard blue eyes, a full mustache, and a take-charge attitude that let nothing interfere with the business of the LAPD. His gun drawn and flak jacket in place, Gallagher didn't expect much in the way of real resistance.

"Roll over and don't move," he ordered Thomas. "We have a warrant for your arrest."

Thomas, who was well acquainted with the drill, complied lazily but without hesitation. Shanique was another matter. The sight of two armed white cops—Gallagher and Jim Rowinski, who had quickly followed his superior into the bedroom—sent her into a state of uncontrollable panic.

"What the fuck is going on?" she cried, sitting bolt upright, top sheet pulled over her chest. "We ain't done nothing. Can't you people leave us alone?"

Rowinski, who had not experienced the pleasure of slapping a suspect for at least a week, reacted eagerly. "Shut up," he barked. "I said shut the fuck up." When she continued to sob and shout, he backhanded her across the face, using the force he usually reserved for OGs like Thomas. The blow sent her flying against the wall, dropping the sheet, her last measure of dignity against the white invaders, to her thighs.

This was more than even the established protocol of the drug bust allowed, and Thomas reacted instinctively. Naked and unarmed, he charged at Rowinski, who, with a four-inch and fifty-pound weight advantage, met him head-on in the middle of the floor. It was another easy victory for the LAPD, a quick takedown, followed by a closed fist to the face that brought a stream of blood from Thomas' nose and persuaded him to relinquish thoughts of further resistance.

Rowinski, for his part, seemed disappointed at the sudden surrender. "Go ahead, you fucking nigger," he screamed, holding his handgun to the side of Thomas' fade, "give me a reason."

"That's enough," Gallagher interceded, placing a hand on Rowinski's heaving shoulder. "You want to screw up the whole operation, let some faggot defense attorney bring a motion to dismiss?"

Rowinski released his prey and stood up as other members of the search team entered the room. He was chastened but without apology. "Just doing my job," he muttered.

"Get this motherfucker dressed," Gallagher ordered, staring at Thomas' naked body with the kind of sneer most people reserve for insects and other lower life-forms. "The bitch, too," he added roughly, gesturing toward the bed.

Gallagher watched as Thomas and Shanique struggled into their clothes and were led away by a phalanx of officers. Standing in the bedroom, thinking he was alone, Gallagher was surprised to find Officer Mary Delgado, an athletic-looking woman of black and Latino heritage and the lone female member of the arrest team, positioned by the door. He sensed immediately that she had witnessed the scene with Rowinski, and he also knew she wasn't above filing a complaint with Internal Affairs or making some other kind of noise. For the moment, however, he chose not to broach the subject.

"I thought you were supposed to find the gun," he said.

"I already have, cowboy," she replied in a voice completely devoid of respect. "You do your job and I'll do mine."

After showing her identification and answering a few embarrassing questions, Shanique was released and ordered to go home. As much as Gallagher would have liked to arrest her, it isn't a crime to fuck someone accused of murder.

Juan Thomas, of course, was far less fortunate. He was placed in the back of a squad car, read his *Miranda* rights, and driven off to be booked, printed, and photographed. The process was even more perfunctory than Thomas had remembered, and by 11:00 A.M. he was on his way to a cell in the "High Power" maximum-security module of the men's central county jail.

It was also 11:00 A.M. when the alarm clock sounded in John Solomon's Silver Lake apartment. "Sleeping in," he had alerted his answering service the night before in the event any business calls came his way the following morning. "Sleeping it off" was how the wisecracking operator on the receiving end logged his instructions to monitor the office phone until he checked in.

The fierce buzz of the alarm was enough to pierce the deepest of stupors, and Solomon stirred grudgingly to life. He sat up in bed, smoothed back his hair, and took in the chaos of his domestic life. The inexpensive Picasso and George Grosz prints from the county art museum adorning the walls had sagged to thirty-degree angles. A single sleeve from an old sweatshirt hung lazily out of the top drawer of his dresser like a dying man adrift in a raft at sea. Three feet away, two weeks of laundry lay heaped on an old red leather chair, the one personal possession he had insisted on keeping when his marriage unraveled five years earlier.

It really wasn't a bad apartment. A third-floor one-bedroom perched atop a steep hillside, it featured a separate dining area, a balcony, and a magnificent view of the city. To be honest, he was lucky to get it. He had moved in just after his separation from Jennifer and about a year before he resigned from the DA's office. The marriage was a casualty of his wife's failed pregnancy, a stillborn child, followed by an emergency hysterectomy and the realization that she would never bear children. The blow devastated them both, creating a wound that neither counseling nor talk of adoption could heal. In the end they parted painlessly, vowing, in the vernacular of 1980s psychobabble, to "remain supportive." By now their contact consisted of little more than a perfunctory exchange of birthday cards and an occasional phone call.

The rest of Solomon's apartment wasn't so much of a mess as it suffered from a look of abandonment. A thin layer of dust covered the dining table while large gray clumps of dust, like miniature tumbleweeds, had collected along the baseboards. Outfitted in a lumpy corduroy sports jacket, Solomon walked past the dining area and into the living room, taking no notice of the chest-high stack of un-packed boxes containing the collection of college textbooks he refused to discard. His breakfast—a half-consumed pepperoni pizza, seeping grease in its red and white box—lay on a side table by his sofa. Solomon stepped into the kitchen, to share the morning meal with his house cat, Earl Warren.

Earl, however, was nowhere to be seen, and Solomon, for once, had business to attend to—a twelve-thirty appoint-ment, with a paying client no less. A quick swig of beer and a vitamin C and he was out the door and into his '66 Mus-tang convertible heading for the Santa Monica office of Dr. Irv Weinberg.

The freeway, as usual, was jammed with lunchtime traf-fic, giving Solomon plenty of time to prepare mentally for his conference with the doctor. Depending on your political point of view, Weinberg was either an American success story or, as the Jews from his old neighborhood of Boyle Heights used to say in Yiddish, a *gonef,* a thief. Located in the heart of East L.A., Boyle Heights was once home to one of the largest concentrations of Jews in the United States outside New York. Today it was nearly a hundred percent Hispanic. It was also run-down, poor, and plagued by van-dalism and crime.

The middle child of a large extended family, Weinberg had put himself through community college, earned a degree in podiatric medicine, and made a fortune, opening up a chain of clinics. As his bank account fattened, he joined the exodus of nouveau riche and left the old neighborhood be-hind for the west side, eventually constructing a seven-thousand-square-foot Mediterranean villa in the Palos

Verdes Estates. He had maintained his ties to Boyle Heights, however, by purchasing the apartment house he grew up in and adding the title of "slumlord" to his long and growing list of credits.

After years of neglect, Weinberg's building was still turning a profit but was becoming a headache, with mounting repairs for plumbing, electric, pest control, and a new breed of tenants who had actually filed a complaint against him with the city attorney. That was where Solomon came in.

"Sit down, Mr. Solomon," Weinberg said as a receptionist dressed in a white hospital uniform led him into the doctor's office. In other sections of Los Angeles, Weinberg's Yiddish inflections would have seemed incongruous, but in Santa Monica they blended in perfectly. "You want something to eat?" Weinberg asked as he chomped away at a corned beef and slaw sandwich behind his large black desk.

"No, thanks," John answered, and took a seat in a client chair across from Weinberg. The cold pepperoni was the only cause for heartburn he needed at the moment.

He waited for Weinberg to swallow, knowing that with a three-hundred-dollar-per-hour podiatry practice to attend to, Weinberg would make the meeting as brief as possible.

"I want those people evicted," Weinberg shouted, his face reddening at the thought of the ungrateful tenants who had fallen behind on their rent. For a man who had long since passed the sunny side of sixty-five, he had enormous energy, which was always harnessed to his advantage.

"I've already drawn up the papers and the quit notices. All you have to do is serve them," Solomon assured him in his best professional manner.

"What, I'm some kind of a schmuck? I hired a lawyer who advertises in the classified pages." He shook his head with theatrical incredulity. "Listen to me, boychick, I'm not serving *bobkes*. You are."

"But that wasn't part of our agreement," Solomon reminded his client.

But the old man remained steadfast, sensing that Solomon, who was already beginning to shift uneasily in the seat before him, would eventually yield to his pressure. "So sue me," he said. "You want your money, you get those peasants out of my building. Now get out of here. I've got patients to see."

Solomon fought back the urge to tell him where to stick his *putz* and took a deep breath, realizing he had lost the war of words. "Okay, I'll see to it myself."

As he closed the door to the doctor's office, he heard Weinberg mutter, "Next time I'll hire a goy."

Weinberg's apartment building was on the corner of a crowded street just off Brooklyn Avenue and was even worse than Solomon imagined. A four-story walk-up, sixteen units in all, trash strewn across the front steps, no lock on the entry door, no names on the mailboxes, and the sounds of crying children emanating from every open window. Solomon pushed open the front door and was sent reeling from the overwhelming stench of urine in the foyer, a telltale sign that the building was doing double duty as a late-night latrine for the community's expanding army of vagrants.

He knocked on the door of unit 1A, checking the apartment off on a tenant list attached to a clipboard that he carried. He could hear the words of a Spanish-language deejay booming sonorously with an echo chamber effect over the shuffling sounds of people moving around inside. He knocked again and announced, "Mrs. Martinez, I have a three-day notice from your landlord, open up."

The rustling from inside the apartment grew louder, and the door opened. The face of a young Hispanic woman peered through the crack created by the safety chain. "*No dinero,*" she said with sad, sunken eyes. "I lose my job."

Solomon could see that she was carrying an infant in her right arm and stroking the head of a small girl, no more than three years old, with her free hand. The voices of at least two more children could be heard in the background. He tore off an eviction notice from the clipboard and almost handed it to her. He took another look at Mrs. Martinez, hesitated, and stuffed the notice in his jacket pocket. "In that case, just pay when you can," he said, and turned to leave.

"*¿Mande?*" Mrs. Martinez asked in a confused voice.

"*Está bien, señora,*" he replied, heading out the front door. "*No se preocupe.*"

He shoved the clipboard inside a reeking Dumpster at the side of the building, climbed into his Mustang, and drove down Brooklyn Avenue, wondering how long it would take Weinberg to find another two-bit lawyer to throw Mrs. Martinez and her kids into the street.

CHAPTER 4

Howard Ainsworth stood at the lectern, his blue eyes shifting from his notepad to the poker-faced visage of Superior Court Judge Larry Nagai, garbed in black judicial robes on the upraised dais in front of him.

"I have prayed on my knees for Carlos Hernandez," Ainsworth said, pointing to the defense table, where a public defender sat beside a young Chicano, who, for the moment at least, seemed more interested in stroking the gang tattoo on his left forearm than contemplating the all-expenses-paid vacation he was about to receive to Folsom state prison. "Because in some ways he is just as much a victim as the young man he shot and killed—a victim of the soul, who hasn't had the moral decency to show one ounce of remorse or regret."

Ainsworth was approaching the climax of the standard

speech he delivered at sentencing hearings in noncapital murder trials, the point where he threw in the special twist about the Almighty. Having secured a conviction but unable to charge the defendant with a statutory "special circumstance" that would bring the death penalty into play, Ainsworth would ask the court to fix the sentence at twenty-five years to life, plus an additional two years for use of a handgun—all for the spiritual benefit of the prisoner.

"It is up to us to show this young man the error of his ways and help him make his peace with God," he told Nagai, who, like nearly all California judges in the age of law and order, was a former deputy district attorney and still very much a prosecutor at heart. "That is why I ask Your Honor to give him the maximum sentence under the law. It may not benefit him in this life, but it certainly will in the next."

"I'm not sure I share your faith in the hereafter, Mr. Ainsworth, but I can't argue with your legal position," Nagai announced, and proceeded with the formalities of pronouncing judgment.

It was another in an unbroken string of courtroom triumphs for the man who had succeeded John Solomon as the DA's chief deputy for major trials and had been assigned to represent "the People" in the "Joe Richards, Mustang Club" murder case. The gaggle of TV reporters who descended on him outside the courtroom came as no surprise. Ainsworth had his share of critics—particularly the "left-libs" of the defense bar who scoffed at his religious convictions and dubbed him the archbishop of prosecutors—but he was the odds-on favorite to become the next district attorney in the November elections.

"Is it true that Simon Lasker has endorsed your candidacy for district attorney?" the woman reporter from Channel 2 asked as he walked calmly down the corridor toward the elevator.

"I have not only Simon's backing but the support of over half the voters. The people want a man of competence and conviction," he said, pausing to smile confidently at the camera. With his closely cropped salt-and-pepper hair and his suntanned good looks, Ainsworth had the undeniable image of a winner—an asset he exploited with smug self-satisfaction.

"What about the claims that the police nearly executed the defendant accused of shooting Officer Richards outside the Mustang Club?" another reporter asked.

"With all the racial tension, how will the defendant receive a fair trial?" yet another demanded.

"He'll get far more fairness than Joe Richards got," Ainsworth told the throng, and continued his march toward the elevator.

"Now that the public defender is off the case, who will represent the defendant?" the Channel 2 reporter pressed as the elevator door opened and Ainsworth stepped resolutely inside. The door closed before he could reply.

The same question was very much on the mind of District Attorney Simon Lasker, whose fourth and final term was about to expire. Lasker was a lifelong Republican, and he wanted desperately to cap his career as a highly paid partner at a downtown law firm and a behind-the-scenes power broker in party circles. To make his exit from public service on a winning note, he had given the highly publicized Richards case to Ainsworth, whom he had summoned to his office on the eighteenth story of the Criminal Courts Building for the important meeting that was about to begin.

"This violence will be the end of us unless we join together," Ainsworth intoned, looking out at the late-morning sun falling over the San Gabriel Mountains.

"That's exactly why we're here," Lasker snapped, loosening his tie as he sank into the high-back leather chair behind his desk. A tall, lanky man, with a fringe of gray hair and a sharp, aquiline nose, Lasker was a widower with a perpetual look of impatience that made many of his subordinates cringe at the thought of encountering him in person. While other men of his stature might have taken to wearing toupees to cover their baldness or learned to modulate their voices to seem more agreeable, Lasker believed his public image depended on one thing and one thing only: his office's conviction rate.

Lasker finished jotting down some random thoughts on the yellow legal pad in front of him and turned his attention to the puffy-looking fifty-year-old man fidgeting in his seat on the other side of the desk. "Are you going to change your mind on this or not, Burton?" Lasker asked gruffly.

"Dammit, Simon, I'm the judge in this case," Burton Lawler shot back. "I shouldn't even be here, and you know it."

"Whoever said this meeting took place? Don't be so paranoid, you're not being taped," Lasker said, barely concealing his annoyance. Lasker knew it was only a matter of time until Lawler caved in. Two years earlier he had intervened to derail an ethics probe of alleged improprieties committed by the judge's reelection campaign, and it was time for Lawler to return the favor.

"The goddamn prelim's tomorrow. Why did the PD wait until yesterday to declare a conflict?"

"That was already explained on the record," Lasker said. "The public defender represented our eyewitness on a prostitution bust four years ago. They were ethically bound to conflict out as soon as they discovered the grounds. Come on, it's not surprising it took them awhile; it was a small misdemeanor. It just fell through the cracks."

"If I appoint him, I'll come under a mountain of criticism. You know the man's no longer qualified."

"Please, Burton," Ainsworth interrupted, moving next to Lasker, assuming the supplicating posture of a loyal son. "Let's not forget our kindness. He was once a part of this office, and I believe he's still a good attorney."

Lawler's eyes began to roll with the rhythm of Ainsworth's clichés. "Tell that to the ACLU and the NAACP."

"He needs this chance to redeem himself," Ainsworth moralized. "He might not get another."

"Okay," Lawler relented. "I'll announce the appointment in court this afternoon—on *your* recommendation. If he screws up, I expect you to shoulder the blame."

Ainsworth stared coolly at the judge, as if passing judgment upon his moral worth. Finally he said, "Your lack of faith, Burton, saddens me deeply."

Briefcase in hand, Jimmy "Stretch" Johnson pushed open the front door of Swanson's just as the after-work crowd was thinning out. "Corner booth?" he asked, catching sight of Linda as she collected her tip from a deserted table.

"He's had his tush nailed to the seat cushion for the past two hours," she replied matter-of-factly.

Stretch's nickname dated back to his salad days as a small forward on the USC basketball team and, later, as a benchwarmer for the Lakers. Although his pro career passed in a blink—just three seasons, to be exact—he made the best of his "time on the pine," as the Lakers' radio announcer described life as a second-stringer, finishing up his B.A. and completing sixteen units toward a master's in criminal justice before becoming an investigator for the DA's office. The forty-five-year-old black man had gone private three years earlier, in search of bigger paychecks, but he quickly became bored with the divorce and missing person cases that were coming his way in ever-increasing numbers. He missed the excitement and high drama that only high-profile criminal cases could generate. He also missed the teamwork involved.

"You look like shit," he said as he wedged his six-foot-six-inch frame into the bench opposite from Solomon.

"I look even better than I feel," Solomon said sarcastically, doing his best to conceal the fact that he was glad to see an old friend.

"You waiting to be served, or is this another of your liquid meals?" Stretch cracked a grin, deliberately provoking John, whom he knew from their days together in the major trials division.

"Is this a social visit, or are you just here to point out my virtues?" Solomon asked.

"Strictly business," said Stretch, coming straight to the point. "Burton Lawler's appointed you on that gangbanger case."

Solomon's confused look told Stretch he had missed the reference.

"You know the one," he reminded him, "the vice cop gunned down outside the Mustang Club. The judge expects you to start tomorrow morning."

Stretch opened his briefcase and tossed a thick case file on the table.

Solomon suppressed the urge to laugh. "Bullshit, I'm not even on the court-appointed list anymore. Besides," he added, trying to jog his memory, "I thought the defendant was some kind of dealer. Why can't he afford his own lawyer?"

"I'm not jivin' you," Stretch insisted. "The cops found

only five hundred dollars in the defendant's bedroom, and the man doesn't own any retirement accounts." He pointed to the case file for confirmation. "The public defender was appointed, but now they're off the case. They need someone else."

Solomon mulled the matter over. The defendant, he thought to himself, probably spent his drug money faster than he could get his hands on it and now was stuck with whatever legal defense the justice system would mete out. "Who's the prosecutor?" Solomon asked.

"Ainsworth."

"Well, tell him I don't need any new opportunities." Icy at the mention of the name, Solomon quickly drained his glass of beer.

"No, you'd rather be doin' hundred-dollar evictions, chasing ambulances, and feeling sorry for yourself."

"He's the reason I'm doing that in the first place," Solomon argued, pouring himself another tall one.

"No, you're the reason," Stretch shouted, and stood up to leave. "Look, man, I'm not tellin' you what to do. But from where I'm standin', you need this case."

John suppressed the urge to answer back and then began to reconsider. "Tomorrow morning?"

"The prelim's set for nine A.M., and Lawler won't be happy if you ask for a continuance."

"What kind of crap is that?"

"I was in Lawler's court this afternoon on another case when the judge made the appointment. I told him and Ainsworth you'd be ready. Don't look so surprised," he said, surveying the astonished expression on Solomon's face. "It'll be just like the old days. You as the mouthpiece and me as the gumshoe." Stretch flashed a wide smile. "That's right. I've been named your court-appointed investigator. How do you think I managed to score the PD's file?" he asked rhetorically, pointing again at the as-yet-unopened manila folder in front of John.

Stretch stood up and threw a couple of bills on the table. "One more thing," he added before walking off, "they're going for the death penalty on this one. Remember, nine A.M."

"Is that all?" Solomon muttered, and began leafing through the file.

CHAPTER 5

Except in cases initiated by a grand jury indictment, the preliminary hearing is the first major event in a felony prosecution in California. Conducted before a Municipal Court judge, the hearing serves as sort of a dress rehearsal for the trial, except that there is no jury and no finding of guilt. The judge's role is to hear the prosecution's witnesses and decide if there is "probable cause" to commit the defendant to Superior Court for trial.

For many judges, the defendant's mere presence in court is sufficient reason to send the case upstairs. As a result, defense attorneys rarely call witnesses of their own at a prelim. Their approach instead is to use the hearing as an opportunity to obtain discovery, or information, about the prosecution's case and test the People's witnesses on cross-examination.

Solomon knew the strategy and tactics of a preliminary hearing about as well as he knew the logo on a can of Budweiser. As a deputy DA he had put on hundreds of prelims and had never failed to win a commitment order. The outcome of virtually all prelims was predetermined. That was why, he tried to persuade himself, it wouldn't really be malpractice, even in a death penalty case, to go forward with the hearing without asking for a continuance. Besides, Stretch had represented to the court that he would be ready to proceed, and Judge Lawler had a well-publicized policy against postponements. Either he went ahead with the prelim or he could kiss the appointment good-bye.

Solomon settled into the red leather chair in his bedroom to study the case. He had known other attorneys who had handled prelims with as little as fifteen minutes of preparation. It was a technique called winging it. He'd at least have all night to prepare, and he'd get to pick up a sorely needed paycheck for his trouble.

He opened the file and began to read through Juan Thomas' rap sheet and the police and ballistics reports. As he flipped through the pages, the urge to sleep was strong. If only he hadn't chased the second pitcher of Bud with a shot of J & B. If only he hadn't blown his career. If only his life hadn't taken a nosedive for the toilet. But sleep was a refuge, an old friend offering solace and absolution, a seductress who could not be resisted. He closed his eyes.

But for Earl Warren jumping in his lap, licking his face with a sandpaper tongue, he might have slumbered through the morning. When he looked up, the digital display on his alarm clock read 8:15.

Judge Lawler's courtroom on the fifth floor of the Criminal Courts Building was packed to capacity with an assortment of TV and newspaper reporters, members of victims' and civil rights groups, and a handful of curiosity seekers. A squad of six deputy marshals was also on hand to maintain order, and a mobile X-ray unit had been set up outside the courtroom to screen all who entered to make sure that no one decided to exact justice the old-fashioned way.

Ainsworth, conservatively dressed in a dark blue suit, sat at the prosecution table, notepads at the ready, next to Lieutenant Tom Gallagher, who had been named his investigating officer, a role that entitled him to remain at Ainsworth's side throughout the proceeding. Stretch, who held the equivalent position for the defense, sat alone at the defense table, wearing a look of undisguised irritation.

At precisely 9:00 A.M. the bailiff called the court to order. "All rise. Division two seventy of the Municipal Court of the state of California for the county of Los Angeles is now in session, the Honorable Burton Lawler, judge, presiding."

Judge Lawler, looking considerably less like the scared bureaucrat he appeared to be in front of Lasker, ambled confidently to the bench from the side door that led to the court's interior offices. "Be seated and come to order," he said, surveying the courtroom. "This is the time set for the preliminary hearing in the case of the *People of the State of California versus Juan Javahn Thomas*. Are we ready to proceed?"

Ainsworth shifted uncomfortably in his seat and stood up to address the court. "We're waiting for Mr. Solomon, Your Honor. He seems to have been delayed."

"In that case, Mr. Solomon has just delayed himself right off this case," Lawler responded, sensing an opportunity to ease out of the backroom deal he had made. Not that he objected on principle to colluding with the prosecution. He was just scared shitless that he might get caught. After spending half a lifetime in the legal profession, he knew that secrets and lies habitually resurfaced long after they were thought to be dead and buried.

"Your Honor," Ainsworth pleaded, "I'm sure there is a valid explanation."

Growing more impatient by the second, Lawler looked down at his daily calendar. "I'm sure it's quite valid, Mr. Ainsworth." He turned to his clerk and ordered, "Give me the appointment list."

Though Lawler was determined to halt the comeback of John Solomon before it got under way, Ainsworth was equally determined to hold the judge to his commitment. Another attorney might not have risked offending the court; but Ainsworth was the chief trial deputy of the largest prosecution office in the country, and he and Lawler both knew they were in this one together. "May I remind the court that it was Your Honor who chose Mr. Solomon in the first place."

"You can remind me of anything you want, Mr. Ainsworth, but this case is going ahead."

Lawler scanned the appointment list, and the gallery came alive with speculation on who would be the next whipping boy for the defense. The buzzing died down immediately as Solomon entered the courtroom and slid into the seat next to Stretch under Lawler's watchful glare.

"Ready whenever you are, Your Honor," Solomon said, smiling at Lawler and doing his best to look under control.

"What's with you, man?" Stretch whispered, suspecting that Solomon's affinity for the bottle might have left him in less than mint condition.

Solomon turned toward Stretch, but Lawler interrupted before he could answer.

"We start on the hour, Mr. Solomon. You think you can remember that?" the judge asked. Solomon nodded, but

Lawler's judicial temperament remained unappeased. "Any reason I shouldn't hold you in contempt?"

"The same good judgment you used in appointing me to this case," Solomon retorted, deciding to call what he hoped was Lawler's bluff. Sometimes the only way to gain a judge's respect was to prove that you were prepared to hold your ground.

Lawler glowered and bristled, shuffled his papers, and turned to the bailiff. "Bring out the defendant," he ordered.

If appearances count for anything in a court of law, Juan Thomas might have mailed in the results without ever leaving the fifth-floor holding tank. He came in with two chunky deputies, one on each arm. In his jail jumpsuit and with his hands cuffed, it was hard to believe that in the eyes of the law, he was presumed innocent. His mood was one of pure defiance.

The deputies marched Thomas over to the defense table, removed the handcuffs, and eased him into the seat next to Solomon. "Who the hell are you?" Thomas asked, and looked contemptuously at Solomon.

"John Solomon. I'm your lawyer." Solomon held out his hand.

"This is bullshit, man," Thomas said to himself, but loud enough for the court personnel, including Lawler, to overhear.

"What did you say, Mr. Thomas?" Lawler inquired.

"I said this is bullshit," Thomas shouted, pointing at Ainsworth. "First you motherfuckers give me a public defender, and then you stick me with this piece of garbage." He motioned menacingly in Solomon's direction. "I want a real lawyer."

"Mr. Thomas! Mr. Thomas!" Lawler banged his gavel

angrily, wishing for a moment that he had been assigned to probate cases at the civil courthouse.

Thomas jumped to his feet and turned to the arresting officer, Gallagher. "You should've just shot me when you broke into my house. Save us all a lot of time."

Solomon also rose to his feet as a trio of deputies approached Thomas and pushed him back into his chair. "Mr. Thomas," Lawler yelled, his face almost blue with rage, "I suggest you shut your face and sit down."

"Your Honor, I request a recess to confer with the defendant," Solomon interjected between the fireworks as he sat back down.

"I don't want no conference. I want a real lawyer." Thomas scowled and stared straight ahead.

"I think it's a good idea," Lawler remarked, regaining his composure.

"I ain't talking to no dump truck," Thomas shot back, eyes fixed on Solomon.

"In that case," Lawler said, with some hesitation, "you may proceed, Mr. Ainsworth."

Even a first-year lawyer knew that forging ahead without any client consultation was reckless and ill advised. But the decision was Lawler's, and Solomon elected not to protest further, thinking he might preserve the ruling as a ground for a pretrial writ petition to the Court of Appeal, alleging denial of Thomas' right to counsel.

"The People call Lieutenant Gallagher," Ainsworth announced.

Gallagher strode to the witness stand and took a seat, steely-eyed as ever, like a windup toy soldier dressed in an outdated sports coat. He raised his right hand as the clerk, a plain-looking white woman in her late thirties, recited the oath from memory. "Do you solemnly swear that the testimony you give in the cause now pending before this court shall be the truth, the whole truth, and nothing but the truth, so help you God?"

Gallagher answered in the affirmative. Ainsworth approached the lectern, and the festivities got under way.

"Mr. Gallagher, where are you employed?" Ainsworth began.

"I'm a lieutenant with the Los Angeles Police Department, Homicide Division." The title sounded impressive, even to a judge sitting without a jury.

"Lieutenant, I'd like to direct you to the early-morning hours of June the fifteenth," Ainsworth said, cutting straight to the pertinent issue. "Did you have occasion at that time to respond to a particular location?"

"We received a call from a nightclub in West L.A." Gallagher proceeded to describe the crime scene and the body of Joe Richards that he found on his arrival.

"Were there any witnesses?" Ainsworth inquired.

"One of the club's dancers, a Ms. Sally Sutton." Gallagher and Ainsworth both paused, anticipating a hearsay objection from Solomon. Hearing none, Gallagher continued. "She claimed to have been talking with Richards at the time of the shooting."

"And could she describe the assailant?" Ainsworth asked, readying himself for another hearsay objection that never came.

"She described him as a black male, aged twenty-five to thirty, with a fade haircut, the kind with the closely shaved sides and the hair piled on top." Lawler raised his head and took silent notice of Thomas' 'do.

"Was Ms. Sutton asked to make an identification?"

"Later that same day she picked out an individual from a notebook of police mug shots I showed her. Two days later she picked out the same individual in a live lineup."

Ainsworth strolled casually behind the defense table, turned, and fired the final question. "Do you see that individual in court today?"

"The defendant," Gallagher boomed, pointing a thick, accusing finger at Thomas.

It had been a typical Ainsworth direct examination: short, to the point, and deadly. "Cross-examination," a much happier Judge Lawler intoned.

Solomon stood up and adjusted his tie. Like a prize-fighter suffering from ring rust, he shuffled the papers scattered before him on the counsel table. "Lieutenant Gallagher," he began finally, "you participated in the arrest of my client on June sixteenth, is that correct?"

"Yes," Gallagher answered, warming to the combat.

"That was just one day after Officer Richards was gunned down. That's pretty fast work, isn't it, Lieutenant?"

As a rule, Gallagher hated defense attorneys, all defense attorneys. But he reserved particular vitriol for those who chose to address him with mock deference as "Lieutenant." He also looked upon Solomon, a former prosecutor, as something of a traitor. "The murder of a police officer gets our highest priority, Counselor."

"A dozen uniformed officers descended on my client's house, isn't that right?"

"Yes."

"And you personally led the charge?"

"So what if I did?"

"Isn't that a little irregular for a homicide lieutenant?"

Ainsworth voiced a halfhearted objection, more to let his witness know he was ready to protect him than to disrupt the cross-examination. The objection was overruled, and Lawler ordered Gallagher to answer.

"I *asked* to lead the charge. Joe Richards was once my partner."

One of the cardinal rules of cross-examination is never ask a question to which you don't know the answer—unless, of course, you don't mind looking at the wrong end of a malpractice claim. Solomon was taken aback by the revelation that Gallagher had a personal interest in the case. It wasn't the sort of information that would be routinely disclosed in discovery, but then again he hadn't actually studied the discovery. He did his best to recover. "Tell me, Lieutenant, what was Officer Richards doing at the club that night?"

Although the question improperly called on Gallagher to speculate about Richards' state of mind, Ainsworth elected to forgo an objection, confident in the knowledge that Solomon had just made another colossal blunder.

"Working," the witness answered, a cunning half smile directed at Ainsworth. "If you had bothered to read through the case file, Counselor, you'd know the Mustang Club is a notorious hangout for gangbangers and drug dealers. Officer Richards was on assignment."

Although John hadn't known about the club's reputation, he knew full well that the killing of a police officer in the performance of his duties was a "special circumstance" under Section 190.2 of the Penal Code that made Juan Thomas eligible for the death penalty. By eliciting the testimony himself from Gallagher, John had saved Ainsworth the trouble of calling other witnesses to prove that Richards was on duty when he was shot.

It was an embarrassing mistake, and rather than risk more damage, John decided to cut his losses. "No further questions," he said, and sat down.

Thomas grumbled silently to himself, and Stretch slowly shook his head, wondering if divorce cases really were that bad after all.

"The People call Sally Sutton," Ainsworth announced.

For a woman whose livelihood was earned by making entrances, Sally's debut as a witness was decidedly understated. Attired in a conservative green suit and white silk blouse, she could easily have passed as the secretary of a senior partner at a major law firm. Still, she turned the head of every heterosexual male in the room as she took the stand, her luxuriant blond hair arranged in a neat chignon.

Ainsworth knew that a beautiful woman on the witness stand was a powerful asset, but one that had to be handled carefully in order to keep the court's attention focused on the evidence. Examining Sally from a seated position, he casually led her through the standard preliminary questions, eliciting her name, age, and job description at the Mustang Club, before taking her up to the point where the driver of the getaway car rolled down his window to speak with Richards.

Then he stood, and with a sense of drama that comes only with years of pleading cases, he asked the crucial question: "Did you actually see the gunman fire the shots that struck Officer Richards?"

Sally, who had performed well under the stress of testifying, nodded, struggling against tears. "I saw him reach through the window and fire three times. It was awful. All I could do was scream."

Whether a witness tells the truth is far less important than whether she *appears* to be lying. Sally sounded sincere to everyone in the courtroom except the defendant, who, in his first attempt at communicating with his counsel, leaned over to Solomon and muttered, "Lying strawberry bitch."

Fortunately Thomas' remarks went unnoticed, and Ainsworth proceeded with his questioning. He had Sally establish the gunman's distinctive hairstyle, race, and approximate age. Then, sensing that Sally could be trusted to field an open-ended question, he asked, "And apart from his hair and age, did you notice anything else about the gunman?"

"His eyes," she said, pausing for an instant, "like he'd killed before, like it didn't mean anything to him."

The courtroom stirred as she delivered her remarks, which were patently objectionable, based on speculation, and, as far as Juan Thomas was concerned, factually untrue. "Move to strike," Solomon objected.

"So ordered," Lawler responded. "The witness is instructed to confine her testimony to facts within her personal knowledge."

It was a minor victory, akin to drawing a bases-empty walk with two out in the ninth inning of a game you're losing by ten runs. Nonetheless, it served to let Ainsworth know that at least Solomon knew it was the ninth inning. Rather than let Sally's imagination wander further, Ainsworth concluded her examination. "Do you see the gunman in court today?"

"That's him over there," she answered confidently, pointing at a visibly disdainful Juan Thomas.

"Your witness," Ainsworth said, resuming his seat.

"They sell alcohol at the Mustang Club, don't they, Sally?" John began his cross-examination. It was a stupid question, and he realized it almost as soon as he asked it. But he was committed to developing some angle at impeaching Sally's testimony, and if he could show she was even a little high, he might be able to discredit her identification of Thomas.

Sally shifted uneasily in her seat, slightly nervous yet attracted by John's suddenly serious demeanor. "Yeah," she answered, almost flirtatiously, slowly crossing her legs in a provocative manner.

"Did you have any drinks the night of the shooting?"

"Maybe two or three."

"Two or three—isn't that a lot?" It was another dumb question. Yet another rule of cross-examination is never give a wise guy a straight line unless you're looking for a career in stand-up.

Like most of the major participants at the hearing, Sally had heard of John's fondness for the suds, and she couldn't resist a good comeback, even if it came at the expense of a cute guy. "You'd know better than me," she said with a faint smile.

The entire gallery broke into audible guffaws. Even the wire-service reporters snickered. It wasn't that the joke was all that funny, but in the airtight tension of a murder case even the slightest humor comes as a great release.

Lawler banged his gavel and instructed Sally to answer the question. "Two drinks is nothing while I'm dancing," she said. "It's hard work."

"Harder than prostitution?" John asked, determined to take his revenge.

Lawler sustained Ainsworth's objection and began to pound his gavel again as Sally shouted, "At least if *I* screw someone, they know what they're getting." Her meaning was not lost on Juan Thomas, who looked at John and shook his head in disgust. Thomas had received many a screw job in his hard-luck life, but none as complete as the one he was getting now from his court-appointed lawyer.

Stretch gently tugged at John's jacket, signaling that it was time to let Sally off the stand. "No further questions," John announced. He watched Sally's every move as she walked past the counsel tables and out the courtroom door.

Ainsworth was in the stretch run now and heading for home. Just one more witness to tie up the murder weapon, and he'd have more than enough proof to send the case to trial. "The People call Mary Delgado," he said.

John dropped his pen and turned around in his seat to reassure himself that what was happening was real. Even in her dark blue uniform, Mary was an attractive woman, athletic and well proportioned, about five feet six inches, with a flat stomach, firm, contoured breasts, and a high, round rump that was a continual distraction to her male coworkers. Younger-looking than her thirty-two years, she was known in police ranks for her street smarts and self-reliance—qualities that served her well in the department. Being black and Latina, she had often been snubbed not only by the LAPD's white establishment but by its minority employee associations as well. Although at times she felt isolated and resentful, such feelings fed her competitive edge and honed her well-recognized determination to succeed.

But as she settled into the witness stand, her air of confidence was visibly shaken. She sat, looking half stunned, her unblemished light brown skin framed by a crown of reddish brown curls, her eyes locked on John.

"Are you all right, Officer?" Lawler asked in an avuncular voice.

"Yes, I'm fine," she answered.

Even Ainsworth, who was well acquainted with the reason for Mary's distraction, was surprised by the magnitude of her reaction to seeing John Solomon for the first time in four years. Two years earlier, when Ainsworth had interviewed Mary for the newly created position of liaison officer between the LAPD and the DA's Major Trials Division, he asked whether she still harbored any feelings toward Solomon. Mary assured him that the "affair," while inexcusable, had been a momentary indiscretion and that nothing would ever again interfere with her duties as an officer. Ainsworth believed her. He concluded that she had been the victim of Solomon's indecent sexual advances, and he offered her the position. Since then he had come to rely increasingly on her efficiency, her knowledge of internal police practices, and, above all, her ability to be deployed in the field and supervise search-and-seizure operations. He regarded her as an indispensable member of his holy law and order crusade, fancying himself a redeemer to her Magdalen.

Noticing Mary and John react to each other brought an inexplicable sadness to Ainsworth, an emotion he rarely experienced and therefore distrusted. He decided to make his examination brief. "Officer Delgado, did you take part in the arrest of Juan Thomas?"

"Yes," Mary answered, recovering her equanimity. "I helped prepare the warrant for the defendant's arrest and led the search for the murder weapon at his residence."

"What, if anything, did you find?"

"We retrieved a three-fifty-seven magnum from under the front porch of the home. The weapon was booked into evidence and turned over to ballistics for testing."

Ainsworth approached the witness stand and handed Mary a handgun the size of a small cannon. "Is this the weapon you retrieved?"

Mary examined the evidence tag attached to the gun. "Yes."

"The People move the gun into evidence, Your Honor," Ainsworth requested.

"The gun shall be received," Lawler remarked. "Cross-examination, Mr. Solomon."

John, deep in thought, failed to respond. Like Rick in *Casablanca,* he was lost in a haze of self-pity and regret. It was a hell of a time to freeze, and the entire courtroom sensed that something was wrong.

"Mr. Solomon, do you have any cross-examination?" Lawler asked again.

John shook himself back to the present. "No, Your Honor."

"The witness is excused," Lawler announced.

Mary's eyes avoided both Solomon and Ainsworth as she left the courtroom.

"Your Honor," Ainsworth said, "the People offer to stipulate that the gun found by Officer Delgado was test-fired by the LAPD ballistics lab and determined to be the weapon used in the killing of Joe Richards."

"So stipulated," John said weakly.

Ainsworth moved that the defendant be bound over for trial on the charge of murder with special circumstances, and Lawler dutifully announced the appropriate findings of probable cause.

"Mr. Thomas," Lawler added gravely, "you shall be held to answer for trial in Superior Court, Judge Rosten's department. Arraignment is set fifteen days from today."

As the crowd began to file out, two bailiffs approached Thomas to lead him back to the lockup and the return bus ride to County Jail.

Although he offered no physical resistance, he was determined not to go meekly. "Fuck you," he called out. "The cops planted that gun." Turning to John, he added, "Why didn't you ask any questions, you worthless piece of shit?"

The bailiffs marched Thomas out of hearing range as John, overwhelmed and defeated, sat at the counsel table. A torrent of questions raced through his mind. Why hadn't he demanded a continuance? Why had he taken the case in the first place? Was a lousy county paycheck worth the humiliation, or had he really believed he could pull off some of his old courtroom magic?

Judge Lawler looked at Solomon from on high and pounded his gavel for the last time. "This hearing is adjourned," he announced as he stepped down from the bench and retreated to his chambers.

CHAPTER 6

John sat at the counsel table a good ten minutes while the spectators and court personnel filed out for the noon recess. He and Stretch made plans for the late afternoon to interview Juan Thomas, and then Stretch left for a business lunch with a divorce client. Except for the bailiff, John was the last to leave Lawler's courtroom. As he reached the exit doors, he turned and took a last look at the counsel tables, the witness stand, and the bench. The courtroom looked the same as any number he had performed in over the years, but he had never felt so out of place.

He walked down the deserted fifth-floor corridor and pressed the up arrow for the elevator. When the car arrived, he pushed the button for the eighteenth floor, headquarters of the district attorney's office. He knew what he had to do.

Externally at least, not much had changed in the four years since he occupied a prize corner office in the oversize suite. "SIMON LASKER, DISTRICT ATTORNEY" was still printed in raised gold letters on the forbidding mahogany-stained wooden doors that opened to the seat of prosecutorial power. The same numeric keypad was mounted on the wall to the side of the doors. During John's tenure, each supervisory employee had been assigned a confidential four-digit personal identification number, a PIN code, that would release the doors for off-hours entry. For now, however, the doors were unlocked, and an assortment of well-dressed men and women, some alone, others in pairs or larger groups, filed out of the office in search of quick meals. John waited for the last group to make its exit before opening the doors and stepping inside.

Gloria Alvarez, a plump fifty-year-old career civil servant from East Los Angeles, sat at the reception desk, reading a romance novel and answering the phones. One of the senior clericals, Gloria had long since graduated from reception duty but was not above providing lunchtime relief while the regular staffers took their noon break. She was a team player and a good sport.

John and Gloria were also good friends. They went back to the days when John was a rookie assigned to screening felony complaints. Gloria ran the overflow secretarial typing pool and with a wry sense of humor dispensed pointers on motion drafting to the newcomers. She was genuinely pleased to see John and waved him through the reception area without requiring him to sign the visitors' sheet.

"Mr. Solomon, long time, no see," she declared with feigned formality as she hurried out of her sentry station and gave John a big hug. "What brings you to this awful place?"

"I'm here to see Howard; we have a case together," John

replied, smoothing back his hair, doing his best to appear like a moderately successful member of the bar or at least to avoid being taken for one on the verge of bankruptcy. "Is he in?"

"You know Howard always takes lunch in his office when he's in trial. I didn't know it was you on the other side. I hear it's a death penalty case," she said with a look of interest and concern. "I'll buzz him and tell him you're on your way back."

"Thanks, Gloria, it was really good to see you again."

John squeezed Gloria's hand, smiled, and turned away. He crossed through the secretarial pool and opened an inner door that led to the corridor housing the offices of the deputy prosecutors. Most of the office doors were closed, and some of the nameplates affixed to them looked unfamiliar.

But there was nothing unfamiliar about the door at the end of the corridor. John reached for the handle and had to stop himself from opening it involuntarily. For a moment it seemed that *his* name, not Howard Ainsworth's, was still imprinted in the center of the door. He knocked, heard Ainsworth call, "It's open," and stepped inside.

The expression on Mary's face, as she sat on a couch across from Ainsworth, betrayed nothing of the surprise she had exhibited in court. It almost seemed that she and Ainsworth were expecting him.

"Sorry, I didn't realize you were busy," John said, preparing for a quick exit.

"We were just finishing," Ainsworth assured him. He and Mary stood up to greet him. "You remember Officer Delgado."

John and Mary shared a long, awkward look. Finally John said, "Of course. I heard you were doing great things."

Mary smiled nervously. "Depends on who you've been

listening to." She wanted to say more but thought better of it. "Well, I've got to be going. Nice to see you again."

"Be right with you," Ainsworth said to John as he walked Mary out the door and down the hall.

Alone in Ainsworth's office, John noticed just how much things had changed since he held the chief deputy post. The old wooden desk that he once sat behind was gone, replaced by a sleek black lacquered model that Ainsworth must have custom-ordered. A worn leather-bound Bible lay on the desk next to pictures of Ainsworth and his wife and three kids on a skiing vacation. The walls were tastefully decorated with expensive biblical art prints by the old masters, complemented by a selection of antique lamps, expensive client chairs, and a large Persian rug. It looked like the office of a senior partner from a downtown law firm—a far cry from the thrown-together frat house motif the room had sported when Solomon was the tenant.

As John walked over to the desk to retrieve one of Ainsworth's business cards, his eyes fixed on an old news clipping carefully framed on the rear wall next to an assortment of photographs showing Ainsworth glad-handing local community leaders. AINSWORTH REPLACES SOLOMON IN DA SHAKEUP, the headline read. Although John hadn't seen the story since his dismissal as head of Major Trials, he felt an ironic measure of justice and symmetry in finding it here, where his career had fallen apart at the seams.

It was Simon Lasker himself who had delivered the fatal blow, calling him into his office for an "urgent" conference late one afternoon. He entered to find Mary seated in one chair at the foot of Lasker's desk and Ainsworth pacing nervously behind the old man. Knowing full well what was about to unfold, John hurried into the chair next to Mary.

"Not only was it unethical," Lasker screamed at the top

of his lungs, "it's all over the goddamn papers. We'll be lucky if they don't get a mistrial because of this."

"What do you want me to say, Simon?" was the best reply John could manage.

"I want you to tell me it never happened," Lasker thundered. "I want you to tell me there was a sane reason my chief deputy slept with the arresting officer in the biggest case of his career." He turned his anger toward Mary and continued. "And what the hell were *you* thinking? You think you can drop your panties whenever you feel like it?"

"I'm sorry, but it's not what you think." Mary tried to explain.

"Back off, Simon, it was my fault," John interrupted.

"That's the first thing right you've said all day," Lasker said. He turned again to Mary and ordered her to leave. She gave John a last look of sympathy and affection as she shut the door.

Lasker paused for a moment, considering his words carefully. "I want you to tell me why I shouldn't fire you."

"Because I'm the best lawyer you have," John answered honestly.

"That's not good enough," Lasker concluded. "As of today, Howard is taking over the case."

Ainsworth walked over to Lasker's side, looked directly at John, and spoke as if reading from a script. "I've already reviewed the files and lodged the necessary motions with the court," he said. "I've also arranged a press conference for tomorrow afternoon where I'll announce you're taking an extended leave of absence for stress-related reasons."

"You're really enjoying this, aren't you, Howard?" John said angrily, noticing that Ainsworth had pulled out a legal pad and begun taking notes.

"Don't make this harder than it has to be, John,"

Ainsworth replied. "We have no other choice, and you know it."

John looked at Lasker, hoping for a last-minute reprieve. "After all we've accomplished together, you're just going to dump me?" he asked. Lasker turned away, his silence louder than words. "You'll have my resignation by the end of the week," John said.

"The paperwork's already done," Lasker said softly, gesturing with his hands that the meeting and John's career as a prosecutor both had come to an end.

John was still staring at the news clipping when Ainsworth reentered and took a seat behind his desk. "Mary's become a very valuable asset to the DA's office," he said with a sincere smile.

"She's working with you now?" John asked. Somehow he had sensed a bond between Mary and Ainsworth that transcended that of prosecutor and police witness. Now he knew why.

"She's the LAPD's special liaison with the Major Trials Division of our office; it's a new position created last year. She's one smart woman. I'm encouraging her to go to law school." Ainsworth glanced at his watch and decided to cut matters short. "So what's on your mind?"

"I want a deal," John said, trying not to sound as if he were begging. "Drop the death penalty, and we'll plead to a straight first-degree murder."

Ainsworth savored the thought of his former rival groveling at his feet, but he had no intention of plea bargaining. The case was too high-profile and far too easy to prove, a "slam dunk" in the parlance of the trial bar. "You must be joking," he said.

"Come on, Howard," John implored. "Thomas is a drug

dealer, not a killer. Besides, you've got no prints on the gun, and your eyewitness is a hooker."

Ainsworth rocked back in his chair, as if considering John's pitch. "You know, I pulled a lot of strings to get you appointed to this case."

John had fully expected Ainsworth to reject his plea, but this came as a total shock. So it was a setup. Both he and Stretch had been set up. He was the used-up patsy handpicked to roll over for the great Howard Ainsworth, and Stretch was just thrown in as his investigator to make the massacre look like a fair fight.

"I thought Judge Lawler . . ." John stammered.

Ainsworth shook his head slowly. "It was my doing. I was the one who convinced Lawler," he said. "I knew you'd hit bottom, and I felt you deserved a second chance. No, this one's going to the jury whether you like it or not." He took another look at his watch. "You're going to have to see this through. And now I'd appreciate it if you'd leave before you start to embarrass yourself."

John let himself out the door. He was a reluctant conscript in a war he couldn't win.

CHAPTER 7

Even when he was a DA, John Solomon was awestruck by the immensity of the men's central county jail on Bauchet Street in downtown Los Angeles. A stone's throw from the main post office and the train station, it was an urban fortress, home to some seven thousand inmates. Some were serving out misdemeanor sentences, but the majority were criminal defendants who were awaiting trial or sentencing on nonbailable offenses or were otherwise unable to raise the bondsman's 10 percent surcharge.

Now that he was a civilian, Solomon could no longer park in the lot reserved for law enforcement personnel but was relegated to the run-down and poorly lit underground structure adjacent to the jail. Even in the daytime you took your chances wheeling into the cavern. If your car wasn't whacked by one of the many overage, uninsured, large

American vehicles favored by the jail's legions of indigent visitors, you had to keep your eyes peeled for the packs of gangbangers who occasionally congregated in the parking structure to pick up a newly released homeboy.

Luckily Solomon found a parking spot near the concrete steps that led to the jail's front entrance. As he got out of his Mustang, the stench of urine stung his nostrils. A large, angry-looking message—"LAPD 187"—was scrawled in red spray paint on the wall to his left. Solomon knew that "187" was a street reference to the Penal Code section for murder and that the slogan was a death threat aimed at the police department, right here in the citadel of law enforcement itself. Solomon took a quick look to his rear and proceeded up the steps.

Inside, the lobby was relatively uncrowded. Two deputy sheriffs stood behind the counter, fielding questions from a couple of lawyers who were trying to find their clients' booking numbers in the multivolume computer printout that listed the inmates by their names, booking numbers, the charges against them, and the modules where they were housed within the jail. While the vast majority of prisoners were kept in the mainline sections of the facility, some— such as rival gang members, incorrigible defendants, ex-cops, homosexuals, and jailhouse informants—required special handling and had to be housed in segregated units.

John found Juan Thomas listed in the "High Power" module on a no-bail hold and filled out a booking slip. He walked through the X-ray booth that screened visitors for weapons and presented the slip to the deputy who operated the sliding steel door that led to the attorney interview room. The deputy waved him through, and John stepped forward as the door clanged behind him. It was a sound that most lawyers hardly noticed but that never failed to send a slight shiver down John's legs.

The interview room was filled with the usual assortment of lowlife inmates dressed in blue jumpsuits. They were seated on stools arranged along two narrow counters directly across from their harried-looking defense attorneys, who busied themselves asking questions and furiously scribbling on yellow legal pads their clients' claims of alibi, self-defense, and mistaken identity. The fluorescent lights and cream-colored walls gave everyone an otherworldly pallor.

John looked to his left and was relieved to find Stretch sitting in one of the Plexiglas booths off to the side of the room. True to his word, Stretch had arrived early and secured one of the few spots where a truly private interview could be conducted.

"So how'd it go with Ainsworth?" Stretch asked as John entered the booth and sat down.

"He's set on going to trial."

"Are you surprised?"

"Shit, no," John answered, "but I'm sure as hell gonna try again."

Stretch gave John a look of disappointment as two guards led Juan Thomas into the booth. Shackled at the legs and cuffed at the hands, Thomas looked even meaner than he did in court, scowling at the deputies as they guided him into a chair across from John and Stretch and removed the handcuffs.

"They treating you okay?" John asked, trying to break the ice.

"Just like a fuckin' country club," Thomas answered, his body tense with anger.

"Look, I know you don't like lawyers and the system is full of shit," John started to explain, hoping to make peace and get through the interview with as few disruptions as possible.

But Thomas was in no mood to be mollified. " 'Bout the

only thing you got right all day," he said with a sneer. "How much they payin' you to throw this case?"

"Hey, there's no call for that," Stretch interjected, showing Thomas his best don't-fuck-with-me expression.

"My homies say he used to be a DA." Thomas laughed. "Looks to me like he still is."

Like most of the other felony defendants John had met in his career, Thomas professed to be completely innocent, despite overwhelming evidence to the contrary. The plain truth, however, was that as inefficient, racist, and occasionally corrupt as some cops were, innocent men in jail constituted a species even rarer than honest personal injury attorneys.

John paused for an instant and considered his next move. He had known that talking to Thomas again would be unpleasant, but he had no idea to what degree until now. He decided to screw the interview and get straight to the point. "I'm not going to waste your time, Juan," he said. "I went to see Ainsworth about a deal."

Thomas appeared genuinely shocked, as if he actually thought his uncompromising bad-ass demeanor had somehow managed to convey his innocence. "A deal? For what? I didn't kill nobody, and they know it!" he shouted.

"Look, I'm not going to bullshit you," John said, barely able to conceal his own anger. "You're black, you're a gangbanger, and you look like shit in court. It'll be a fucking miracle if you don't end up sucking gas." John stood up to leave, then added, "So unless there's something new you can add, you better pray I can make a deal."

Now that Thomas was faced with John's imminent departure, his expression for the first time became stone-cold serious. For a brief moment John swore he saw a look of fear and desperation on his client's face. "I didn't kill that cop," Thomas said softly. "Dupree did. BJ Dupree."

Neither John nor Stretch was particularly impressed. Although they had finally penetrated Thomas' macho facade, they weren't about to fall for what was known derisively in legal circles as the old SODDI defense, the claim that "some other dude did it." Not when the other dude—BJ Dupree—once topped the list of the county's most notorious jailhouse informants. Dupree was something of a household name inside the jail, and he was often blamed by desperate defendants who had never met him as the source of their problems with the law.

Solomon had never worked on a case in which Dupree had testified, and would not have recognized him if Dupree were standing in front of him right now, but he knew the man had a well-earned reputation for delivering the goods on felony defendants, often in devious and unpredictable ways. In one case, if he remembered correctly, Dupree had even secretly tape-recorded a meeting with an attorney and his client by posing as a potential defense witness. The problem was that Dupree hadn't set foot in a courtroom in years and had no known prior involvement with Thomas. For all John knew, Dupree either had gone out of state or had caught a bullet and was buried in some godforsaken place where his body would never be discovered.

Stretch stroked his chin with the long fingers of his powerful right hand and slowly shook his head on hearing Thomas' implausible claim. "Yeah, and I've got a tryout with the Knicks next week," he said. "Come on, man."

"I'm not shittin' you," Thomas pleaded, looking more pathetic by the syllable. "Dupree worked for the cops. My homies and me paid direct to him. They was kickbacks, so the man would leave us alone to deal our rock. Richards got in the way."

"You know what I think, Juan?" John said, deciding to let Thomas know exactly where he stood. "I don't think there was any kickback thing. I think Richards found out you were one of the biggest crack dealers in South Central, so you decided to take him off the police payroll, all by yourself. How does that story sound?"

"Sounds like you're a boned-out ass kisser, like everybody said." Thomas spat in cold rage. He reached across the table and grabbed John around the neck. It took all of Stretch's strength and the assistance of two deputies to pull him off. "It's Dupree," Thomas yelled as he was dragged away. "It's Dupree, motherfucker. You find Dupree."

If Solomon thought that having Thomas' hands around his neck was a major inconvenience, he soon forgot all about it when he found the windshield of his Mustang shattered in the jail's parking lot. Someone must have taken a crowbar and smashed it just for the fun of it because there was nothing missing, just shards of glass strewn across the seats. Fortunately Stretch was still in shouting distance and put in a call to a nearby tow yard from the car phone in his new Ford Taurus. Divorces may have been a pain in the ass for Stretch, but they paid for the rent and a few little luxuries like the phone.

Within a half hour a tow truck rumbled into the lot. It was driven by an affable Mexican, who promised to replace the windshield in three days for only $250. For another hundred he'd also see that Eddie's Tuck 'n Roll Shop, located just next door, replaced the old seat covers. John wrote out a check, was given a receipt, and watched his Mustang disappear through the gate. "It's been a long day," Stretch said, placing a consoling hand on John's shoulder. "Come on, I'll take you home."

As they made their way through the downtown section, Stretch's silence signaled his annoyance with the afternoon's events. He was bothered not just by the fracas with Juan

Thomas but even more by John's eagerness to get off the case. Instead of chattering away as he usually did about the weather, the Lakers, and his latest female conquest, Stretch stared straight ahead, saying nothing.

"Look, I'm not changing my mind on this," John said finally. "I should've never taken this case in the first place."

"You hear me say anything?" Stretch replied.

"Your silence is enough." As he spoke, John noticed that Stretch had taken a turn to the south. Either this was some kind of new shortcut to the hills of Silver Lake or Stretch had other plans in mind, like dumping him somewhere in the middle of gang territory. "This isn't the way to my house," John added a little nervously.

"That's because I'm not going to your house," Stretch answered with exaggerated patience.

Stretch wheeled around a corner and came to a stop next to a small neighborhood park. He reached into the backseat, grabbed a gym bag, and, after removing his coat and tie, walked off in the direction of a well-kept outdoor basketball court. Sensing a game of hoops was unavoidable, John threw his jacket and tie on the front seat and followed after Stretch.

The ragtag assembly of neighborhood kids who were already on the court parted for Stretch like the Red Sea for Moses. Though none of them was old enough to remember Stretch's playing days with the Lakers, they knew his reputation and had seen him in action in pickup games. Yielding the court to him was the ultimate sign of respect, and Stretch, for his part, knew how to show his appreciation. He took a few dribbles, then swooped to the basket for a dazzling slam dunk, eliciting a chorus of oohs and aahs from his small audience.

John walked onto the court, feeling out of place and

looking decidedly out of shape. "Don't tell me you buy that horseshit from Thomas," he said. "The guy was lying."

"Probably," Stretch said amiably as he popped in a twenty-foot jumper.

"So who gives a shit if I quit or not? The case is a total dog. Why do you think we were appointed? We're expected to lose."

Stretch stopped shooting and fired the ball at John, who barely managed to catch it before it hit him in the chest. "*I* give a shit," Stretch said, "and I don't care what anybody else expects. You quit this case, man, and I'm through with you. I don't know you anymore."

John fired the ball back at Stretch. He hadn't appreciated just how much Stretch wanted back in criminal law. This case was his ticket, and now it was about to be taken away. "I didn't ask for this," John said in a voice attempting reasoned calm. "I already begged that son of a bitch Ainsworth. I don't know what the hell I'm supposed to do."

"Tell you what," Stretch said, his voice and demeanor softening. "Play you best of ten and spot you eight. You win, you quit the case. I win, we check out Thomas' story."

Stretch handed John the ball and took a quick look at his crowd of young admirers. John took advantage of the momentary lapse and drove past him for an uncontested layup. "Who said white men can't jump?" he chided.

"Time to get serious," Stretch replied, snuffing John's lights out on his next move to the basket and taking the ball home for an easy score.

The rest of the game was a clinic: a slam dunk here, a spin move there, a couple of high archers from fifteen feet, all punctuated by a reverse jam that left John exhausted and panting on the asphalt.

"That's ten." Stretch grinned and extended his hand to

the fallen lawyer. "You know you've never beaten me," he added as they walked slowly off the court.

"I know," John said. He also knew that Ainsworth couldn't possibly stomp him any worse than his old friend had. The big difference, of course, was that the stomping he'd get from Ainsworth was the one that counted in the standings.

CHAPTER 8

Agreeing to try a death penalty case is like signing on to fight a guerrilla war; prevailing in one is like winning a revolution. Despite his long years in professional exile, Solomon had not forgotten the building blocks of victory. To the contrary, in the time since Stretch had kicked his ass in basketball and secured his commitment to the case, he and Stretch had done just about everything a competent capital defense team could do. Stretch undertook the unenviable task of interviewing the members of Juan's Crip set, while John concentrated on banging out a paper blizzard of well-written legal briefs, including a motion to suppress the alleged murder weapon on grounds of illegal search and seizure.

The Superior Court judge assigned to hear the trial, the Honorable Joseph Rosten, took the suppression motion under submission for two days before denying it. Had the motion been granted, the People's case might well have collapsed.

With Rosten's ruling, however, the prosecution's position remained as strong as it had been at the prelim. Thomas' alibi—some bullshit tale about attending his cousin's birthday party into the wee hours of the morning—evaporated into thin air when it turned out that the cousin had moved out of town before the shooting.

Nor was there any trace of the elusive BJ Dupree. Records from both the LAPD and the state Department of Justice listed the informant under his formal name of Robert James Dupree. As far as John could tell from such sources, Dupree had dropped out of sight four years ago after completing his last sentence for cocaine possession. And if Juan's homies knew where Dupree was hiding, they were keeping his whereabouts to themselves. Trying to link the murder to Dupree seemed at best a dead end.

It was now a Friday night in the middle of September. John and Ainsworth had spent the entire week picking a jury. To Solomon's surprise, he had come away with a panel that actually appeared capable of giving Juan Thomas a fair trial: four blacks, two Latinos, an Asian, and five Anglos. But as matters stood, even a fair jury would have little difficulty returning a guilty verdict. There would be a short readiness conference with the judge on Monday, and the trial would begin on Tuesday with opening statements.

Behind the wheel of his Mustang Solomon drove west on Temple Street from his downtown office with no particular destination in mind. As had become his custom in moments when he had no answers to life's more immediate challenges, he began drifting back to his childhood, this time to his early teens and the days of friction and discord when his family struggled to adjust to the overcrowded conditions of the run-down old apartment house.

One of the things he remembered best about that era was the late-night pizza run he and his father made every Saturday. As the midnight hour approached, his old man and he would pile into the family station wagon and head for Pat's, a little hole in the wall on Broad Street in North Philly owned by a former sailor with an honest-to-goodness anchor tattoo on one of his forearms and a chipped front tooth that Solomon swore he found one night in a slice with extra cheese. They'd stop at a corner newsstand to pick up the early Sunday edition of the Philadelphia *Inquirer*, and then they'd stop again, always at a deserted phone booth, rain or shine, winter or spring, to allow the old man to call his bookie.

"Gotta see a man about a dog," his father would say evasively as he got out of the car. Every member of the family knew he was still placing bets, even after his gambling had cost the family their home, but no one, not even John's mother, knew the name of the bookie or his location. It was a secret his father took with him to the grave, not unlike the secret Juan Thomas would take to his if he didn't let on soon about what really happened the night Richards was killed.

As John ruminated on his past, he slowly realized that he had driven into the west side and was approaching the well-kept middle-class neighborhood where Mary lived. Although he hadn't thought about her for years until the prelim, he knew he still wanted her, not just because he was lonely and his life was empty, not just because he hadn't been laid in six months (though that was reason enough), but because he truly believed they had had something special together, something which, in a period of despair and weakness after his forced resignation, he had let slip away.

He found his way to her house and parked halfway down the block on the other side of the street. Except for a new coat of paint, some expensive landscaping, and the red Mercedes parked in the drive, the place looked much the same as it had on those brief but precious weekends when they stole away to spend rapturous hours laced around each other, intoxicated with passion and thoughts of building a future together. As John sat and stared at the house, the front door opened. Mary, dressed in evening clothes and looking better than he'd ever seen her, stepped outside. At her side was a well-dressed Howard Ainsworth, all smiles and Sunday school manners. If John hadn't known better, he'd have guessed the fundamentalist bastard had a sexual interest in her, the way he solicitously helped her into the Mercedes.

The sight of Ainsworth and Mary together made John's stomach congeal. "Things change," he told himself, "but only for the worse." He reached under the seat and pulled out his emergency pint bottle of J & B. He undid the cap and took a long deep hit, then gunned his engine and headed for home.

It was eight o'clock the next morning when the phone woke him up from a deep, dreamless sleep.

It was Stretch, full of piss and vinegar and plans for the case. "Get your lazy ass out of bed," he said. "I'll be over for you in an hour. Got a witness to interview."

Although John wanted nothing more than to sleep in, he knew he couldn't disobey an enormous black man barking marching orders into a telephone, especially when the man was his only real friend.

If there was anything John had learned from his years of working with Stretch at the DA's office, it was to trust his investigator's instincts. As an up-and-coming prosecutor

John had called on Stretch many times not just to ferret out the facts but to soothe the fears of crime victims and potential witnesses. Like the time Stretch had convinced the brother of a murdered high school baseball player that he could testify without fear of retaliation from a neighborhood gang, or the time he had held a four-year-old girl in his arms as her mother took the stand to identify her father's killer. Stretch had a gift for dealing with people, and John counted himself lucky to have him in his corner.

John hung up the receiver, staggered to the bathroom, put his head in the sink, and turned on the tap. He knew that in all likelihood Stretch would arrive for him ahead of schedule.

Estelle Richards lived in a modest wood-frame house in one of the better neighborhoods of South Central. Normally Stretch would never have suggested interviewing the wife of a murder victim, but none of the normal leads in the case had panned out. "Let me handle the intros," he told John as they walked up to the front door.

Mrs. Richards was a plain-looking black woman of thirty-five with a pleasant broad face and straight dark hair cut just above her shoulders. When she opened the door, it was clear from the puffiness around her eyes that she had been crying. Although it was midmorning, she was still dressed in her housecoat, a telltale sign that the depression over her husband's death had not abated.

"Mrs. Richards?" Stretch asked with a smile, extending his hand.

"Yes. What can I do for you?" she answered warily.

"I'm Stretch Johnson, and this is John Solomon." Stretch gestured toward John, who did his best to affect the image of a nonthreatening white man on the black side of town.

Mrs. Richards' consternation was immediate, but she

chose to direct her anger solely at Stretch, thinking that as a black man he at least should have known better than to come snooping around her home. "What is it with you lawyers? I told you on the phone that I have nothing to say to you," she said impatiently.

"Please, just five minutes," John interrupted. "It was my idea," he lied, allowing Stretch to maintain his good-guy profile.

Mrs. Richards frowned, let out a deep sigh, and then stepped back to let them enter.

Mrs. Richards' three school-age children, two girls and a twelve-year-old boy, were sacked out on the living room couch and armchairs, watching what was left of their favorite Saturday morning shows. She shooed them into the backyard and gestured for John and Stretch to sit down. The interior of the Richards house was clean and well furnished, with family portraits hanging on the living room walls and a handsome set of clear pine bookshelves stocked with an assortment of hardbacks ranging from biographies of black Americans to a family medical guide and a collection of academic tomes on criminal justice and race relations in America.

"I know this is a difficult time for you, and I know how you must feel," John said, sounding like the bureaucrats Mrs. Richards had encountered at the Social Security office while applying for death benefits for her kids.

"What do you know about how I feel?" she snapped back, taking a seat across from them. "When all this is over, who's going to be here for my children?"

Neither John nor Stretch had an answer to the question, and the three of them sat there for an instant sharing a knowing silence. Finally John pressed on with the interview. "Had your husband ever mentioned the Mustang Club to you before his death?"

"I never even heard of the Mustang Club before Joe was shot," she answered.

"Did he have any enemies—on the street, I mean?" Stretch added.

"Everybody liked Joe," she said, choking back indignation.

"What about inside the department?" John asked.

The question clearly struck a nerve. Mrs. Richards hesitated, as if choosing her words very carefully. "No. I told you, everybody liked Joe—everybody."

To all intents and purposes, the interview was over. Before her visitors could leave, however, Mrs. Richards' son came bounding inside through the back door. He was a bright-eyed, neatly groomed boy with short hair and a body that already displayed the first signs of athletic promise. "Say," he shouted to Stretch, "didn't you used to play for the Lakers? Can I have your autograph?"

"You got a pretty good memory, little man," Stretch replied with a mixture of satisfaction and astonishment. It had been a long time since anyone had commented on his playing days, let alone a kid who hadn't even been alive the last time he suited up.

As the boy quizzed Stretch on what it was like to be in the NBA, John quietly asked for permission to use the bathroom and was directed to use the toilet in the master bedroom since the kids' bath in the hallway was, as she put it, "too messy for visitors." John's real purpose, of course, was not to empty his bladder, which had become hardier than an Australian beer drinker's from all those pitchers at Swanson's, but to catch a glimpse of the rest of the Richards home. If he could gain a better understanding of the kind of man the deceased had been, perhaps he'd find a clue to explain the widow's evasive response to his question about her husband's enemies.

To John's surprise, the interior seemed completely devoid of Joe Richards' personal effects. There were no men's clothes in the bedroom closets or dressers, no men's magazines or toiletries on the nightstands or the bath, no sporting equipment, no spoor of adult male presence anywhere. Except for a manila file with the notation "Joe Richards—Medical" on it, lying on top of an otherwise empty desk in a corner of the bedroom, there was nothing to indicate that the place had ever been shared with a fully grown man. Richards' wife had clearly gone to great lengths to purge the house of any trace of his presence, out of grief or anger or a combination of the two.

John eavesdropped a moment as Stretch held forth about his exploits on the hardwood, and then opened the file. The interview with Mrs. Richards might have yielded nothing, but the file offered the first concrete lead since he had agreed to take on the case. After a brief perusal he set it back on the desk, entered the bathroom to flush the toilet, and returned to the living room, where he and Stretch said their good-byes to Mrs. Richards and her kids.

As they drove down Century Boulevard toward the Harbor Freeway, John took a three-page document out of his jacket pocket and waved it in front of his face. Stretch waited for him to explain himself, but John just sat in the passenger seat with a shit-eating grin.

"Okay," Stretch said finally. "What is it?"

"It's a medical report from the widow's bedroom. Nine months ago another cop broke two of Richards' ribs in a fight."

"I knew she was holding back," Stretch said, pulling onto the freeway.

"You didn't know shit." John laughed. "You were too busy signing autographs for that kid."

"What cop?" Stretch asked.

On this point the report was silent. "Maybe the one we're looking for," John answered. "Maybe the one BJ Dupree was funneling the kickback money to."

CHAPTER 9

Howard Ainsworth and his wife, Teri, lived in a wealthy hillside section of north Glendale. They had a well-appointed ranch-style house, with five bedrooms, a wood-paneled study, a big backyard with a covered patio and pool, and a two-car garage that sheltered Ainsworth's Mercedes and Teri's Range Rover from the sun and smog. Ainsworth and Teri had bought the property twenty years earlier, just after they had returned to Los Angeles from the small Arizona college where they met as religious studies majors. Land values were low then, and the purchase proved a wise investment, like most of the ventures Ainsworth had chosen in his life.

Ainsworth and Teri were a model couple. To make ends meet in the early days of their marriage, Teri postponed the joys of childbearing and supported Howard through law school, working long hours as a grade school teacher at a fundamentalist Christian school. Her sacrifices were well rewarded. After graduation Ainsworth joined the DA's office and, with an Old Testament zeal for the jugular, quickly ascended the prosecutorial ladder. With Teri's constant encouragement, he had become the consummate prosecutor, a man with an unlimited future and a candidate for public office.

Teri handled the role of the candidate's devoted spouse like a Stepford wife in overdrive. A pert five-foot-four-inch bundle of brunette energy, she was blessed with a relentlessly cheerful disposition and always made a positive impression at public appearances, even on those rare occasions when Ainsworth's evangelical shtick seemed phonier than a constipated smile. Like a well-seasoned First Lady, she knew when to involve herself in Howard's affairs and when to keep a supportive distance. Above all, she was a devoted mother to their three children: two boys, ages twelve and ten, and an eight-year-old girl.

Glendale had a well-earned reputation for being staid, white, and conservative, and that suited Ainsworth and Teri just fine. It was, in fact, the ideal community for them—far enough removed from the dangers of downtown to raise a family yet close enough to the office to allow Ainsworth to work the long hours expected of a high-level trial attorney and still make it home in time to lead the bedtime prayers and tuck the kids in.

Glendale was also the home of the world-famous Forest Lawn, a three-hundred-acre cemetery theme park of rolling green meadows that regularly pitched its pathways to the afterlife on the radio and was the final resting place of numerous Hollywood celebrities. Ainsworth and Teri had long since placed their down payment on his and her burial plots on a quiet hillside that caught the last rays of the afternoon sun.

Ainsworth's attention today, however, was not on the hereafter but on the here and now—specifically, the November election. With less than two months left in the campaign, the latest polls had him as the clear front-runner. According to the experts, the election was his to lose. To maintain his momentum, however, he had to keep on campaigning, making himself available to the media whenever possible, delivering his patented speeches on law and order and family values before civic organizations and church groups across the county.

Today, on a brilliant Saturday afternoon, he was hosting a backyard barbecue and photo shoot for a select group of major contributors. At least a dozen local business leaders were on hand, along with Simon Lasker and some high-ranking senior deputies from the DA's staff, three members of the City Council, a handful of partners from L.A.'s blue-chip law firms, and a collection of representatives from religious organizations and victims advocacy groups. Teri had hired a catering crew to prepare an all-American cookout of hamburger, chicken, and fish while she supervised the decorations of bunting, balloons, and strategically placed campaign posters. Thanks to her efforts, their home struck just the right balance of domesticity and affluence that reassured Ainsworth's backers of his worthiness.

While Ainsworth's boys tossed a football in the backyard, he stood by the barbecue, shirtsleeves rolled up and spatula in hand, fielding questions from reporters and posing for the cameras. Most of the inquiries dealt with standard matters like his views on the death penalty—he was a strong supporter—and his plans for the DA's office: He intended, among other things, to put an end to plea bargaining and crack down hard on welfare fraud.

Ainsworth answered all the queries as he had many times in the past, with glib good humor and a calm professional-

ism that announced to the world that he was a dedicated
public servant and a man who could be trusted to turn back
the tide of lawlessness that had transformed a once-God-
fearing city into a human cesspool. "For starters, I would
insist on basic sentencing reform," he began to say when he
felt a tugging motion at his belt.

It was his little girl. Scissors and a half-cut sheet of paper
in hand, she was oblivious of the media event she was dis-
turbing. Shyly she asked for Daddy's help in cutting out a
set of paper dollies. "Of course, sweetheart," Ainsworth
said, turning the diversion into an impromptu opportunity
to display his well-honed family orientation. He was, as his
supporters had expected, becoming a real politician.

The image of domestic bliss imprinted on the Ainsworth
household might have endured without a blemish but for a
sudden disruption around six o'clock at the side gate.
Ainsworth excused himself and walked over to find Teri
speaking with Lieutenant Gallagher. Gallagher may have
been an important cog in God's army, but he wasn't on
the guest list and was about as welcome as a turd in the
punch bowl.

"I'll take over from here, dear," Ainsworth told Teri in
an affable tone. Greatly relieved, Teri retreated to resume
the role of charming hostess as Ainsworth turned his attention to Gallagher. "I thought I told you not to come here.
This had better be important," he said with unconcealed
anger.

"We've been served with a subpoena for Richards' personnel file," Gallagher answered matter-of-factly, acknowl-
edging the inconvenience yet refusing to kowtow to
Ainsworth's imperious manner. "I thought you'd want to
know."

Even on this special occasion, Ainsworth thought, the legion of evil was hard at work. "Get the file to my office to-

morrow afternoon," he said, shifting gears from candidate to legal strategist. "I'll draft a motion to quash the subpoena for Monday's readiness conference." As Gallagher turned to leave, he added, "And you'd better make sure nothing's missing from the file."

Furious at both the disruption and Solomon's nerve, Ainsworth walked back over to the barbecue and dropped the half-cut paper dollies into the flames.

Judge Rosten's courtroom on the fourteenth floor of the Criminal Courts Building was no bigger than Judge Lawler's, but even the most unsophisticated person could tell it was far more important. This was the Superior Court, with an emphasis on "Superior," the place where those accused of felonies were sent for jury trials after preliminary hearings, where defendants were found guilty of mayhem, rape, and murder, and where, in capital cases, they were condemned to die.

Like Lawler, Rosten was a former prosecutor, but with the United States attorney's office, not the DA's. It was a distinction that, together with a law degree from Yale, gave him an air of arrogance and a certain measure of independence. The picture image of a judge, with a full head of straight white hair and a deep suntan earned during repeated vacations he spent climbing tall peaks in the Canadian Rockies, Rosten was fond of quoting himself, saying that he favored neither the prosecution nor the defense but hated both with equal fervor.

In practice, however, his evenhanded ill will seemed to fall more regularly on the defense, as in the burglary prosecution that had made its way to the top of the courthouse rumor chart last year after Rosten had threatened to jail a deputy public defender for not wearing a tie in his courtroom. The watchwords for attorneys entering his kingdom were: Dress professionally, speak respectfully, act deferentially, and cover your ass at all times.

It was midmorning, at the outset of the readiness conference, when Ainsworth's motion to quash came on for hearing. With the afternoon scheduled for racquetball and the trial set to begin on Tuesday, Rosten wanted to keep things brief and was in no mood for last-minute delays. Last-minute delays, Rosten believed, had turned the system into a travesty, inflated the fees of fat-cat attorneys, and enraged the rabble to the point where they were actually holding recall elections to vote judges out of office. Still, there was no telling how Rosten would rule, especially since Ainsworth had produced Richards' file an hour earlier for the judge to review in camera, giving him ample time to prepare his ruling. Rosten was known for being unpredictable and deviating from established protocols.

John and Ainsworth avoided looking at each other as Rosten took the bench. "I've had an opportunity to study the personnel file of Officer Joseph Richards, and I'm not sure I see its relevance," Rosten grumbled. "Mr. Solomon, perhaps you can enlighten me. And while you're at it, you can also explain why you haven't followed the procedures set forth in the Evidence Code for obtaining these records."

John could tell from the judge's tone that Rosten wasn't about to release Richards' file without a strong showing of good cause. Under state law, a party seeking discovery of police personnel records was supposed to file a written motion, with at least fifteen days' advance notice to the prosecution and the police. John was clearly in default of those procedures.

Taking due note of the judge's somber appearance, John gathered his notes and the affidavit he had appended to the subpoena and stood to address the court. "Nine months ago," he said, "Joe Richards was sent to the hospital with two broken ribs by another officer. He had enemies inside the department, very dangerous and determined enemies. I only acquired this information two days ago, so I chose to proceed by serving a subpoena."

"And you think there might be some connection between this fight and the death of Officer Richards?" Rosten interrupted, suddenly sounding unconcerned with Solomon's failure to observe the rituals of the Evidence Code.

It was Ainsworth, not John, who answered. "This is just a fishing expedition designed to buy time and postpone the trial," he said, rising to his feet, hoping to avoid a decision on the merits and coax the judge into quashing the subpoena solely in order to avoid a time-wasting continuance.

Ainsworth's strategy, however, was a little too obvious. If he had just sat back and let Rosten come to his own conclusions, the judge would probably have quashed the subpoena on purely procedural grounds. But the last thing Rosten wanted in his courtroom was a lawyer who presumed to know what he was thinking.

"Nonetheless," Rosten said with considerable consternation, "the records do bear out Mr. Solomon's claim of a fight between Richards and Officer Rokowski."

"That's Row-in-ski, Your Honor," Ainsworth corrected, bringing an angry mauve hue to the judge's face. "Officer Richards' estate has a privacy right in preventing disclosure of those records."

"Whatever right his estate has," Rosten nearly shouted, "is outweighed by the right of the defense to present its theory of the case. A copy of the records shall be turned over forthwith. That's my ruling, gentlemen."

Rosten had closed his file and prepared to rise from the bench when Solomon, buoyed by his unexpected victory, spoke again. "Your Honor, with the trial set to start tomorrow, I'd also like to request a continuance to interview Officer Rowinski."

"I knew that's what you wanted," Ainsworth fired back, a look of vindication on his face.

"I have every right to interview police personnel. What are you hiding, Howard?" John countered.

"You want to interview Jim Rowinski, be my guest," Ainsworth said matter-of-factly. "I'll tell you where to find him—in the morgue." He paused for a damage assessment, taking in every wrinkle of Solomon's incredulous visage, then added, "Funeral arrangements have been made for this afternoon. I expect tomorrow's *Times* will run a story."

John stood at the counsel table, staring blankly, searching for words he couldn't find.

Ainsworth closed the lid on his briefcase and stood to leave, confident that providing John with a copy of the Richards file would do nothing to compromise his case.

Judge Rosten, whose long career presiding over murder trials had left him anesthetized to reports of violence in Los Angeles, glanced impatiently at his watch, fearing he'd miss the first set of his racquetball match. To him it was just another day at the office, and he wanted to get it over with. "Unless either of you cares to add anything, I'll see you tomorrow for the start of trial," Rosten said. He pounded his gavel and disappeared into his chambers.

Solomon arrived at Swanson's just ahead of the regular lunch crew. He settled into his private booth and called over to Linda for a scotch and a Bud chaser. He took his head in his hands and ran his fingers through his hair, realizing that Ainsworth had been toying with him in court. Ainsworth didn't really care about disclosing Richards' personnel file. What Ainsworth really wanted was to prevent the trial from being postponed, and that was exactly what he'd gotten.

"I thought you were preparing for your big case," Linda said as she delivered the liquid amber.

"I am preparing," John assured her, grabbing for the scotch and downing it in one hard swallow. "Bring me another, Linda."

By the time Stretch found him, John was well into his third round of drinks. Solomon may not have done anything to aid his client, but at least the fees he had gotten from the court for going through the motions paid the tab for drowning his sorrows.

"I heard about Rowinski," Stretch said with a worried look, taking a seat on the other side of the booth. What concerned him, however, was not the death of a cop known throughout the force as a budget Rambo but John's impending collapse on the eve of trial.

"Too bad for him, too bad for Juan Thomas, too bad all around," John said, affecting the slurred speech of the truly drunk.

"Don't you even want to find out what happened to Rowinski?" Stretch asked, the tone of disappointment in his voice verging on resignation.

"He was killed outside his apartment. The police have no clues. It's a dead end," John answered, uttering the last sentence slowly and deliberately to underscore the futility of his position.

"This has got to be your last," Linda said as she arrived with another round.

"He's already had too much," Stretch told her sharply.

"You mean I haven't had enough," John quipped, reaching up for the shot glass on Linda's serving tray. "Bring me another." She disappeared in the direction of the bar with no intention of complying.

Stretch stared at John, knowing he could say nothing to exorcise his demons. Stretch was no shrink, and his attempt at basketball therapy had, at least for the moment, exhausted his psychological repertoire. In the end all he could manage was an exasperated "What the hell's your problem?"

"You're the one with the problem," John replied. "Are you afraid of what you see?"

"I don't even know what I see anymore," Stretch said with grim honesty.

"That's because you don't know yourself," John explained, having reached the stage of inebriation where drunkenness gives way to delusions of intellectual prowess and heightened erudition. "You never really know yourself until you're evicting single mothers with five kids. This is who I am. At least I know that." John downed the dregs of his last beer and started for the door.

"You're not gonna drive?" Stretch called after him.

John either didn't hear or chose not to respond. He walked out the door without looking back, leaving Stretch to ponder how the haunted figure that had just departed could ever have been one of the city's top litigators.

He hadn't been there in almost five years. All that time he had purposely avoided the place, hoping to escape the pain and anguish he feared would overcome him if he ever set foot inside its gates. It was funny, especially for someone as stewed as he was and whose sense of direction even when sober would have made Laurel and Hardy look like Indian scouts, but he still remembered the way. He took the Highland exit off the Hollywood Freeway, nearly sideswiping a UPS truck in the process, and headed west. A few quick turns later he pulled up in front of the small Jewish cemetery where his daughter was buried.

The place hadn't changed a bit, he thought to himself, as he traversed the rows of headstones bearing names like

Goldberg, Farber, Pincus, and Levy. Annabel's tiny plot was tucked away in a far corner and was marked by perhaps the smallest stone in the entire yard. It also bore the simplest inscription, noting only her name and, unlike all the others, a single date, that cold morning in February when she both entered the world and left it as another infant mortality statistic for the county archives. She was, as John recalled one of the maternity room nurses saying insensitively, the baby without a brain. The official cause of death was listed as anencephaly.

John must have stared at Annabel's headstone for nearly half an hour before he became aware of the tears streaming down his cheeks.

CHAPTER 10

The coroner's office operated twenty-four hours a day, seven days a week, on a first-slain, first-on-the-slab basis. Normally a body brought in during the morning had to wait its turn in cold storage behind those that had arrived the night before. Jim Rowinski was an exception, partly because the death of a cop always gets top priority and partly because the county coroner himself was urged to put a rush on the case by its investigating officer, Lieutenant Thomas Gallagher, and Chief Deputy District Attorney Howard Ainsworth. Rowinski's body had been discovered slumped over the steering wheel of his Trans Am by an *L.A. Times* paperboy early Sunday morning. The forensics team had little difficulty ascertaining the cause of death: a single gunshot wound to the back of the head. The autopsy was completed by nightfall.

The expedited autopsy, together with a few phone calls from Ainsworth and a financial guarantee offered by the LAPD's pension fund director, enabled Rowinski's friends inside the department to schedule a memorial service for late Monday afternoon at Forest Lawn. Unlike the little forlorn function the Solomons had held for Annabel, Rowinski's final sendoff was a military dress affair, complete with rifle salvos and stilted commemoratory orations from Gallagher and others who had served alongside the fallen hero.

Among the speakers jockeying for a mug shot from the political paparazzi was Ainsworth, somberly attired in a dark blue suit, pressed white shirt, and red tie. With Mary at his side and Sally Sutton, dressed in widow's black and fighting off a wave of graveside tears, he was at his evangelical best, reviewing the sorry state of Western civilization, extolling the virtues of the thin blue line holding the last vestiges of society together, and finally reciting the good works of the dearly departed. "When Jim Rowinski took his oath to protect and to serve," he said in a singsong preacher's rhythm, "he knew that even with God as his protector, death was always an imminent possibility. In the final reckoning, however, death for Jim Rowinski was surely a path to greater glory."

Or another human sacrifice to the drug trade, thought Solomon as he watched the proceedings from behind one of the park's old oak trees. The forty-minute drive from Annabel's burial plot to Forest Lawn was another Mr. Toad's ride, full of more near misses than a year's worth of traffic at a busy airport, but God protects idiots and has-been lawyers, and Solomon arrived woozy but in one piece. Still trailing the stale odor of booze, he pushed his way through the crowd of departing mourners and walked up to Sally, who remained at the grave, sobbing softly. "You knew the deceased pretty well, I take it," he said politely.

Before Sally could answer, John felt a sharp shove between his shoulder blades that nearly knocked him off his
feet. He turned to meet the glowering face of Gallagher no
more than six inches from his own. The lieutenant's breath,
the casualty of a souvlaki sandwich, reeked of garlic, but it
wasn't a farewell kiss that he was after. "What the hell's the
matter with you?" Gallagher asked, sounding like a de-
ranged Eagle Scout. "Don't you have any respect?"

Had he been completely sober, John might have answered back in the voice of a frightened soprano. But
whether it was the alcohol or the sense that he had nothing
left to lose except a few teeth (which he didn't need for
swigging beer or sipping the more potent stuff), he felt no
fear. "I've got a right to talk to the lady," he snapped.

"You've got five seconds to get out of here," Gallagher
informed him. A phalanx of beefy colleagues stepped up to
prove the point.

John stood his ground and refused to back down.
"What's the matter, Lieutenant?" he shouted. "Are you
afraid that your witness might say something if you let her
out of your sight?"

Thinking that John had made his day, Gallagher flashed
a Clint Eastwood grin and balled his right hand into a men-
acing fist when Ainsworth suddenly interceded. Ainsworth
waved Gallagher away and put his arm around Solomon,
playing the role of peacemaker like a kindly brother. "This
isn't appropriate, John," he scolded. "Please, you should
leave." Together they watched as Gallagher led Sally to a
waiting limousine. "We've got a trial date tomorrow, remember," Ainsworth added. He squeezed John's right arm
and gave him a long, sincere look, the kind reserved for lost
souls and orphans, then headed for his car, leaving John
alone to pay his last respects to Rowinski and the secrets he
took with him into the next world.

* * *

John spent the rest of the afternoon waiting for Mary Delgado to arrive home from work. It was nearly eight o'clock when she pulled into her driveway. The weather had turned cool and cloudy, and a rare September rainstorm appeared on the way. When John finally summoned up the courage to knock on her door, about an hour later, he found himself in the midst of a steady downpour.

He rang the doorbell and waited in the rain for what seemed like ten minutes. He was already wringing wet when Mary answered. She had just stepped out of the shower and was dressed only in her slippers and a red bathrobe that was slightly open at the top, exposing the smooth, inviting upper contours of her breasts. With her hair combed straight back and her hazel eyes sparkling in the reflected glow of the porchlight and the rain, she had nothing of the tough-cookie veneer she adopted while on duty. Whoever said female cops were all butch had never met Mary. John fought the urge to take her in his arms.

They stared at each other, sharing a moment of surprise and indecision. Finally she broke the silence. "What are you doing here?"

"I thought you'd want this," John responded lamely, reaching into his jacket to retrieve an old Billie Holiday cassette. He handed her the tape.

"Why are you giving me this?" she asked suspiciously.

"I came across it the other day at my place," he lied. "You must have left it." He studied her stiff reaction, then lied again. "It was always one of your favorites; I thought that you should have it."

Smooth technique with the ladies had never been one of Solomon's strong suits, and this awkward exchange on the porch was no exception.

"How would you know what I liked?" Mary asked,

sounding like a seasoned cross-examiner. "You weren't around long enough to notice."

It wasn't at all what he wanted to hear, at least not while standing in the rain with his back still aching from Gallagher's ministrations. "You were the one who didn't want me around. As soon as I lost my job, it was like I didn't exist." He stopped himself before he said something more provocative and blew his chances entirely.

"You don't miss a trick, do you?" Mary countered. "What do you want?"

"Can I come in?" John asked in a conciliatory tone, the rain forming tiny rivulets as it migrated from his forehead to his chin. "Just to dry off?"

She hesitated, then stepped back, clutching at her robe to prevent him from copping a cheap peek. She left him alone in the entry while she went to find a dry towel.

Like many single women, she had decorated her walls with photographs of family and friends. There were pictures of her mother and father, her sister's kids, a couple of shots of her graduation from the police academy, even one of her in a pair of tight shorts whacking a softball. John perused them quickly until he came to two black-and-white prints mounted side by side—one of Mary and Ainsworth toasting punch glasses at what looked like an office Christmas party, the other of himself and Mary, hand in hand and wearing a pair of shit-eating grins, taken more than four years ago on a bracing autumn morning at the Santa Monica Pier. As he stared at the photo, he wondered if he could ever feel that close to anyone again.

Mary returned to see him looking at the picture. Feeling an uneasy combination of nostalgia and annoyance, she handed him the towel. "I think you should go," she said.

"I need your help," John confessed, handing the towel back to her. It was clear he was referring to the case, not his personal life, which in any event seemed beyond anyone's ability to repair.

"Are you crazy? I'm set to testify in this case, or have you forgotten? I shouldn't even be talking to you."

"Something's wrong." John fumbled for the right words. "I'm not sure Juan Thomas shot Richards. Something's going on inside the department. I think my client's been set up."

It was difficult for Mary to measure the greater insult: being lied to by an ex-lover or being asked to betray the department by a drunken lawyer desperate to help a guilty client. For a moment she considered showing Solomon the techniques she had picked up in her martial arts classes. She settled instead for a firm rebuke. "I knew you didn't come here to see me. I'm not going to let you into my life again and ruin it for me."

"Whatever happened was just as much your doing as mine," John said.

"What did happen, John? You tell me."

"We made a mistake."

"The only mistake was my going to bed with a guy who wasn't ready to have a relationship with a black woman."

She had played the ultimate trump card, like a personal declaration of war. He knew that answering back would only throw gasoline on the fire, but he couldn't control himself. "Is that what you tell Ainsworth?" he said with a sneer.

"Get out," she shouted, her eyes glazed with an anger he had never seen. "Now."

He opened the door and took a backward step outside. "Look, I'm sorry. I didn't come here to fight." He did his best to apologize, but Mary would have none of it. She slammed the door in his face, leaving him on the threshold, once again in the rain. "It wasn't because you were black," he said barely audibly. "It was never that."

---

* * *

He sat in his car outside Mary's house another good hour, taking slow sips from the pint bottle of J & B, thinking not about what had just happened but about the night so long ago when he and Mary first made love.

It was his last big case as chief trial deputy, the execution-style murder of the manager of a Burger King. Mary had recently been assigned to Robbery-Homicide and was named as his investigating officer, a position that required them to work closely together.

The night before the prelim she came to his office to go over her testimony. It was hot, and he was tired, not just physically but emotionally drained from Annabel's death a year before and the divorce that followed.

They began the prep session around seven, went for an hour, then paused for a ten-minute break. John walked down the deserted hallway to the coffee room and returned to find Mary sitting behind his desk, fanning herself with a magazine. She had unfastened the top two buttons of her blouse and had her eyes closed and head thrown back. He tried not to stare, but there was no denying the attraction he felt. It was the first time in months he had felt much of anything but grief and anger. It was a welcome, almost liberating sensation.

"Okay," he said, as much to announce his presence as to get back to work. "Let's go over your testimony again." He took one of the client seats in front of her and smiled. She seemed to smile, too, but in a different kind of way, as though she also felt some kind of attraction. He resisted the idea and continued, outwardly all business. "I'll ask you to state your name, your rank and describe your general job responsibilities in the department. Then we'll get into the details."

She only pretended to listen. "It's really hot in here, don't you think?" she asked. She smiled again and raised her right hand to move her reddish brown hair off her neck. The maneuver caused the opening in her shirt to widen, exposing a portion of her breasts and violet bra.

"They turn off the air-conditioning at six," John answered, eyes fixed on her cleavage. "You want something cold to drink?"

"No, I'm fine," she assured him, continuing to smile.

"Okay." Distracted by the mounting sexual tension, he began to fumble through his papers like an absentminded professor. "Did something unusual happen on the night in question?" That wasn't exactly the way he had phrased the question at the outset of the prep session, but for the moment he was too rattled to stick with the script.

"I saw a man," she answered.

"Good," he said, trying to get back on track. "Can you describe him?"

"He was tall, well built, dark hair." As she spoke, she got out of the chair, walked over to the window, and looked briefly at the downtown lights. Then she twisted the miniblinds to a closed position and sat down in the client chair next to John.

"Anything else?" John checked his notes. He could smell her perfume.

"He was kind, gentle, incredibly smart, and very attractive," she said, lightly touching his cheek with her hand. "And one day he was going to be a very powerful man."

It was Mary's script now, and John willingly decided to play along. "And did you approach this man?" he asked, taking her hand in his.

"At first I was afraid to." She looked directly in his eyes, as if to assure him she knew exactly what she was doing.

"Did something change your mind?"

"I decided to take a chance."

"And what did you do?"

"I did this," she whispered. She leaned toward him and kissed him softly on the mouth. He felt Mary's breath against his face and savored the aroma of her perfume, sweet sensations he had almost forgotten in his period of mourning. He took her head in his hands and felt the soft thickness of her hair. They kissed again, slowly at first, then passionately, eagerly, almost greedily. She undid his shirt and tie. He unfastened her blouse and bra and pressed his face against her breasts. They slid to the carpet and made love at the foot of the desk underneath the nameplate that read "John Solomon, Chief Trial Deputy."

For the next two months they were practically inseparable, bunking in one night at her place, the next at his. Animated by the adrenaline high that only new love can generate, they took in the latest movies, strolled along Venice Beach at sunset, and sampled the city's best cuisine over late-night candlelight dinners. Above all, they made love—fast and furious, soft and slow, free and uninhibited. The fact that she was black and he was white, and that it was the first interracial encounter for either, made it all the more exciting.

It was as though the emotional wreckage had been cleared from Solomon's life. For the first time in recent memory he felt happy. Then it all came crashing down, harder than ever, the afternoon he was summoned into Simon Lasker's office and Mary again became a stranger.

Solomon drained the last drops of the J & B and threw the bottle into the street, where it landed with a loud crash that sparked a chain reaction of barks and howls from the neighborhood dogs. He started his engine and pulled away from the curb, too drunk to notice the late-model Camaro that tailed him all the way home.

CHAPTER 11

The overnight rain purged the sky of a summer's worth of smog, and as dawn broke, the city woke up bright and clean. For the first time since last winter's storms, the second range of the San Gabriels was visible from downtown office buildings. It was a perfect day for cruising along Pacific Coast Highway with the top down, checking out the latest fashions on the secretaries, catching the Dodgers' home stand at Chavez Ravine, or just delighting in the forgotten art of breathing fresh air.

For Juan Thomas, it was the first day of a trial that would determine if he lived or died. Of all the legal controversies decided in American courts of law, none compared with a death penalty trial for procedural complexity, cutthroat advocacy, and sheer emotional wallop. Capital trials were particularly gut-wrenching for the twelve bewildered citizens whose status as registered voters resulted in their reluctant conscription as members of the jury.

Unlike other criminal cases, in which the jury could head for home after deciding on guilt or innocence, death penalty trials were divided into two separate segments or phases that required as many as three critical verdicts. During the guilt phase the jury was charged with deciding not only whether the defendant had committed first-degree murder but whether any statutory special circumstances charged against him were true. At the time of the Thomas trial there were no fewer than nineteen special circumstances set forth in section 190.2 of the California Penal Code, ranging from felony murder to murders carried out by destructive devices. Juan Thomas was charged under section 190.2 (7) with the murder of a peace officer, Joseph Michael Richards, in the performance of his duties.

The grand prize for the defense, of course, was to win the guilt phase or at least to avoid a specials finding. Failing that, the case moved on to the dreaded penalty segment, in which the jury was directed to balance such matters as the circumstances of the crime and the defendant's record against any mitigating aspects of his background and general character.

Prevailing at the penalty phase meant a sentence of life without the possibility of parole rather than death in the gas chamber or by means of lethal injection. To avoid the death penalty, a defendant had to fill the witness stand with reputable relatives, friends, teachers, and doctors capable of explaining his cold-blooded behavior as the product of a deprived childhood, fetal alcohol syndrome, or some other nonculpable factor. The goal was to "humanize" the defendant, to transform him into a person the jury would decline to condemn.

The trouble with Juan Thomas, as Stretch's investigation

had shown, was that he had no reputable friends, teachers, or associates, and the two psychiatrists appointed by the court diagnosed him as a remorseless sociopath. Thomas' entire world was his 'hood and his homies. In his case the penalty phase would be a mere formality, the last step on the conveyor belt to "the row" at San Quentin.

Knowing that he had no penalty case did nothing to brighten Solomon's worldview as he entered the crowded courtroom. He had no guilt case either. His plan, if it could be called one, was to follow a slight modification of the old trial lawyer's adage: "When the facts are against you, argue the law. When the law is against you, argue the facts. When they're both against you, go for the balls and see who screams." He had managed to pull himself together and arrived in a mood to do battle.

Stretch recognized the change in John immediately. There was a difference in the way he walked. The bounce in his step was back as he pushed open the swinging wooden gate that separates the spectators from the courtroom interior, the "playing field," as Stretch liked to call it. There was a difference in the way he dressed. In place of the rumpled sports jacket, he had on a dark pinstripe suit pressed so crisply he might have passed for an investment banker. There was also a difference in the way he eyed Ainsworth as he took a seat at the defense table. He had a look that seemed to say that the outcome might be inevitable, but he was going to make the prosecution sweat bullets before it was all done. There would be no rolling over.

Stretch felt like giving John a high five but settled instead for a professional handshake. "You look ready," he said, eliciting a knowing smile from John.

Ainsworth and Gallagher were also ready, the latter outfitted in his trademark police-issue sports coat and the former in his customary first-day-of-trial three-piece. They conferred quietly and did their best to avoid further eye contact with John and Stretch as Judge Rosten took the bench and the bailiff called the session to order.

"Are we ready to proceed, Counsel?" Rosten inquired. He had a tired look on his face, the result of a late night in the sack with one of the new female members of his rock-climbing club. More than twenty-five years older than his playmate, the judge was barely able to climb out of bed in the morning and had yet to recover fully. After receiving the obligatory affirmative responses from the lawyers, Rosten ordered the defendant brought out.

The accused has a constitutional right to be tried in civilian clothes and Stretch had gone to great lengths, even shelling out $150 of his own money, to have a new charcoal gray suit specially tailored for Juan Thomas. It was a good investment. As he was led into the court, Thomas looked nothing like the angry gangster who had been dragged, kicking and screaming, into the preliminary hearing. With a blue shirt, a red tie and his hair grown out, he was the best-dressed jailbird in the courthouse lockup.

The jurors were the last to enter and were by far the least comfortable as they filed into the box. In one of the justice system's great legal fictions, they had been admonished during the voir dire that they would have to put all thoughts of the death penalty aside during the guilt phase of the trial. Although they promised to do just that, the admonition was akin to a circus ringmaster telling the crowd not to think of an elephant as the houselights go down in the big top. The anxious expressions on their faces showed that only now did they fully appreciate that in this orderly, rule-governed proceeding they were being asked to play God.

No matter how long he had been a judge, at the outset of every trial, Rosten invariably experienced an odd mixture of jealousy and relief. The relief stemmed from the fact that apart from making evidentiary rulings and instructing the jury, he would be turning over the hard work of trying the case to the lawyers. The jealousy came from the realization that he would no longer be the center of attention. The conflict accounted at least in part for Rosten's ill-tempered demeanor on the bench.

"Ladies and gentlemen," Rosten told the jury, then cleared his throat and took a swallow of water. "We're now going to hear the opening statements of counsel. As you listen to them, please remember that an opening statement is not itself evidence and you should not consider it as such. Rather, it is what counsel anticipates the evidence will show after it has been presented." He cleared his throat again, took another swallow, and ceded the floor to Ainsworth.

Trial attorneys have always disagreed on the strategic importance of opening statements, just as they have always disagreed about right and wrong, night and day, black and white, and the subtle difference between proper courtroom decorum and in-your-face aggression. Some regard the opening as the most vital part of the trial, as an opportunity to make a winning first impression on the jury and entice its interest in the evidence to come. To such advocates, opening statements are to a trial what foreplay is to penetration: You either win or lose on the quality of your first move. To others, they are little more than ritualistic formalities capable of seducing the unwary attorney into promising more than the evidence can deliver, a cardinal sin that an attentive jury will neither forget nor forgive.

There was little disagreement, however, that Howard Ainsworth made some of the best opening statements in the business. Ainsworth liked to begin his openings from a seated position, giving the impression of folksy candor and informality, a technique that placed the jury at ease and set the stage for the more theatrical gestures he liked to employ once he really got rolling. This morning was no exception.

"This is a case of right and wrong, good and evil, life and death," he told the panel, looking directly, as was his custom, at the juror he believed most likely to question the prosecution's case. David Avila, the young El Monte postal clerk who had voiced some trepidations about capital punishment during voir dire, made eye contact with Ainsworth and did not turn away. Ainsworth took the reaction as a positive sign. "In that respect, the case is by no means unique," he continued, rising to his feet on the last syllable to make his way over to the jury box. "Evil and death stalk us every day of our lives, tempting us, challenging us, daring us to do right and avoid wrong." He paused to survey the twelve faces before him, decided they were buying his rendition of Jeremiah in a Brooks Brothers suit, and began to recount the facts of the case.

"In the early-morning hours of June the fifteenth, the forces of good and evil brought two men together in a terrible encounter that left one dead and the other charged with murder. Those men were Joseph Michael Richards, now deceased, and Juan Javahn Thomas, the defendant seated at counsel table." He paused again to point an accusing finger at Thomas, who squirmed noticeably in the seat next to John.

"Who was this man Joseph Richards, and how was the gift of life taken from him that June morning?" Ainsworth looked again at Avila and then at the other jury members as though engaging each in a heartfelt personal colloquy. "Joseph Richards was a policeman, a fifteen-year veteran of the Los Angeles Police Department, assigned to the Vice and Narcotics Division.

"Every police officer leads a life of danger but none more

so than those whose job it is to seek out the users, runners, and dealers of illegal drugs—drugs like heroin and cocaine—drugs that have become the mainstay of the street gangs terrorizing our communities, drugs that are seducing and poisoning the minds and bodies of our youth."

Like a televangelist selling the last tickets for the final train to heaven, Ainsworth exuded confidence. In any other locale, his cornball rhetoric might have seemed comical. In the controlled environment of a courtroom, it was positively commanding. He paced deliberately along the length of the jury box, carefully shifting the inflections of his speech, pounding his right fist in his left hand at all the appropriate junctures, as he told the jury of the murder at the Mustang Club and the evidence that would prove beyond a reasonable doubt that Juan Thomas unmistakably was the killer.

Although Solomon had always aligned himself with those who believed opening statements were overrated, it was easy to see that Ainsworth was running away with the jury's hearts and minds. A few more earnest references to good and evil and another forthright forefinger aimed at the defense, and the case would be over before the first warm rump descended on the witness stand. Deciding to object to an adversary's opening, however, is a delicate matter, a bit like walking in on someone using the toilet. Unless it's urgent, you're better off waiting your turn. John decided it was urgent. He rose to his feet and shouted the first thought that came to mind. "This isn't an opening statement; it's a sermon."

As objections go, it wasn't particularly well worded or even well founded. Rosten took less than ten seconds to deny the protest, but the disruption was well worth it. For the first time since he swaggered into court, Ainsworth was put on the defensive, his forward momentum and timing thrown unexpectedly off-balance. Suddenly losing his place, he asked the court reporter for a "read back" of the last two sentences of his speech, a request that cost him another ninety precious seconds.

By the time Ainsworth resumed his oration, the steam and passion were gone. A once-brilliant beginning was reduced to a pedestrian summary of the witnesses the prosecution planned to call and the testimony each would offer. Ainsworth promised to conclude the People's case by the week's end, urged the jurors to remain faithful to their responsibilities, and thanked them for their time and attention. It was a creditable opening but by no means measured up to his usual standards. As Ainsworth made his way back to the counsel table, he realized he had committed the kind of error in judgment that law students who have yet to set foot in court are repeatedly warned of: underestimating the opposition. He swore silently it would not happen again.

John's objective as he stood to deliver his own prefatory comments was less to educate the jury in the nuances of the evidence—which in any event were unfavorable—than to keep the prosecution in a negative light for as long as possible.

"This may be the first and last time in this trial that Howard Ainsworth and I agree on anything," he told the panel, eliciting outright smiles on at least three faces and traces of the same on the remainder. He moved in front of the jury box and continued. "This is indeed, as the prosecutor says, a case of life and death, and your responsibilities are awesome.

"But this case is even more than that. It is also a search for truth." Exactly what kind of truth he wasn't prepared to say, but the phrase was always compelling, and he could tell the jury was duly impressed. "Sometimes, however, the search is difficult. The truth is not always what it appears to be.

"Sometimes"—he raised his voice for dramatic effect—"in our rush to right a terrible wrong—and there is no question that the killing of Joe Richards was a terrible, terrible wrong—we accuse the wrong man. Sometimes, in our desire to uphold what is good and crush what is evil, we forget our own humanity. We give in to the urge to close a case, to move on with our careers." He lowered his voice to a near whisper, as if sharing a dirty secret. "We give in to our urge to win an election."

The words brought Ainsworth out of his chair faster than a hemorrhoid sufferer. "Move that the jury be admonished, Your Honor!" he sputtered. Under other circumstances he might have asked for a mistrial, but with such a strong case, that was the last thing the prosecution wanted.

Rosten instructed the jury to disregard John's remark and ordered him to stick to the evidence. John feigned contrition and turned again to face the jury. This time the jurors stared back poker-faced. It was impossible to tell if his latest gambit had won them over or convinced them he was just another sleazy defense attorney. He decided to play it safe.

"Contrary to what the prosecution has told you, the evidence, ladies and gentlemen, will not show that Juan Thomas is guilty of murder. Far from it. The evidence will show that Joe Richards is dead, but it will also show that his killer is still very much at large. Thank you." His comments were short, sweet, and on the money. He returned to his seat a new believer in the power of opening statements.

The remainder of the day was devoted to what trial lawyers call routine housekeeping matters. Ainsworth closed the morning session with the crew chief of the paramedic unit that attended to Sally Sutton in the parking lot of the Mustang Club and later drove her to a nearby hospital, where she was kept for a few hours for observation and then discharged under police escort.

The afternoon featured the halting testimony of a rookie patrol officer who was called to identify pictures of Richards' body. The rookie and his older and considerably less enthusiastic partner were the first to arrive at the crime scene and undertook the tasks of roping it off with yellow police tape, clearing it of rubberneckers and radioing headquarters for the homicide squad led by Lieutenant Gallagher. The rookie was followed by one of the deputy county medical examiners who performed the autopsy on Richards. A young female doctor who had only recently passed her state boards and spoke with a distinct southern drawl, she fixed the time of death as approximately 2:30 A.M. and the cause as three gunshot wounds through the heart, chest, and lungs. John allowed them to testify without objection, and Rosten called it a day at half past four.

Avoiding the press at Swanson's was never easy, and John and Stretch had to invoke their own version of the Fifth as they pushed their way past two bourbon-breathed reporters to Solomon's corner booth. Although he had worked through lunch, John was wound up tighter than a CPA at tax time and had no thoughts of eating. He ordered black coffee, pulled out a well-worn case file, and began poring through the police reports on the search of Thomas' home. He knew he had lost a pretrial suppression motion, but he couldn't help thinking the gun had been found a little too quickly. Somewhere there had to be an angle for cross-examination. His frustration was evident.

Stretch noticed the lines of tension etched on John's face but chose to ignore them as he plowed his way through an enormous plate of roast beef and mashed potatoes and perused the latest issue of the *L.A. Weekly*. The *Weekly* was one of those quintessential L.A. phenomena, a trendy left-leaning tabloid whose editors liked to think of it as a West Coast equivalent of the *Village Voice* but whose readers— like Stretch—were mostly drawn to the record and film reviews, the sexually suggestive tanning, body sculpture and lingerie ads, and, above all, the provocative personals.

What passed as dinner for two was capped off by a less than leisurely four-block stroll to John's office south of Swanson's, an area of town where Spanish served as the native tongue not just on the lips of pedestrians but on everything from storefront signs and restaurant menus to movie marquees. The tiny two-room office, all two hundred square feet of it, was a third-floor walk-up in an old brick building that had barely escaped the wrecking ball in the city's last ineffective crackdown on unreinforced structures. According to the seismologists at Cal Tech, such buildings were earthquake disasters waiting to happen. The "big one," the killer quake that was due any day to turn the San Fernando Valley into beachfront property and drop the rest of Los Angeles into the Pacific, would flatten them like unleavened bread.

They spent the next three hours under the cheery glow of an overhead fluorescent light debating the merits of every sentence in every report and motion in the case file. When they came for the fourth time to the affidavits Mary and Gallagher had executed in support of the search warrant, Stretch saw a serious problem in the making. John still hadn't eaten. Five strong cups of black coffee had left his hands shaking like a junkie's as he studied photographs of the murder weapon, Richards' body, and the Thomas lineup under the light. John's frustration had metamorphosed into a kind of manic anxiety made all the more desperate by the dismal surroundings.

The first day of trial was behind them, and John had performed far better than expected; but Stretch had seen it in other lawyers many times before. John was already showing the signs of burnout. Whether it was just the coffee, the years of physical neglect, or the pressure of the case didn't really matter. If he continued like this, he'd be a basket case by Friday morning. Stretch looked at John sitting bent over at his desk and considered the delicacy of the situation. "You need to loosen up a little," he said. He lifted his copy of the *Weekly* out of his briefcase and plopped down on the small cloth-covered couch across from John.

"Thanks for the advice. I'll remember it next time you get me appointed on another winner," John replied without looking up.

Stretch ignored him and turned his attention to the *Weekly*. "Maybe what you need is to get laid," he said matter-of-factly.

It was a remark from left field, deep left field, but it was right on the mark, and it succeeded in getting John's attention. John put down his pen and closed his file. "What did you say?"

"You heard me." Stretch feigned a deadpan expression and pointed to the personals. "Look, here's one for you. 'DWF,' that's divorced white female, 'fond of rock musicians and hard up, sorry-ass attorneys, any shape, any size, your office or mine. Must be a professional.' " He let his eyes roam across the page like a shopper in a department store. John was not amused, but Stretch was determined to continue. "Here's another. 'Attractive feminine, submissive adventuress. Seeks visionary dominant SWM. Let me feel your warmth.' That's you, baby, especially the dominant part. You know about those exotic escapades." He made a mildly obscene gesture with his tongue and forefinger.

A reluctant smile broke across John's face, and he began to laugh. He knew the case file inside and out, and he knew Stretch was right, not about the submissive adventuress or exotic escapades—as far he could remember, Stretch liked his women tall, full-breasted, and straight—but about the need to conserve his energy for "crunch time," as Stretch put it in yet another basketball reference. The redoubtable Stretch Johnson, he thought to himself. All he needed was a bowl of chicken soup, a sex change, and a shave, and he'd qualify as the world's tallest Jewish mother.

CHAPTER 12

Outfitted in a neatly pressed uniform, with her badge pinned over the left breast pocket of her short-sleeved dark blue shirt, Mary looked and sounded the part of the police professional. Nonetheless, Ainsworth proceeded cautiously. Mindful of the way he had been upstaged the day before, he had decided to play things conservatively, at least at the outset. He took Mary on a slow-developing direct examination, having her explain her career assignments in the department, her current position as special liaison to the DA's chief trial deputy, and her role in reviewing and helping to prepare the search and arrest warrants.

It was all very competent but lacked the usual fanfare John had come to expect from Ainsworth. Throughout the Q&A Mary's eyes shifted between Ainsworth and the jury but studiously avoided John. She seemed otherwise calm and natural, however, and John regarded her behavior as a sign of contempt, confirming that his impromptu visit in the rain had made him yet another enemy.

Finally, Ainsworth came to the inherently dramatic moment in any homicide trial when the prosecution introduces the murder weapon. As cautious as he might have felt earlier, it was clear he would exploit this phase of the examination for all it was worth. He picked up the .357 magnum from the prosecution table and held it in his right hand, pausing briefly to allow the jury to catch a clear cross section of the firearm. Even those jurors who had begun to tire from the morning's slow pace were suddenly wide-eyed and attentive.

Ainsworth requested permission to approach the witness, handed Mary the gun, and asked her to identify the weapon. "And where was this gun when you found it?" he asked.

"Underneath the wooden steps of the front porch of the defendant's home." In her small hands the magnum looked especially sinister and deadly.

"What was its condition?" he continued, still standing within an intimate distance.

"It had been thrown in the dirt, but otherwise it was fully operable." She reflected on her use of police jargon, then added, "It was in good shape."

"And what did you do with it?"

"The weapon was booked into evidence and turned over to ballistics for testing."

Mary handed the gun back to Ainsworth, who took it back to the counsel table and put it carefully next to his notepad, in full view of the jury. "Your witness," he said, looking in John's direction.

John studied his own notes and stood to begin his cross from behind the defense table. Deciding where to stand while examining a witness is an art in itself. While many attorneys routinely station themselves behind the lectern that divides the counsel tables, a position that imparts a professorial air to the questioner, others prefer to stand close to the jury box in an effort to force the witness to look directly at the men and women whose task it is to assess the witness's credibility. Still others prefer to roam between the box and lectern, firing their questions like motormouth gunfighters shooting from the lip.

John's decision to remain at the counsel table was designed to force Mary to look squarely at him. The maneuver made her noticeably uncomfortable.

"Officer Delgado," John said, "you don't know *who* put the gun underneath the porch of my client's home, do you?"

It was a typical cross-examination question, geared to extract a concession that seemed much more important than it really was. Still, Mary had no choice but to answer honestly. "No, I don't." She folded her arms defensively, the muscles in her jaw tightening.

"In fact, there were no fingerprints on the gun, were there?"

Mary thought the question over, waiting to see if Ainsworth raised an objection. Technically the question called for a hearsay answer because the pistol had been dusted by forensics and she had nothing to do with its report. Hearing no protest from Ainsworth, she guardedly offered what she knew. "I believe that's correct."

John pressed on with his attack. "So for all you know, the gun could have been placed under the porch by someone else?"

"That's possible," she conceded, her discomfort level rising.

"Could have been a neighbor?"

"That's possible."

"Could have been another gang member?"

"I don't know about that," she replied sharply.

"Might even have been a cop?" John said in an accusatory tone that served the dual purpose of rattling Mary's chains and planting the idea of a police setup in the minds of the jurors.

"Objection, no foundation!" Ainsworth boomed like a morally aggrieved Sunday school teacher. To his astonishment, however, Rosten ordered Mary to answer.

"Absolutely not," she shot back, not knowing whom she loathed more at the moment, John for impugning her integrity or Ainsworth for failing to protect it.

"Exactly how long did it take you to find the gun?" John asked, broaching the subject that had dogged him from the preliminary hearing.

"Maybe fifteen minutes," Mary answered, determined to keep her remarks as brief and unrevealing as possible.

"Only fifteen minutes?" John asked incredulously. "Sounds like you knew where to search."

"I'm an experienced officer," Mary replied. She had a look of hatred in her eyes so intense it could have made water boil.

"I'm sure you are," John replied mildly. "Nothing further," he added coolly as he returned to his seat, leaving Mary seething on the stand. The jurors had been treated to an exhibition of cross-examination at its furious best. They had no idea that they had also witnessed a lovers' quarrel spawned by the conflicting loyalties of the criminal justice system.

For the first time since John ripped into his special liaison, a smile crossed Ainsworth's lips. Standing at the counsel table, Ainsworth guided Mary through redirect, exuding calm and confidence. "Is there a reason why you first searched outside the defendant's home?" he asked.

"Yes," she said, sensing the strategy behind Ainsworth's laid-back approach. "In the last ten gang cases I've worked on, we've found guns outside the home, hidden on the property."

"And why is that?" Ainsworth inquired, glancing at John.

"The gangs have gotten smart. They can always claim that somebody else planted the guns there. Either that or their lawyers can."

It was the perfect answer, and John realized to his chagrin that his attack on Mary had only set the stage for it. He thought briefly about objecting but quickly reconsidered when he caught a glimpse of Stretch shaking his head in disgust. John had "opened the door" to the volatile and otherwise inadmissible subject of Thomas' gang connections on cross-examination, hoping to lay the groundwork for his theory about the gun. Now that the door was ajar, he had no legal basis in the rules of evidence to complain about Mary's testimony. Ainsworth had given him a long rope to play with on cross, and he had unwittingly hanged himself. It was that simple.

John declined to question Mary further, and she was excused. She walked out of the courtroom, casting a barely perceptible glance in John's direction.

Ainsworth used the next witness to erase any doubts that the magnum was in fact the murder weapon. John Seymour was a small, bespectacled man in his early fifties with a fringe of thick dark hair surrounding a bald head that glistened with the reflection of the courtroom's ceiling lights. Dressed in a quiet gray sports coat and with a multicolored array of lead pencils and ballpoint pens fastened to the left breast pocket of his plain white button-down shirt, he looked like an underpaid high school physics teacher. Actually, he was the most senior firearms examiner on the LAPD's payroll.

He and Ainsworth had worked together on several homicides and had the routine down like a pair of ballroom dancers. John and Ainsworth had "stipulated" to Seymour's findings at the preliminary hearing, thereby avoiding the need for Seymour to testify in Municipal Court before Judge Lawler. But Ainsworth had no thought of entering into a "stip" in a jury trial. He wanted the jury to hear every word that Seymour had to say.

The examination began in the familiar way with a recitation of the witness's credentials. Seymour explained that he had a Bachelor of Science degree in physics, earned twenty years earlier at Cal State Long Beach, after he had been placed on extended medical leave following an encounter with an angel-dusted robbery suspect that left him with a deep gunshot wound to the left thigh. He was a young and spry patrol officer back then, but the wound made it impossible for him to carry out the duties of a street cop. Not wishing to leave the department, he apprenticed himself to one of the sergeants in the criminalistics section and discovered he had an affinity for the science of ballistics.

"And how long, Mr. Seymour," Ainsworth continued from behind the lectern, "have you been a firearms examiner with the LAPD?"

"Exactly seventeen years this month," Seymour answered, adjusting the glasses on his nose.

"And can you tell us, sir, what a firearms examiner does?"

"It's my job to decide if a particular bullet was fired by a particular gun. In most cases the bullet is one recovered from the body of a human being, a crime victim, and the gun is one police suspect of being used to perpetrate that crime."

Ainsworth took a moment to set up the two-by-three-foot poster of a standard gun barrel and cartridge that Seymour used to illustrate the basic principles of the science. With Rosten's permission, Seymour stepped down from the witness stand, picked up a pointer, and, in response to occasional inquiries from Ainsworth, explained that every cartridge, or casing, actually contained two distinct explosive charges. The first, called the primer, is ignited on contact with the gun's firing pin. The primer, in turn, sparks the propellant, which releases a surge of highly compressed gas that forces the bullet, or slug, out of the cartridge, through the spiral ridges of the barrel, and into the air. When he was finished with the lecture, Seymour, confident that his class had mastered the fundamentals, looked at the jury, tapped the pointer lightly in his hand, and returned to the stand.

Ainsworth retrieved the magnum from the counsel table where it had remained since Mary's testimony and approached the witness. "In this case," he asked, handing the gun to Seymour, "did you conduct any tests to determine if this was the gun used in the homicide of Police Lieutenant Joe Richards?"

Seymour examined the evidence tag, collected himself, and answered thoughtfully, "I conducted a standard test firing and a microscopic comparison of a bullet of the same caliber with one retrieved from the body of the deceased."

"And what in particular were you looking for?"

Seymour adjusted his glasses again as he prepared to deliver another professorial exegesis. "What we call lands and grooves, the distinctive markings etched on a bullet by the ridges of the barrel as the bullet spirals forward."

"And what conclusions did you reach?" Ainsworth asked, raising his voice slightly.

Seymour took off his glasses and held them in his right

hand near his cheek. "There's no doubt about it: Whoever shot Joe Richards used this gun."

John stood up for cross-examination, knowing his time at the lectern would be brief. Seymour had conclusively tied the magnum to the murder, and it would have been foolhardy to attack his qualifications, so John settled on the only available option: arguing that someone other than Thomas pulled the trigger.

"Of course," he asked, "there's no way of telling who fired the gun, is there, Mr. Seymour?"

"Not from the tests I performed," Seymour conceded, his back stiffening to meet whatever challenge John might throw his way.

"And there were no identifiable prints on the weapon, were there?"

Not being a "print man," Seymour technically lacked the credentials to respond. But once again Ainsworth failed to interpose an objection, and Seymour reluctantly answered, "That's my understanding."

John closed his cross on what seemed to be a high note, but Ainsworth moved quickly to negate any defense gains. It was a carbon copy of the maneuver he had pulled off with Mary, and John, in truth, should have seen it coming.

"Tell me, Mr. Seymour," he said, holding the magnum high in his right hand, "how difficult would it be to wipe fingerprints from a weapon like this?"

"It wouldn't be hard at all," Seymour replied. "Even a shoeshine rag would do the trick."

It didn't take a genius to see that the jury swallowed the firearm examiner's testimony like Sunday morning Gospel.

The morning clearly had been a triumph for Ainsworth, boosting his confidence and restoring the momentum he had lost on the first day of trial. But momentum in a trial can be difficult to sustain, and the problem Ainsworth proposed to tackle in the afternoon session—proving the special circumstance that Joe Richards was killed while in the performance of his duties—was one of the trickier aspects of the case. In a jury trial he couldn't rely on Gallagher's knowledge of the Mustang Club as a hangout for dopers and whores, as he had done at the preliminary hearing. Since Gallagher had had no personal contact with Richards on the night of the murder, his testimony would never prove the special beyond a reasonable doubt. Nor did Ainsworth feel comfortable relying solely on Sally, at least not when he had another witness available to corroborate the reason for Richards' visit to the club. That witness was the club's owner, Joe Hidalgo.

Hidalgo arrived in court as he usually arrived everywhere—overdressed in an eight-hundred-dollar white double-breasted suit and blue silk shirt, with perspiration glistening on his forehead. The expensive threads were the result of too much money and too little taste, while the perspiration was the lingering aftereffect of a bout of tropical disease he had contracted as a young man in pre-Castro Cuba. The combination of gaudy dress and sweat made the dark-haired Hidalgo a decidedly unappealing figure as he sat on the stand, daubing his swarthy brow with a pale pink monogrammed handkerchief. Still, he had valuable evidence to offer in support of the People's case, and Ainsworth was determined to see that it was received.

Ainsworth took up his position behind the lectern, both to assume a professional pose and to place as much psychological distance between himself and the witness as possible. Hidalgo answered Ainsworth's questions in the thick Cuban accent that his customers at the Mustang Club had grown accustomed to but that the jury found both amusing and occasionally difficult to decipher.

After establishing that Hidalgo was the sole owner of the

club and that he was on the scene the night of the Richards homicide, Ainsworth asked the witness to explain the nature of the club's business. "It's a nightclub." Hidalgo shrugged with a show of nervousness. "A place of, I suppose you would say, adult entertainment." He looked to the jury for approval but found only blank stares.

"The club sells hard liquor and features erotic nude dancing, does it not, Mr. Hidalgo?" Ainsworth inquired.

"It's a legitimate operation," Hidalgo stammered, wiping his forehead again. "A man's got a right to make a living in this country, doesn't he? This isn't Cuba."

Ainsworth ignored Hidalgo's protestations and turned a page in his legal pad. "Prior to the night that Officer Richards was shot, had members of the vice squad ever made any arrests at the club?"

Hidalgo took a couple of deep breaths. "I can't help it if some of my customers carry things they're not suppose to. We have a big sign—'no drugs allowed.' " He made a sweeping motion with his hands to emphasize the immensity of the sign, looking at the jury for approval. "We cooperate always with the LAPD. I'm a businessman, strictly legitimate," he said, trying to sound convincing.

"And one of the officers you cooperated with was Joe Richards, isn't that right?" Ainsworth continued.

"Yes. Joe Richards was a good man. We talk all the time. Very friendly. Whatever the police want, Joe Hidalgo is ready to help. Always."

"In fact, you spoke with him on June fourteenth, the day before he was shot, didn't you?"

"Yes."

"Tell the jury, Mr. Hidalgo, what Officer Richards said to you," Ainsworth commanded.

John stood up to make a hearsay objection but just as quickly returned to his seat, realizing that Ainsworth could qualify Hidalgo's answer under a time-honored legal doctrine known as the state of mind exception to the hearsay rule. Normally the hearsay rule prohibited witnesses from repeating what third parties had said outside the courtroom. But there were so many exceptions to the rule that a skillful lawyer could almost always find a way around it. Under the state of mind exception, Hidalgo would be permitted to relate what Richards told him as long as Richards' comments were offered into evidence to explain why the officer had come to the club the morning he was shot. The proposed line of questioning went to the heart of the special circumstance alleged against Thomas and was indisputably relevant.

Ainsworth took no notice of John's calisthenics and stared at Hidalgo, a form of silent communication that let him know he'd be facing the dark side of a perjury complaint if he strayed even slightly from the truth.

"Officer Richards, he come to my office the day before he was killed. He say he would be at the club next night," Hidalgo answered. He paused to take another deep breath.

"And what else did he say?" Ainsworth interrupted.

"He tell me he was looking for someone, who I don't know. He ask me to make sure we close on time, that he be there, at the Mustang Club, that he intend to make an arrest."

"Is that all?" Ainsworth asked sternly.

"Yes, I cooperate fully," Hidalgo pleaded. "I'm just a businessman."

"Thank you, Mr. Hidalgo." Ainsworth smiled and returned to his seat.

John dug through his briefcase and pulled out the discovery file the prosecution had turned over to him prior to trial. In addition to the police reports on the case, the file contained the rap sheets on Juan Thomas and Sally Sutton, which set forth the legal histories of their convictions and arrests. The file also contained a New York State rap sheet on Joe Hidalgo.

"Tell me, Mr. Hidalgo," John asked, "before you came to Los Angeles, you lived in New York, didn't you?"

Hidalgo, who believed the worst was already over, was shocked at the mention of the Big Apple. "I own a nightclub there, but that was more than ten years ago," he said.

John glanced at Hidalgo's rap sheet as he walked over to the jury box. "What happened to your New York club?" he asked.

"I sold it," Hidalgo answered, looking in Ainsworth's direction for help.

"Why?"

"I don't know," Hidalgo responded, wiping another wave of perspiration this time not only from his brow but from both cheeks as well. "I wanted to move to L.A. I like the climate here," he added, looking, despite his professed love of the local weather, like a plantation owner suffering from heat stroke. He smiled, attempting to make friends with his interrogator.

John scanned the jury, then quickly turned back to Hidalgo. He had no intention of accepting the witness's olive branch. "Did it have anything to do with your indictment by a New York State grand jury for insurance fraud? That was ten years ago, too, wasn't it?"

Hidalgo took a hard swallow but was spared the embarrassment of an answer as Ainsworth rose from his chair to demand a sidebar conference. The jurors watched attentively as Ainsworth and John came forward and crowded in close to the bench to prevent them from overhearing the discussion.

"What's all this about insurance fraud?" Rosten asked, wishing to keep the exchange as brief as possible.

"It's right here in his rap sheet," John answered, handing the document to Rosten. "He was charged under section 176.25 of the Penal Law of New York."

"But it doesn't matter," Ainsworth quickly interjected. "The case was dropped. In fact, this witness's rap sheet shows only two prior misdemeanor convictions for driving under the influence. So unless the defense has some independent proof of the alleged fraud, counsel's questions are improper."

Rosten mulled the matter over. It was a complicated issue. A ballot initiative ratified by California voters in 1982—the so-called Victims' Bill of Rights, the first in a series of law and order measures that had transformed the face of the state's criminal justice system since the early 1980's—had changed the state's law pertaining to the impeachment of witnesses in criminal trials. Under a section of the initiative dubbed "truth in evidence," a witness could be impeached simply by showing he had committed "prior bad acts." It was no longer necessary to show that such acts had resulted in a felony conviction as long as the prior acts could be proved and were found relevant to the witness's credibility.

"Can you prove your fraud allegation, Counsel?" Rosten asked John. When John conceded he had nothing but the rap sheet to fall back on, Rosten shook his head slowly. "In that case the court will exercise its discretion to exclude the question. It just opens up a can of worms better left closed."

"A can of worms, Your Honor?" John asked, a touch of irritation in his tone.

"You heard me, Mr. Solomon, a can of worms," Rosten said again. "Long unconstitutional ones that the Supreme Court hates to find in trial records." He flicked the fingers of his right hand, simultaneously ridding himself and the case of the annoying annelids. His patience was wearing thin with the two lawyers hovering close enough to kiss him. It was nearly four-thirty, and Rosten had a six o'clock dinner date in Santa Monica with his lady rock climber. Invoking his judicial prerogatives, Rosten declared it was time to move on.

Ainsworth and John returned to their seats, and Rosten instructed the jury to disregard the entire subject of Hidalgo's indictment. Knowing that the panel would be able to do no such thing, John decided to let Hidalgo step down and slink his way into the late-afternoon sun as the day's proceedings came to a close. Whether John had accomplished anything more than proving that Hidalgo was as big a sleazebag as he appeared to be remained an open question. For the time being at least, Ainsworth had "proved up" his special circumstance allegation and was proceeding as scheduled toward a clean sweep of the guilt phase.

CHAPTER 13

There comes a time in every hotly contested trial when an advocate pauses to appreciate the skills of his adversary. As John inched his Mustang forward on the southbound Harbor Freeway, fighting his way through the evening rush hour, he couldn't help admiring Ainsworth's performance. From the trap he laid for John in his examination of Mary to the seamless Q&As with Seymour and Hidalgo, Ainsworth showed both a mastery of the rules of evidence and a sense of strategy that John never knew he possessed. Solomon couldn't have done a better job himself, even in the old days.

The examination of Hidalgo, however, gave John a minor opening, one he and Stretch had debated over corned beef sandwiches at Swanson's. If Hidalgo and Joe Richards were well acquainted, how was it that the officer's wife,

Estelle Richards, had never heard of the Mustang Club? Both he and Stretch knew that Estelle was holding back on them. That much was clear from the medical file John found in her bedroom. The question was, Why she was holding back, and why hadn't she shown up at the trial?

With box seats for the Dodger game and a hot date to go with them, Stretch urged John to hold off on the mysteries of Joe Richards until tomorrow. But the advice wasn't worth the fifteen seconds it took to deliver. John was never one to wait. Not when he was a little kid looking forward to the start of another football season, not when he was married and anticipating a two-week vacation somewhere with lots of white sand and palm trees, and, most of all, not now. He left Stretch picking his teeth at Swanson's and decided to pose the questions himself directly to Estelle Richards.

Even though it was only early evening, a well-dressed white man venturing into an all-black neighborhood in South Central L.A. stands out like a nudist on a street corner. The residents can spot the intruder a block away and instinctively sense he hasn't come for a social visit.

Estelle Richards no doubt would have been keenly annoyed at Solomon's return if she had been home. But the lights were out at the small wood-frame house, and five minutes of pounding on the front door succeeded only in rousing her next-door neighbor. The voice of the old man, who had crossed over to the Richards yard and moved within a few feet of the door, caught John by surprise. "What's the trouble here, mister?" the man asked with just a touch of rancor.

John turned quickly and prepared for the worst, a surge of adrenaline coursing through his body. He raised his fists defensively as the old man began to hiss and cackle with unrestrained laughter. "I've seen better moves on Aunt Emma.

Didn't anyone teach you? You got to lead with your left."
The old man flashed a toothless grin. Standing there in a
flannel nightshirt, snapping the set of red suspenders that
supported his baggy gray pants, the only threat he posed
was to the bottle of fortified wine he had been working on.

John's fear subsided and gave way to embarrassment.
"I'm looking for Estelle Richards," he stammered, trying his
best to put on a businesslike front.

"Well, you lookin' in the wrong place." The old man
continued to smile, thoroughly enjoying John's obvious
discomfort.

"Doesn't she still live here?" John asked incredulously.

"Mrs. Richards went to St. Louis, visiting her momma."
The old man snapped his suspenders again and, thinking the
show was over, shuffled off across the lawn.

John hurried off the steps in hot pursuit. "When?" he
shouted, spinning the old man around by the shoulder. Up
close the man looked at least seventy-five, his hair and
beard a seamless patchwork of gray and white. John relaxed
his grip and caught his breath. "It's important. I've got to
know."

"What do I look like, the yellow pages?" The old man
began to turn away as John reached into his pocket and
fished out a twenty-dollar bill. The old man shot back a
look of disgust. "I don't need your money. Nobody down
here does." He gestured at the neighborhood with a majes-
tic sweep of his hand as he crossed into his own yard.

"I'm sorry," John called after him. "I didn't mean any
offense."

The old man took a seat on a wicker chair on his porch
and watched John head slowly for his Mustang. As he
reached for the driver's side door, John heard the old man
yell out, "Last Thursday she left for the airport. A big old
nasty white man with a brown mustache and the angriest

eyes this side of Sonny Liston come to take her and the kids."

John looked up to thank him, but the man had already disappeared inside. The description fitted Lieutenant Gallagher down to the last scowl.

John caught sight of Ainsworth just as the prosecutor stepped off the elevator en route to Rosten's courtroom early Thursday morning. "We've got to talk," John snapped.

The glare in his eyes told Ainsworth a potential brouhaha was in the offing. Puzzled, but hoping to avoid a public confrontation, Ainsworth suggested they step into the men's room.

The architects who drew up the plans for the Criminal Courts Building must have saved the rest room specifications for last, knowing that the remaining funds on the county contract would be practically exhausted when it came time to install the fixtures and appointments. Either that or they knew that the suffering multitudes who, over the decades, would relieve themselves in the stalls and urinals would leave them looking like the johns at a downtown bus station. There was the same institutional light brown tile on the floors and walls, the same cracked and broken mirrors, the same backed-up toilets. Only the graffiti was different, interspersing vulgar observations on the quality of American justice with the usual salacious commentary about the preferences of white women for jumbo-sized black genitalia and the thrills of anal intercourse.

Fortunately it was still very early, not yet 8:30 A.M., and with the exception of a teenage cholo combing his hair at one of the sinks, the room was deserted. The kid took a look at John and Ainsworth, figured a law enforcement confab was about to begin, and did a bad-ass strut out the door.

"I'll give you five minutes," Ainsworth said, looking at his watch. His tone was brusque and unfriendly, but in his own mind he was behaving nothing short of magnanimously in relinquishing even a second of preparation time to hear John's complaints.

"This case stinks, Howard," John began.

"If you're referring to the murder committed by your client, I entirely agree," Ainsworth replied pompously.

"I'm referring to your case, Howard. It's phony—just like you." John took a step toward Ainsworth and for a moment considered throwing a punch. "The only reason you dragged this into court was so you could grandstand before the press. Your campaign is probably saving a fortune in free publicity."

"Now you have four minutes," Ainsworth replied, refusing to retreat. "This case is here because your client is guilty and for no other reason."

"Then tell me why Gallagher shuttled Estelle Richards out of town. How is it that the widow of a murdered man would skip on the eve of trial? What does she know, Howard?"

A look of surprise came over Ainsworth as if he were impressed at John's resourcefulness in following Mrs. Richards' trail. He paused to collect his thoughts. "I think it had something to do with her father's heart attack. Bad timing." He smiled in a half-smug, half-sympathetic manner. "I appreciate your effort, John, I really do, but conspiracy theories are an insult to us all." He turned and walked away, leaving John to twist on his words and stare back in angry silence.

By any measure, Sally Sutton was the key to a prosecution victory. On Ainsworth's advice, she showed up for trial looking even more prim and proper than she had at the prelim, dressed in a borrowed blue business suit, a dignified strand of white pearls draped over her gray sweater. But there was no way to conceal her sexual magnetism, and there was no way to avoid the fact that she was a former prostitute who had once been placed on probation for cocaine possession.

Rather than let Solomon bring out her record on cross-examination, Ainsworth had Sally testify on direct about her career as a topless dancer and a call girl. For the men on the jury, this seemed to present no particular problem. They smiled reassuringly at Sally's nervousness and tried not to be too conspicuous in the way they stared at her mouth and breasts. The women were a different matter, folding their arms defensively, shaking their heads ever so slightly as Sally recounted the tawdry details of her life. In an odd twist of form, Ainsworth found himself thinking like a defense attorney, hoping that the jurors remained true to their oath and based their verdict strictly on the evidence rather than on their personal views of Sally's character.

With the facts of Sally's steamy past behind him, Ainsworth zeroed in on the murder. "Ms. Sutton, what time did you get off work on the morning Officer Richards was shot?" he asked, standing at the midline of the jury box, acting as a buffer between his witness and the panel.

"I finished dancing about two A.M. and went to my car around a half hour later," Sally recounted convincingly.

"What happened then?" Ainsworth inquired, hoping that she would stick to the story she had related previously.

"Officer Richards asked to speak with me."

"And what exactly did he say?"

Sensing that the payoff was at hand, Sally cleared her throat. "He introduced himself as a vice and narcotics cop—I mean, officer—and asked if I had seen a young black man with one of those fade hairdos hanging around the club." She raised her hands and pressed them to the sides of her hair to illustrate the stylized coiffure of the suspect. The movement of her arms caused her jacket to open, exposing the silhouette of her breasts. The men on the panel smiled with wide-eyed approval.

"And what did you say?" Ainsworth continued.

"Before I could even answer," Sally replied with a tremulous voice, "a car pulled up alongside of us. Officer Richards walked over to the driver." She choked back a rush of tears. "That's when it happened."

Even the women jurors were feeling sympathy for Sally now as they prepared to hear the gory details of a killing committed before a young woman's eyes. Sensing the tide of emotions had turned in his favor, Ainsworth asked gently, "Tell me, please, exactly what you saw."

"I saw the driver of the car shoot Officer Richards." Her voice broke as she revisited the horror. "Officer Richards fell back on the parking lot. There was blood everywhere."

The courtroom became absolutely still, the only movements those of the court reporter pecking away at her transcriber.

"I know this is painful," Ainsworth said, breaking the silence. He walked back to the prosecution table and continued. "Do you see the driver of that car in court today?"

"Yes," Sally sobbed, pointing through her tears at a somber Juan Thomas. "Over there."

Ainsworth asked to have the record reflect Sally's identification of the defendant and passed the witness on for cross-examination.

"It was two-thirty A.M. at the end of another long night of dancing when Joe Richards was shot, isn't that right?" Solomon asked, with more than a modicum of menace. There was no particular reason to treat this witness with kid gloves. If the jury swallowed Sally's testimony, the guilt phase was all but over. In any event, the jury was unlikely to regard John as a brute for coming straight at Sally. She wasn't an aggrieved widow, and she was hardly the girl next door, unless you lived in a neighborhood unfit for small children and stable marriages.

Sally composed herself and answered in the affirmative, bracing for the anticipated verbal combat.

"And you were tired, weren't you?"

"I suppose so."

"Dancing is, after all, hard work," John prodded, insinuating that while it might be hard, it couldn't be considered honest, at least not in Sally's case.

"Yes, I told you that before," Sally responded stiffly in a reference to the prelim that the jury could not possibly have grasped.

"And you were on your way—"

Sally refused to let John complete the question. "I was on my way home to go to bed—by myself," she snapped, eliciting a chain reaction of titters and smirks from the spectators and the jury.

John alone was unamused. "Could you please let me finish my questions before you answer?"

"I knew what you were going to say," Sally remarked indignantly, sparking another round of barely suppressed laughter. "I know what you think of me."

"Just answer counsel's questions," Rosten reproved, reasserting control of the proceedings. Sally promised to oblige with a show of exaggerated contrition, and Rosten nodded in John's direction for him to proceed, clearly in no mood to endure a game of one-upmanship between a defense lawyer and a hooker.

John was given permission to approach and walked up to the rail of the witness stand. He had a predatory look in his eyes that made Sally's stomach roll. "Now exactly how long did you have to observe the driver in your tired and sleepy condition?"

As any experienced criminal trial lawyer knows, eyewitnesses often overestimate the amount of time taken to make their IDs. Sally was no exception. "I don't know," she answered, her voice cracking with uncertainty, "maybe a minute, minute and a half."

John pulled a shiny stopwatch from his jacket pocket and held it like a newly minted silver dollar in front of Sally. "I'm going to click this stopwatch on, Ms. Sutton," he instructed, "and ask you just how long you looked at the driver. When you're finished, I'll click it off."

Ainsworth stood up to object, but Rosten enjoyed courtroom demonstrations and was eager to see this one unfold. He ordered the prosecutor to park his posterior in his seat, then gave John the green light with an imperious wave of his right hand.

John held the stopwatch aloft. "Are you ready, Ms. Sutton?"

Sally nodded slowly, all traces of the once-confident witness she had been evaporating in the face of the relentless second hand before her.

"Go!" John shouted like a referee firing a starter's pistol.

Sally paused, looking suddenly thoughtful as the courtroom once more fell into complete silence. Then, just as suddenly, she signaled for John to stop. John clicked the watch again and disclosed the results of the test, his eyes fixed coolly on Sally. "Seven seconds. Seven seconds to identify a man you had never seen before, at two-thirty in the morning, in the midst of gunshots." He walked triumphantly back to the counsel table, announcing he had no further questions.

* * *

News in the Criminal Courts Building travels fast, and by the afternoon break Solomon's cross was already a hot item at the courthouse cafeteria. Located on the first floor with an unrestricted view of the pedestrian traffic on Temple Street, the cafeteria was a last resort for lawyers, court staff, and witnesses with too little time to fight their way to a better eatery through the gauntlet of panhandlers and homeless that patrolled the downtown area. With only forty-five minutes to spare, John and Stretch took their places in line behind a group of dark-suited attorneys engaged in hot debate over the latest war bulletin from the Thomas case.

The youngest member of the crew, a tall, lanky kid no more than two years out of law school, insisted adamantly that Ainsworth should never have allowed the defense to pull off the old stopwatch bit. "He could have kept it out or at least made a stink in front of the jury," he argued pompously, unwittingly betraying his inexperience before his friends.

Another member of the group, more interested in realpolitik than the nuances of evidence, speculated that a prosecution defeat would pose a serious setback for Ainsworth's election bid.

Still another wondered aloud where this guy Solomon had been hiding since his retirement from the DA's office.

Standing inconspicuously to their rear, shielded by his pink plastic cafeteria tray, John remained unnoticed, and the debaters carried on with their discourse, never realizing his proximity. John recognized them as rookie deputy DAs. He'd seen them and a host of other emissaries from the office filing in and out of the courtroom during the trial. They came to observe Ainsworth in action and were experiencing a mild form of cognitive dissonance coping with the reality that their hero was a mere mortal.

John thought briefly about introducing himself but

quickly reconsidered for fear of spoiling the fun of eaves-dropping. It was a kick to hear his name bandied about like the second coming of Perry Mason. Every trial lawyer yearns at some level for notoriety, to be the topic of discussion at bar association meetings, to get invited on radio and TV talk shows, to be eulogized like a Homeric hero. There was something about the profession that attracted not only those who were exceptionally aggressive or committed to social causes but those who, like actors, needed deep down inside to win the approval of others. John was essentially no different.

He took a seat at a small table beside Stretch and began scooping up mouthfuls of meat loaf and pasty mashed potatoes. As he looked out on the room of harried diners, he felt the unaccustomed sensation of professional satisfaction. He was back in the element he loved, working on a high-profile case, and his cross of the state's sole eyewitness had gone far better than he ever expected. What he wanted most was for the feeling to last, but somehow he knew that it wouldn't. "Every winning streak comes to an end," his old man used to say. "The only question is when." The words rang through his mind as he worked his way through the last of the loaf and canned peas.

For Ainsworth, lunch offered neither pasty mashed potatoes nor an interlude for quiet introspection. His eyewitness had taken an unexpected beating, and he faced the unpleasant option of attempting to bolster Sally's testimony with expert psychological opinion. Fortunately he had retained the services of Dr. Joanne Powers for just such a contingency. His original purpose in hiring Powers was to prevent John from signing her for the defense. But now he knew he truly needed to use Powers, who was a recognized leader in the fast-growing field of forensic psychology devoted to exploring the accuracy of eyewitness identification.

Dr. Powers was a plump gray-haired woman in her early sixties, with a good-natured disposition, an easy smile, and a pair of wire-rim bifocals that gave the impression that she spent many an hour reading bedtime stories to small children. She was also an exceptionally poised witness, commanding expert fees of twenty-five hundred dollars a day for her testimony. It was a stiff sum for a contract drawn on public funds, and Ainsworth was forced to spend half an afternoon genuflecting at the feet of Simon Lasker to get it approved.

Lasker balked and protested but in the end gave in. Expert witnesses had come to dominate criminal trials. From the lab men who were able to identify clothing fibers found under the fingernails of cadavers to the microbiologists and population geneticists who could match a defendant's DNA code to that found in sperm specimens taken from rape victims, the prosecution was paralyzed without its legion of experts. Joanne Powers just cost a little more than most.

With Lasker's reluctant blessing, Powers was placed on call, with the proviso that she would keep her calendar open and be ready to drive to the courthouse on two hours' notice. Having already reviewed the police reports and the transcripts from the preliminary hearing, she assured Ainsworth that all she would need was a fifteen-minute update on the progress of the trial. Rosten grudgingly granted a brief recess at the outset of the afternoon session for this purpose, and Powers took the stand ready to go, her files laid neatly in her lap.

"Dr. Powers," Ainsworth inquired, taking up his position behind the lectern, "you are a psychologist, are you not?"

"Yes. I received my doctorate from Harvard, and I'm currently a tenured professor at the University of Southern California." There was a noticeable measure of pride in her response, conveying the impression that this was a woman truly engaged in her work.

"Do you also counsel patients?"

"Heavens no," she replied with a bemused smile. "I gave up my private practice years ago. I never seemed able to cure anyone." She paused to look at the members of the jury, who appeared to warm to her droll sense of humor. "I'm a researcher in cognitive psychology. In addition to teaching, I administer various research projects, perform scientific testing and experiments, and write articles for a variety of academic publications." She turned to look at the jury again, this time affecting the image of the serious professional. "My area of specialization," she added, "is the accuracy of eyewitness identification."

"Have you ever testified in court before as an expert witness?"

"Many times." Powers nodded knowingly. Although a dispassionate researcher, she had a keen sense of irony and appreciated the uniqueness of the present circumstances. "This is the first time, however, that I've been called to testify by the prosecution."

"Oh, and why is that?" Ainsworth continued with mock surprise.

Powers mulled the question over, warming to the opportunity to do a little PR for her profession. "It has only been since the early eighties," she offered, "that the courts have recognized my specialty as a scientific field of expertise that qualified for admission into evidence at trial. And it was the defense bar that convinced the courts of the merits of the specialty, largely out of concern that convictions could be obtained on the basis of inaccurate eyewitness testimony. My role has been to explain the factors that influence a witness's ability to make valid identifications. While I usually do that for the defense, there's absolutely no reason why I can't do the same for the People."

Ainsworth could not have been more pleased with either the substance or the delivery of Powers' explanation. It was clear, concise, balanced, and fair. No matter how the jury felt about the stipend she was receiving for her day in court, they would remember her as an objective scholar. Any attempt Solomon might make to portray her as a prosecution whore would fall flat on its face.

"Tell us, Doctor," Ainsworth continued, "what are the factors bearing upon a witness's identification testimony?"

"There are a multitude of factors, both objective and subjective," she instructed calmly.

"Such as?"

Powers again stopped to collect her thoughts, as if dipping into her own computerized memory bank. "The stress and fear the witness felt at the time of the crime, the lighting conditions, the witness's age and sobriety, and, of course, the length of time the witness has to make her observations. These are among the most significant items."

"What about the length of time that elapses between the crime and the time the witness makes her first positive identification?" Ainsworth prompted.

"That's also quite important," Powers answered, slightly miffed at having omitted such a vital criterion from her checklist. "The sooner the identification is made, the better."

The time had come for Ainsworth to pose a hypothetical question. Since Powers had not been present at the murder and had not seen Sally when she made her pretrial ID's, Ainsworth was required to extract the relevant evidence from the record and organize it in the form of an assumed set of facts for the doctor to evaluate.

"Doctor, assume, if you will," Ainsworth intoned, "that

a woman sees the shooting of a police officer. The lighting is excellent, and within hours of the shooting she makes a positive identification of the gunman. If such a witness had an unobstructed view of the killer and was at no point in immediate danger herself, how much time at the crime scene would she need to make a reliable initial identification?"

"Under those circumstances, maybe three seconds," Powers replied without hesitation.

"What about seven seconds?" Ainsworth asked.

Several members of the jury, still mindful of John's morning cross-examination, sat bolt upright with anticipation. Powers didn't keep them waiting. "Seven seconds, Counsel," she lectured, "would be an eternity."

The courtroom stirred at Powers' remarks, prompting Rosten to pound his gavel and instruct the gallery that it was in a court of law, not a bowling alley. Ainsworth, for his part, was like a man who had just pulled off a seven-ten split. He passed the witness on to John, knowing that whatever the defense might throw at her, she had more than earned her fee.

There was little John could have accomplished on cross-examination. Apart from bringing out the small fortune Powers was paid to take the stand, he probed the added difficulties presented by cross-racial IDs, such as the one that Sally made of Juan Thomas. His questioning was focused and sharp, but he knew the jury would not hold the fee against Powers—Ainsworth had seen to that—and he also knew that the racial angle was a loser, given Sally's ecumenical track record with men of all creeds and colors.

John had already made the return trip from the lectern to his seat when one last subject came to mind. "Doctor," he asked, closing his briefcase and capping his pen, "the hypothetical question that Mr. Ainsworth addressed to you didn't include any mention of the witness lying about her identification. Isn't that an important factor, too?"

"Indeed it is, Mr. Solomon," Powers answered before Ainsworth could mouth an objection. "But I assume that people who take an oath to tell the truth, do so—unless proved otherwise. Don't you?" Her response was more of a challenge than an answer, a challenge that John was wholly unprepared to meet.

On his way out of court John could only wonder how a day that had begun with such promise had crash-landed, courtesy of a witness who looked uncannily like his long-deceased Bubbie. His father had been right again: Every winning streak comes to an end.

CHAPTER 14

John took an early dinner at Swanson's, staying just long enough to watch the third inning of a late-season Angels–White Sox game broadcast from Chicago. With both teams out of the pennant chase, the veterans were just going through the motions. Only the rookies recently called up from the minors and vying for invitations to spring training were putting out any effort, and for the most part they weren't particularly worth seeing, not when there was still work to be done on the case.

The drive home was unusually peaceful, almost serene in the clear evening air after the rush-hour traffic had subsided. Earl Warren greeted him like a half-starved refugee, brushing up against his slacks and wailing for his evening meal before John had taken two steps inside the front door. John walked into the kitchen, opened a can of kitty tuna, and spooned it into the cat's bowl. The ungrateful animal circled the foul-smelling slop and continued to howl until John retrieved a slice of two-day-old pizza from the refrigerator. Like people, he reflected, cats are creatures of habit. He warmed up a couple of slices for himself and headed for the dining room, where he spread out the contents of his case file on the table.

It was the only meaningful thing left in his life, this dog-eared collection of police reports, sworn statements, transcripts, photos and pleadings, and he treated it with the reverence of a rabbi for the Torah. He spent the next hour and a half in true talmudic fashion, scouring through the mound of documents for clues he might have missed the other thirty times he had read through them. Finding nothing new, he tore a piece of yellow lined paper from a legal pad, turned it horizontally, and began to sketch a time line of the case, starting with the shooting and ending with the testimony of Dr. Powers. Below the time line he drew a four-point diagram linking the Richards murder not only to the arrest of Juan Thomas but to the disappearance of Dupree and Estelle and the death of Rowinski:

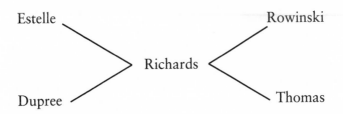

It was only after he had put down his pen that he noticed the message light flashing on his answering machine in the living room. There was a single call, from Stretch.

"Hey, Batman, it's Robin here." Stretch chuckled against a background of bar noise, taking a swallow of what was undoubtedly a draft of Swanson's liquid amber. "Looks like I just missed you here," he continued, shifting to a serious mode. "I hope you get this message before you run out and do something stupid again. You know what I mean. I'm talking about your little trip to Estelle Richards' house. Next time take the butler along. That old man you talked to, he was jivin' your honky ass. He had Estelle's phone number in St. Louis all along. All you had to do was ask. Anyway, I spoke to her. Her father did have a heart attack— right before he died last week. She's coming back in time for the penalty phase and told us to stay the hell away."

Stretch paused again to take another mouthful of beer. "I'll be finishing up those background interviews with Juan's homies I started before the trial. Been trying to find something sympathetic about our client to present to the jury at the penalty phase. But so far I've run into a brick wall. Well, I gotta go. Wish me luck. Tomorrow, brother."

John walked back to his notes and scratched Estelle from the diagram. He circled the entry for Thomas in bright red ink. Next to it, in bold capital letters, he scribbled the word "WHY?" Thomas might be as guilty as the evidence made him appear, but he also seemed too smart to kill a cop, even one who might be out to arrest him, with an eyewitness looking on. Why would Thomas risk his freedom and his life so recklessly? The diagram offered no answers.

Unlike the rest of downtown L.A., not much had changed architecturally in the immediate vicinity of the Criminal Courts Building for at least a decade and a half. The court still occupied the southeast corner of the intersection at Broadway and Temple, with the monolithic Hall of Records standing sentry across the street. The *L.A. Times*, City Hall, the county law library, and the old state office building, all looking just as they had for years, were each within a one-block radius, ensuring that anyone looking for justice or publicity had little distance to travel.

What had changed with time was the number of street people begging for ever-larger denominations of spare change. The area was teeming with them, some released from financially strapped mental institutions, some suffering from AIDS or strung out on alcohol and crack, others just unemployed and chronically down on their luck. A few of the more fortunate and aggressive among them had staked out regular begging locations that they claimed as their personal panhandling turfs. The other homeless seemed to recognize such claims and kept their distance, as they searched for private sites of their own or simply wandered the streets freelancing.

One of the regulars, a white man in his late twenties with thinning red hair, wrinkled leathery skin, and blackened teeth from years of poor hygiene and hard living, had taken up a strategic spot by the masonry wall outside the courthouse along Temple Street. He had caught John's notice each day of the trial, silently thrusting a white styrofoam coffee cup forward to receive quarters and dimes from anyone sufficiently sympathetic or guilt-ridden to part with them. There was something different about the man, John thought, a vague familiarity in the way he made eye contact, the way it seemed he was always on the verge of saying something personal.

Then it happened. As John hurried past the redhead to catch the elevator for Friday's nine o'clock start, the man spoke. "Have a nice day, Solomon," he called out with a sneer.

It was the first time a homeless person had ever addressed John by name. He stopped in his tracks and walked back to the redhead. Up close the man looked angry and ill. "Do I know you?" John asked sheepishly.

The man shook his head with disgust and spat on the ground, barely missing John's right shoe. "Bobby Doherty," he said. "Eight years ago, possession of methamphetamine for sale." He looked at the blank expression on John's face. "You don't remember, do you? You got me sent to Folsom."

The man's face suddenly registered. He was a young street hood back then, one of many busted and sent away during the drug crackdowns of the eighties. It had been a routine case, except for one thing: The kid insisted he was innocent and refused to accept a plea bargain that would have given him a "one-year lid" in the county jail.

"I'm sorry"—John hesitated, at a loss for words—"but I can't help that."

"It don't matter." Doherty laughed derisively as John hurried away. "I shoulda taken the deal. I was guilty, Solomon," he shouted like a man gone mad, "just like the scum you're defending now."

John turned away from Doherty without uttering a rejoinder and headed for the courthouse entrance.

Inside Judge Rosten's courtroom a different kind of madness awaited, the controlled and orderly variety that comes in every death penalty trial when the prosecution wraps up its case, confident of victory. Ainsworth was right on schedule and had only one last witness to present: his cleanup hitter, the ever-genial Lieutenant Gallagher.

Gallagher had sat stoically by Ainsworth's side throughout the proceedings, taking notes, staring balefully at the defendant, and occasionally whispering words of advice and encouragement in the prosecutor's ear. Now it was time to take the stand, and Gallagher warmed to the task. There was no denying he made an impressive witness, walking to the box with soldierlike precision, sitting ramrod straight, and answering counsel's questions without a trace of nervousness or hesitation.

After eliciting a capsule summary of Gallagher's career and qualifications as a law enforcement officer, Ainsworth zoomed in on the essentials. "Lieutenant Gallagher, you were with Ms. Sutton when she made her first identification of the defendant from a set of photographs, weren't you?" he asked at the lectern.

"Yes, I was, at approximately thirteen hundred hours—that's one P.M.—the afternoon following the shooting, at Parker Center." He grinned for the John Wayne enthusiasts he imagined were among the jurors. The military terminology was Gallagher's idea of entertaining testimony. Coming from anyone else, it would have seemed stilted and out of place. Coming from him, it was only stilted.

"How would you describe her condition?" Ainsworth continued.

"Shaken, but she had her wits about her," Gallagher answered, still the voice of authority. "I escorted her home after the incident, and she was able to get a few hours' sleep."

"And were you also present when she picked the defendant out of a live lineup two days later?"

"I was."

"On either occasion," Ainsworth asked, stepping away from the lectern and pausing to glance at the jury, "was anything done to influence her identification in any way?"

"Absolutely not," Gallagher assured the jury.

"On either occasion did Ms. Sutton indicate the slightest equivocation in making her selection?" Ainsworth inquired as if the point had not already been made.

"None whatsoever." The voice of authority had spoken. Sally's ID was squeaky clean.

John stared at an open file, at first appearing to look for something, then seemingly lost in his own thoughts as he fingered through the pages. "Are you with us, Mr. Solomon?" Rosten inquired impatiently.

John shook himself like a tired fighter being worked on between rounds. Ignoring Rosten's question, he looked at Gallagher for an instant, then asked, "The photo spread you showed Ms. Sutton after the shooting consisted of six police mug shots, did it not?"

"It did," Gallagher responded. Like many cops, he was well schooled in volunteering the bare minimum on cross-examination.

"You assembled that photo spread yourself, didn't you?"

The question, though innocuous on its face, made Gallagher uneasy. He couldn't tell exactly where Solomon was going and didn't like it one bit. "Is there something wrong with that, Counsel?" he retorted defensively.

"Not necessarily," John rejoined, suddenly the voice of calm in contrast with Gallagher's ire. "But tell me, Lieutenant, how many police mug shots did you have to choose from for that photo spread?"

Gallagher hesitated. "I've never really counted."

"A dozen, a hundred, a thousand, ten thousand?" John egged him on. "Stop me when I'm warm."

"Thousands, I suppose." There was no concealing the outright contempt Gallagher felt for the defense.

"And out of all those thousands," John continued, moving in for the kill, "you just happened to include Juan Thomas?"

"Not exactly." Gallagher was being deliberately evasive, a fact the jury would surely hold against him.

"Why then?" John asked, gesturing to the ceiling with his palms upturned. "Because he was a gang member? Because he was black?"

Ainsworth stood up to articulate an objection, but Gallagher was in no mood to be rescued by legal niceties. He shouted right through Rosten's attempt at a ruling. "Your client's photo was included, Counsel, because he was the only street punk I could think of with a motive for revenge." The courtroom quieted down, as Ainsworth's objection was forgotten by all concerned. "About five years ago Joe Richards arrested your client's older brother for male prostitution. A few days after the arrest the brother was killed by another inmate at the county jail."

The words fell on John like a sack of nails. He looked at Juan Thomas. Thomas stared back briefly, then turned away. Stretch motioned John to take his seat as the courtroom buzzed with excited conversation.

John uttered the words "Nothing further," making it sound like an announcement of surrender.

"The People rest, Your Honor," Ainsworth proclaimed proudly.

Rosten surveyed the courtroom, pounded his gavel three times to restore calm, and declared the court in recess until Monday morning.

Except for Juan Thomas, the courtroom lockup was empty. The bailiff left John and Juan Thomas alone to allow them to hold a confidential interview, but John was almost too angry to speak as he stood across the bars from his client. "Why the fuck didn't you tell me?" he asked finally.

" 'Cause it's none of your fucking business," Thomas answered. His anger was easily the measure of John's, but there was more to his mood this time than the raw rage that John had come to take for granted. There was something else that John had never seen before, a certain tinge of sadness and remorse.

"Well, it's everybody's business now," John observed sarcastically, "so you might as well let me have the truth. It might help."

Thomas took a step away from the bars and looked to the floor, deep in thought. He had never opened up to anyone since he was a little kid, and he had very few childhood experiences that encouraged him to do so now in front of a middle-aged white attorney like Solomon. But there is nothing like the prospect of a man's own execution to make him reach out in new directions. "Okay, okay," Thomas muttered after a long silence, rubbing his head with his hands. "You think it's all about rock, 'banging, and 'tang, but it's not."

Thomas took a deep breath, struggling against an inner pain, searching for the right words. "We had it hard," he continued. "Our daddy run off; our momma always on wine and shit. I learned to fight and jam, but my brother was different. The homies used to dis him, call him a sissy, but he was still my brother, and I loved him. He had AIDS when Richards threw him in jail. He was raped and stomped by some motherfucker who got away clean, no arrest, no nothing."

"I'm sorry," John said, feeling an empathy for his client that he never thought he would. As his own anger subsided, he began to see Juan Thomas for the first time as more than just a criminal defendant. "But I've got to know: Is that why you killed Richards?"

Thomas backed away and smiled ruefully. "That Richards . . . he was one tough motherfucker. He found out about the dope thing with the cops. He wanted me to make a payoff to Dupree, so he could catch us in the act. It was either that or he was gonna have me busted again for dealing, even said he would see I got a fag jacket in prison." He looked at John as if seeking understanding. "You know what I said to him? I laughed in his bad face."

Thomas walked up to the bars and stared directly at John. "But I didn't kill him. Whoever is running this thing, that's who killed Richards, and Dupree is the only one who knows. I hope you believe me."

Before John could answer, the bailiff opened the side door, signaling their conference time had expired. He released the cell lock, checked the handcuffs on Thomas, and led the prisoner away. John watched Thomas disappear into the service elevator that would take him to the basement and the bus back to county jail. He wanted to believe Thomas, but he had witnessed far too many award-winning performances by guilty defendants protesting their innocence to set his doubts completely aside.

CHAPTER 15

Friday afternoon might have meant early cocktails for lawyers and judges, but for the cops it was a different story. Day in, day out, they had to finish their shifts, keeping pace with the hypes, the kiddie molesters, and the serial killers, who had no intention of knocking off early for the weekend.

For Mary, Friday afternoons were a time for catching up on report writing and working the department's computers. This afternoon she sat behind a PC in one of the workrooms at the LAPD headquarters in Parker Center, using the LAPD's HITMAN program. The acronym was shorthand for Homicide Information Tracking Management Automation Network, a sophisticated computer tool designed for matching and comparing data on homicide cases. With the Thomas case now entering its final stages, she was already working on her new murder assignment, a daylight drive-by shooting in the heart of the Wilshire midtown district. Though hardly the stuff of prime-time drama, computer crunching was a soothing respite from the tensions of the street and court, and the workroom was practically empty, allowing her to concentrate without diversion.

It wasn't just because she personally detested Tom Gallagher that she recoiled at the sight of him as he burst noisily into the workroom on his way back from the Thomas trial. To her way of thinking, Gallagher symbolized the racist and sexist attitudes that were still rampant inside the LAPD.

Gallagher had a young uniformed officer in tow as he loudly recounted the People's day in court. Mary dreaded being forced to listen to the lieutenant's personal account of the proceedings, filled as she knew it would be with ethnic epithets and self-congratulatory asides. On the other hand, she was dying to get a blow-by-blow of the Richards trial from any source, even Gallagher. Since she had been a witness, she was barred from attending the trial and hadn't received an update since a phone call from Ainsworth late last night. She stopped typing and tried to catch the conversation unfolding by the water cooler across the room.

"The kike doesn't know which end is up," Gallagher said to his junior colleague, who seemed to warm to the lieutenant's use of the vernacular. "The way Ainsworth makes the cocksucker squirm is just a thing of beauty. It's hard to believe he used to be on our side." Gallagher poked a rigid forefinger into the chest of his companion in a gesture of manly emphasis. "I'm telling you, Ainsworth's going to make one hell of a DA."

"Word on the street is that the defense is looking for dirt on Richards and Rowinski," the younger cop remarked, proving that he could talk as well as listen. "Something to do with cocaine kickbacks and one of our regular jailhouse snitches."

"Don't believe everything you hear. There ain't no dirt to find." Gallagher crushed a tiny water cup in his massive right hand and smiled. It was the same smile he affected when wringing a confession from a two-bit hood or feeling the rebound of bone against his baton.

Mary remained glued to her video monitor, hoping to escape Gallagher's attention. She stood a better chance of winning the lottery.

Gallagher had spotted her the moment he stepped into the room. He also knew she had seen him and probably had heard every word he'd said, a fact that left him completely unfazed. Her position as Ainsworth's special liaison notwithstanding, he had little regard for Mary as an officer. To his way of thinking she was part of a new privileged class inside the department composed of women, gays, and unqualified minorities, hired and promoted on the basis of affirmative action rather than merit. In the past, when the department was in its glory, things were different. Back then, even the black cops—like his old partner Joe Richards, a man he respected and in his own odd way regarded as a friend—came through the ranks the hard way, the way it should be, just like the whites.

Respect and race were not the lieutenant's concerns, however, when it came to sexual titilation. Affirmative action or not, Mary was an appetizing morsel, and in his impenetrably dense way Gallagher fantasized that she found him equally compelling. He walked over to her desk, approaching from the rear, and began to rub her shoulders, reaching with his big fingers for the straps of her bra. "What's the good word, momma?" he murmured softly, making a pathetic effort to sound hip and soulful.

Mary tensed at his touch and turned around quickly in

her chair, her eyes wide with anger. "Get your hands off me," she shouted loud enough for the civil service clericals down the hall to overhear. "Touch me again, and I'll have your ass before Internal Affairs."

Gallagher backed away, an expression of surprise on his face as though he had been misunderstood. "Just helping to relieve the stress." He smiled as if he really meant it.

"I don't need your help," Mary snapped back, trying to bring the encounter to a close.

But Gallagher had no thought of leaving, not until he had said what was really on his mind. He pulled up a chair and sat down beside her. "I think you do," he said bluntly. He was back to being the hard-ass soldier, an incarnation Mary liked even less than the bigoted suitor. "You know what I'm talking about." He paused to take in her look of incredulity. "I know Solomon came to see you."

"How the hell—"

"It doesn't matter how I know," he interrupted. "The point is, I do." He stared at her closely again, coldly, a portrait of intimidation. "I'd hate to see you do something stupid and get yourself hurt." He laid a hand on her thigh and gave it a gentle squeeze.

"Don't threaten me." Mary was seething as she pushed his arm away. "And get the fuck out of my face." She was like a coiled spring, ready to explode. Gallagher presented a wide and easy target.

Sensing he had overstayed his welcome, Gallagher stood to leave. "Just remember, I'll be watching," he added before stalking off.

Struggling to regain her composure, Mary returned to the computer and typed in a set of commands until the monitor brought up a new file directory. "Richards, J.," it read. She studied the directory, typed in some additional commands, and resumed her work. An hour later she logged off, retrieved some papers from the parallel printer, and left Parker Center in disgust.

The best feature of John's apartment was undoubtedly the balcony. Just off the living room, it faced due south and on clear nights afforded a magnificent panorama of the city, mile after mile of traffic lights, billboards, and signs lit up across a relentless grid of freeways and surface streets stretching to the darkness of the Pacific Ocean. It was hard to believe that a place that sparkled so brightly was home to so much violence and despair.

John sat in an old Adirondack chair, a full glass of scotch rocks perched on one of the oversize armrests. It was the first dram of the hard stuff he'd touched all week, and he felt he'd earned it. He'd given the case his best shot, and to no one's surprise, he'd come up short. The only issue left was whether he'd rest on Monday morning or afternoon. In either case, he'd be ready with some kind of closing argument. He had all weekend to prepare.

For now his thoughts were on the slow-moving airplane overhead, its taillight blinking red against the blue-black sky. Maybe an Aeromexico en route to Puerto Vallarta or a British Air bound for Heathrow. It really didn't matter. Wherever the plane was headed, he wished he were on it, making his escape from L.A. Here he was destined only to be remembered as the attorney who put the final career feather in Howard Ainsworth's cap.

The urge to escape was something else John had inherited from his father. Some of his earliest memories were of his old man leaving home on a never-ending string of business trips through the garden spots of the Midwest, selling lamps and other low-cost housewares to wholesalers in Pittsburgh, Indianapolis, Gary, and especially Chicago. The visits to the Windy City were so frequent—at least twice a month during John's adolescence—that John's older brother started a standing joke that the old man had a second family tucked away somewhere on the city's North Side. It was another secret that his father had taken with him to the great beyond.

Unlike his father's penchant for the country's industrial heartland, John's escape fantasies always pointed south—to places where the sand was white, the palm trees were laden with coconuts, and the bikini-clad women left their inhibitions at home. Maybe, if he ever worked up the courage and a sufficient bankroll, he could find that place of his dreams and start up a small beachside bar. With a little hard work, the bar might expand into a dinner club. That was his idea of heaven on earth, a million miles from Ainsworth, the LAPD, and the wreckage of his personal and professional failures.

He might have clung to his tropical reverie all evening, but an insistent series of determined knocks at his front door brought him rudely back into the present. He downed the last of his scotch, crossed through the living room, and pulled the door back, revealing Mary standing on the other side. She was dressed casually in a lacy white blouse and a pair of tight faded jeans. With her hair tied back off her face and her red handbag slung over one shoulder, she looked as if she'd arrived in a hurry.

John wanted desperately to touch her or at least show how happy he was to see her, but he resisted, convincing himself that he had room for one emotion only: anger. "Was there an insult you forgot to make the other night?" he asked, managing to sound bored and nasty.

Mary looked disappointed and hurt. She hadn't come to fight, but she wasn't about to back down either. Like a fast-spreading virus, his bitterness was contagious. The reason for her surprise visit seemed to dissolve into thin air as she weighed into what promised to be another spirited exchange of words.

"The argument never ends for you, does it?" she asked cattily. It was her way of carrying the fight to him, a nifty maneuver, considering that the battle was taking shape on his turf.

"Is that a philosophical question?" he inquired, stepping back into the living room, knowing somehow that she would brave the storm of barbs and follow him inside. "Because if it is, I'd rather contemplate another J&B." He poured himself a new round, raising his glass in a mock toast.

Mary ignored the comment. She hadn't been inside John's apartment since the night before Simon Lasker turned Solomon's career into Ry-Krisp. She was overcome at the disarray. "When was the last time your housekeeper was here?" she asked, her eyes alighting on the small heaps of Chinese takeout containers and pizza cartons that graced the room like free-form sculptures.

"Last ice age," John answered, lifting the J & B to his lips. "Can I get you a drink?"

"No, thanks." It was clear she disapproved of his fondness for the spirits.

"Drinking never did fit in with your aspirations for middle-class respectability, did it?" He waited for her to respond and was let down to see that she took it in stride. He took another hard swallow, searching his mind for a more hurtful zinger. "Or has Ainsworth turned them into upper-class aspirations?" This one scored a direct hit.

Mary's eyes flashed. She felt like leaving but not before she gave the pampered lawyer she once thought she loved a dearly needed lecture on the hardships of life. "What do you know about respectability?" she asked. "You threw yours away a long time ago. At least Ainsworth works for the respect he gets. He doesn't drown himself in a bottle every time something in his life doesn't go exactly as planned."

As usual, Mary's remarks were accurate and telling. Even in his foul and slightly inebriated state, John found himself reluctantly agreeing with her assessment. "You're right," he conceded, still working on his drink. "I had it all. I went to the right schools, took the right job, and made friends with the right people. Then I threw it all away. So fucking what?"

"You want me to feel sorry for you, don't you?" She looked at him with a mixture of astonishment and annoyance.

"I'm not asking you to feel anything," he told her, reaching for the J & B to pour another round.

"Oh, yes, you are," she said persistently. "You're so busy feeling sorry for yourself you don't realize how easy you've had it."

Whether it was the scotch or her dogged insistence on setting him straight, he felt the need to fight back. "Look who's talking," he said in an effort to silence her. "You got to keep your job, and from what I understand you're climbing the ladder with no end in sight."

"You think it's been easy for me?" she shouted, signaling that silence was the last thing he could expect from her. "You know where I came from. Half my friends were knocked up by the time they were fifteen. You can't imagine what it took to get through the police academy. One minute those assholes were putting their hands all over me; the next they were looking for any excuse to put me down." She was suddenly unable to continue, her voice choking with emotion, her eyes welling with tears.

The sight of her crying caused his anger to dissipate. Whatever hostility he had felt was gone, replaced by an urge to comfort her. "Why are you telling me this?" he asked gently.

"Because you hurt me," she answered bluntly.

John looked at her sadly, recalling the past he had long since discarded. "I know," he said thoughtfully. "But I just couldn't see how we could have a life together. And when I realized that, there was nothing left—nothing for us and nothing for me."

He hoped his confession would soothe her pain, but hearing it only rekindled Mary's rage. "Because I'm black," she shouted. "That's it, isn't it? You couldn't let yourself get serious with a black woman. It's just so convenient to blame it all on me." She looked at him contemptuously and slapped him hard across the face, sending his drink crashing to the floor and Earl Warren scurrying for cover.

John stood in front of her expressionless, a willing recipient of retribution as she slapped him again and again, calling him a hypocrite, a phony, and a patronizing racist. Finally, his face stinging and red from the blows, he grabbed her arms and held her still. They stood for an instant not more than a foot apart, like wrestlers in an uneasy clinch, until he pulled her to his chest. She struggled to free herself, confused and indecisive, then slumped into his embrace.

"I'm sorry," he whispered, stroking her back and shoulders. "I've been dead inside since I left you."

The smell of her perfume, the texture of her skin and hair were just as he remembered. It had been so long since John had shared his bed with her, but they seemed to have lost nothing of the hunger and passion, the softness and solicitude that had once made their sex life a source of both physical pleasure and personal salvation. In the dim light of his bedroom Mary's torso looked like a marbled work of art, her firm, rounded buttocks rising to meet the gentle curve of her back, her stomach muscles tightening and releasing as she straddled his legs and took him inside her. They kissed eagerly, explored each other's bodies with hands and mouths, changed positions, and made love until they lay tangled in the sheets, physically drained and satiated.

For another half hour they remained entwined, in the kind of dreamy half sleep that only the most satisfying sexual encounters yield, oblivious of the world and the professional taboos that their liaison had violated.

Finally Mary broke the silence. "Looks like we screwed up another case," she said. Despite the seriousness of her observation, she wore a satisfied grin that told him she had absolutely no regrets.

John brushed her cheek with the back of his hand, letting his eyes take in the smooth contours of her mouth and chin, the clear sparkle of her wide hazel eyes. He smiled and thought for a moment that Mary would be a welcome addition to his beachside bar in the sun. But reality slowly worked its way back into his consciousness.

"What difference does it make?" he asked with an ironic laugh. "I was handpicked to lose, and that's exactly what I'm doing."

Mary pulled away and propped herself up on a pillow against the headboard. She disliked his defeatist attitude, and her suddenly stiff body language showed it. "Why don't you put Juan Thomas on the stand?"

"Are you kidding? Nobody would believe him," John replied, as if to justify his pessimism. "I'm not even sure I do."

"What did he tell you?" She was determined to find out.

"That it's all a conspiracy," he answered, slightly uneasy in the face of her persistence. She was, after all, still a prosecution witness and an official member of the "other side." He hesitated, then decided to go on. "Thomas claims Richards was blackmailing him to get to a cocaine ring run by the police. Richards wanted him to make a payoff to an informant named BJ Dupree."

"BJ Dupree?" she asked excitedly, letting the sheet slip off her small, well-formed breasts.

"I see that you recognize the name," he remarked sarcastically. "Incredible, isn't it?"

She grabbed him by the shoulders, like a friend shaking a drunk out of an alcoholic haze. "John, BJ Dupree used to be Gallagher's personal snitch." She lay back against the headboard again and stared at the ceiling. "Gallagher threatened me today," she said, looking angry and bitter. "He knew you came to see me the other night and told me to keep away from you. I got pissed off and pulled up Richards' computer files." She turned to face John. "They were completely empty."

"Are you sure?" He sat up at the side of the bed, sensing he might be on to something.

"I have access to all the passwords."

"And you think it was Gallagher?"

"I don't know," she admitted. "Richards could have purged the files himself, but his entire directory was wiped clean. It doesn't make sense. Richards was no neat freak. His desk and locker were so messy it took the clericals forever to box his stuff up after the murder."

"What happened to his stuff?" John asked.

Mary looked confused by the question. "Either his wife has it or it's still in storage at Parker Center. Why?"

"I don't think his wife has it," John commented, remembering that he had seen virtually none of Richards' personal effects on his visit to the Richards home. He slipped into his socks and hitched up his pants. "Let's go down to headquarters and check it out." He slid across the bed and kissed her on the mouth as she looked at him half stunned.

"Wait a minute," she protested. "You want me to take

you to Parker Center? Now how am I gonna sneak a defense lawyer in there on a Friday night?"

"You're not going to have to sneak a defense attorney in," John reassured her. He reached across to the nightstand and fished out a dogeared ID. It was his old flip badge from the DA's office. He displayed it *Dragnet*-style before her. "I told Simon the day after I was canned that I'd lost it. I lied." He flashed a wide, toothsome smile.

Mary shook her head slowly, knowing that resistance would be futile.

CHAPTER 16

When it opened its doors in 1955, Parker Center was the quintessential urban police headquarters. An eight-story glass-and-steel monolith, it bore the name of former Chief William H. Parker, a man praised by his acolytes as the epitome of a police professional and decried by civil libertarians as a cryptofascist. For many years the building had everything the growing LAPD needed: a spacious sixth-floor office suite for the chief, a fully equipped photo and science lab, a motor transport division to service department vehicles, even a bilevel parking structure that made working at the hub of law enforcement one of the easier commutes in the downtown area.

Time, however, had taken a heavy toll on the structure. Although the marble monument to slain officers outside the front entrance had held up impressively, the building itself had begun to deteriorate. From the cracked linoleum tiles in the stairwells and basement to the outdated fluorescent lighting that cast dark shadows on the faces of the detectives and other officials as they crammed into ever more congested offices, Parker Center had acquired the look of a fortress under siege, barely able to hold its own against the tide of the lawlessness enveloping it.

It was nearly ten o'clock when Mary pulled her Honda into the center's parking lot. She showed her badge to the young security guard at the gate and greeted him with the rueful smile of a veteran officer forced to work overtime on a Friday night. The guard looked up from a magazine, stared at her casual attire, and returned the smile. He had begun to wave her through when she rolled down her window. "The driver of the Mustang is with me," she said, motioning to the car behind her. "He's a deputy DA." The young man nodded silently as Mary drove slowly into the lot, casting a nervous look in her rearview mirror, hoping John did nothing stupid to give himself away. As it turned out, her anxiety was entirely misplaced. The guard returned to his reading material, hardly glancing at John's old ID, as he signaled for him to move forward.

With John safely in tow, Mary selected a parking spot in the most deserted section of the lower level. "I told you the ID would work," John remarked as he opened the Honda's driver-side door. He leaned inside and kissed her full on the mouth, as much to assuage her worry as to reassure himself that the magic of their lovemaking had really happened.

Mary resisted the urge to return his affection and pushed him away, an expression of disapproval on her face. "The guard"—she lectured him in a schoolteacher's voice—"is just a flunky. The boys inside aren't quite so dumb." She looked at him with concern, as if she were reconsidering their misadventure. "If they decide to read that ID of yours, we'll be facing some heavy charges. I hope you know that."

"I do," John said grimly, stepping away from the car.

"Just keep your head down and let me do the talking."

Mary led John across the parking lot to a side entrance accessible only to authorized police personnel. The nightlight above the big steel door was out, creating a semidarkness that made Mary feel like a second-story burglar. She fiddled with her key chain for what seemed a small eternity as a string of black-and-white squad cars and unmarked detective vehicles drove past them on their way to the evening's crime scenes. Finally she located the right key, and the lock on the door released.

The entrance opened onto the basement not far from the Property Division's central storage room, where the department warehoused everything from drugs, jewelry, and cash seized from crime suspects to discarded computer and office equipment. If Estelle Richards had indeed failed to claim her husband's personal effects, they would have been boxed up and stashed there.

Mary stopped to consider their options. The huge basement and its labyrinth of intersecting corridors seemed completely empty, but the Property Division was supposed to be staffed twenty-four hours a day. Whether the officer in charge of the storage room was on a coffee break, emptying his bladder, or chatting up the female personnel on duty upstairs, the door to the storage room was closed. The only question was how long it would be until the officer returned. Any way you considered it, they were taking an awful risk. Against her better judgment, she escorted John down the hall, unlocked the steel mesh gate to the room, and flicked on the lights.

Except for the neatly kept log on the front counter, the large room was a study in disorganization, not unlike John's disheveled apartment, she thought with some irony. Row upon row of gunmetal gray filing cabinets stretched from one end of the huge chamber to the other. In between and on top of the cabinets, competing for every available square inch of space, cardboard boxes rose haphazardly to the ceiling. Some of the boxes were tightly sealed; others were completely open in no discernible pattern. They were identifiable only by the crime report numbers scribbled on their tops and sides.

John surveyed the chaos and shook his head in disbelief. "So this is why you guys are always getting sanctioned for losing evidence." He sighed. "And to think I assumed you lost things on purpose."

"It's not as bad as it looks," Mary replied defensively, "once you get used to the system."

"This is a system?" John asked incredulously.

Mary ignored the ill-timed attempt at humor and walked over to a part of the room that seemed reserved for old office furniture and electronic components in various stages of disassembly. She seemed to know just where to start searching. "Over here," she called, pointing to a dual stand of bank boxes marked with proper names. "This is where non-evidentiary items are kept—things the department isn't using but doesn't want to throw away." She stood on a chair and began to lift the top box off one of the stacks, motioning for John to do the same with the other stack.

Before John could find a chair of his own to stand on, he felt her hands pushing into his back. Startled, he turned to find Mary with her right forefinger raised to her lips, silently ordering him to keep his mouth shut. "Get down," she whispered, "we've got company." John scrambled for cover behind a row of filing cabinets, his hand reaching for his old ID, his mind racing for a plausible explanation of his presence in the event he was discovered.

"That you, Jeff?" asked a husky voice from across the room.

"It's me, Dwayne," Mary answered. "Everything's under control." She hopped off her chair and turned to face the man who had preempted her search.

Dwayne Williams was a sandy-haired overweight fifty-year-old white man who had been assigned to the Property Division after a long and undistinguished tenure as a patrol cop in the Mid-Wilshire area and a short stint in Bunco-Forgery. A native of Poteau, Oklahoma, he still spoke with the slow, deliberate twang of the rural poor and was now at the tail end of his career, marking time chasing skirts and knocking back beers until he earned enough service credit to vest maximum pension benefits.

Williams and Mary knew each other just well enough to speak on a first-name basis. They'd met occasionally in the halls and more regularly right there in the main storeroom, where Williams fielded requests to book and inspect evidence from officers returning from crime scenes or on their way to court. Finding Mary inside the storage area rather than on the other side of the counter was a surprise, but if Williams was disturbed by the breach of protocol, he didn't show it. If anything, he looked positively glad to see her, taking careful notice of the hair pulled off her face, the white blouse unbuttoned just above her breasts, and the tight-fitting jeans.

"I'll be out of here in a minute, just had to review something in that new 187 of mine," she fumbled to explain herself. As she spoke, she noticed John's hand sticking out from behind the filing cabinet where he had crouched in a space barely large enough for a man half his size. "Kind of a slow night, huh?" she continued in an effort to make conversation, stepping lightly on John's outstretched fingers to let him know he was in jeopardy of being spotted. With one eye on John holding his now-retracted hand in a mock display of pain and the other on Dwayne, she persisted with the small talk until she was sure there were no lingering suspicions at finding her in the storage room.

"Listen, Mary," Dwayne said after a short and completely inconsequential disquisition on the unseasonably warm turn in the weather, "can you hang on for another minute?" He gave her a slightly embarrassed look that caused her to think momentarily that he might make a sexual advance. "All that coffee I had at the front desk has made my teeth float. Do you think you could hold down the old fort while I take a trip to the rest room? Got to swab the decks." He grinned sheepishly, waiting for her response.

Thank God for the weak kidneys of aging Okies, she thought with great relief. "No problem, Dwayne, take your time." Secure in the knowledge that he thought she was doing him a favor, she gave him her most charming smile.

She paused until she heard Dwayne's heavy leather heels in the hallway before extending a hand to rescue John. He emerged from his hiding place like an old man, holding the small of his back and rolling his head to release the knots in his neck. "Another five minutes, and you'd have needed the jaws of life to get me out," he complained, reaching out for what he hoped would be an affectionate hug.

"No time for that now," she upbraided him, looking all business. "You've got about thirty seconds to get out of here before Gomer Pyle gets back." She grabbed him by the arm and pushed him toward the door. "Wait for me by the exit." She watched, holding her breath as he ran off.

John skulked in the shadows of a side corridor near a bank of service elevators for a good twenty minutes, looking at the second hand making its slow orbit around the dial of his Timex, his anxiety multiplying with each revolution.

As he stared at the watch, he played various disaster scenarios over in his mind about Mary getting caught rifling through Richards' things, about what he would say if she were forced to disclose his role in the evening's escapade, about what he would tell the state bar when it moved to revoke his license. He had barely begun to work his way through the laundry list of potential penalties when a contingent of five uniformed cops in black leather jackets burst noisily through the side entrance. Walking side by side down the wide main corridor, they looked like the interior line of a semipro football team.

The quintet passed within thirty feet of him, engaged in animated conversation over the latest contract negotiations between the police union and the city. John had no idea where they were headed or what Mary would do if she encountered them, but at least they had no interest in taking an elevator ride. For the time being, he remained unnoticed.

In the silence that set in after the group walked by he could hear the Timex's second hand ticking louder and louder as the elevator call light flashed an emerald green. He stood frozen as the lift moaned and groaned to life and climbed slowly to an upper floor. He waited and heard the door of the elevator open above him and shut again as it prepared for its return trip to the basement. He had already decided to bolt from his hiding place when he caught sight of Mary walking to the side door. He hurried to her. She gave him a wild-eyed look like a frightened animal as they stepped quickly outside.

They crossed the parking lot without uttering a word. When they arrived back at their cars on the underground level, he turned to face her and grabbed her gently by the shoulders. "I'm sorry I talked you into this. I should have known better. I was a fool to think we'd find anything."

She pulled away and reached into her bag, avoiding his

eyes. She looked agitated and alarmed, almost in a state of shock. He felt ashamed and guilty at the obvious harm he had caused. After a moment's hesitation she lifted her hand from her purse, her fingers clasping a single sheet of plain white typing paper, neatly creased in the center. "I sent Dwayne on another coffee break. I found this folded inside a spiral notebook at the bottom of a box with Richards' things," she said with a look of amazement.

John took the paper and unfolded it under the dim yellow glow of the overhead lights. It was the continuation page of a two-page document with a running head that read "INTERDEPARTMENTAL MEMO . . . PAGE TWO." Below the header were two sparse single-spaced paragraphs:

> confirming the involvement of officers Gallagher and Rowinski in a cocaine kickback ring.
>
> INFORMANT: B.J. Dupree, age 32, present whereabouts unknown. Because of departmental involvement, request D.A. assistance. EXTREMELY URGENT.
>
> J. Richards

The words were a cry for help from a dead man.

CHAPTER 17

It took John all morning to reach Stretch at the West L.A. racquetball club he had joined a year earlier after finally realizing that his celebrity status in pickup basketball was fading. Though the small ball and the tiny racket were a difficult adjustment, Stretch worked hard to improve his game, using his size and enormous reach to compensate for his lack of experience and finesse. Lately he was spending most of his Saturdays at the club, receiving lessons from a local pro in the morning and huffing and puffing through a series of matches against opponents often half his age until the early afternoon.

The club was also a prime location for meeting lady racquetballers, a pastime near and dear to his heart. Dressed to impress in the most alluring headbands, tight-fitting tops, and Spandex leggings, the female talent was generally friendly and more than able to hold its own on the court. Stretch was just about to start a set with a Vanessa Williams look-alike when he heard his page over the intercom. He reluctantly excused himself and walked over to the front desk. "Johnson," he said in a monotone, picking up the receiver.

"How long will it take you to get to my office?" John asked excitedly.

"Man, don't you even say hello? Today's racquetball," Stretch complained. "We're not due to meet until tomorrow."

"Trust me," John replied. "It can't wait." He sounded unusually determined. There was even, for once, a hint of optimism in his voice.

Stretch daubed his brow with the white terry-cloth towel draped over his broad shoulders, arranged for a raincheck with the Vanessa double, and headed for the showers.

The last person Stretch expected to find sitting across from John's desk was Mary Delgado. He knew Mary only in passing from the end of his tenure as a DA investigator, but what he knew made him instinctively mistrustful. She was widely regarded as bright and competent but also ambitious and calculating. To his way of thinking, she was a relentlessly self-improving individual with no fixed sense of loyalty other than to herself and her career. He had always held her responsible for John's dismissal from the DA's office, and nothing he had seen of her on the witness stand led him to alter his opinion of her in any way.

Mary and John saw the consternation etched on Stretch's face the instant he stepped inside the two-room office.

"I suppose you'd like to know why I pulled you out of your game," John said, hoping to get right down to business and avoid a confrontation over Mary. It was an idle hope.

"You can start by telling me what the hell she's doing

here," Stretch said bluntly, gazing skeptically at both of them as he eased his lanky frame into the vacant client chair next to Mary.

"She's here to help," John responded firmly. He picked up the Richards memo from his desk and handed it to Stretch, waiting to assess his reaction.

Stretch's thick black eyebrows arched quizzically as he perused the document. It was plain to see he wasn't overly impressed. "What the hell is this?" he asked.

"It's an interdepartmental memo to the DA," John said.

"I know what an interdepartmental memo is," Stretch interrupted curtly. "But what is *this?*" He held the memo aloft in his powerful right hand, shaking it like an angry shopkeeper who had just been hit with a summons from the Bureau of Weights and Measures. "It isn't signed, and unless my eyesight has suddenly failed, it's the second page. Where's the first?"

"Hey," Mary broke in, "maybe I should leave." She gave John a look of resignation and started to stand.

John motioned her to sit. He wasn't about to let Stretch's distrust undermine the first big break they'd gotten since he agreed to take on the case. "We found the memo last night at Parker Center hidden in a box of Richards' personal things," he explained. "Mary took a great risk to get it." He saw the muscles in Stretch's face stiffen defensively. "It's true," he went on, doing his best to sound persuasive. "She's here to help."

Stretch settled back for a moment, mentally weighing the odds against an up-and-coming police officer suddenly deciding to switch sides in the middle of a murder trial. Then he sensed the physical connection between John and Mary, like an invisible electrical current. He lowered his gaze and regarded them fully. "This isn't just about the case, is it?" he asked. The shy smiles John and Mary exchanged were the only answer he received, but they were enough to enable him to make sense out of the otherwise improbable turn of events. Shaking his head and sighing deeply, Stretch shrugged his shoulders with resignation. "I hope you guys know what you're doing."

With Stretch at least partially appeased, John reached inside a small manila file on his desk. He pulled out two old color glossy three-by-five-inch mug shots of a young black man dressed in county jail blues, with a short Afro, round, smooth face, deep-set dark eyes, and a sharp, undersize nose. A jail booking number was superimposed across the young man's chest.

"Stretch Johnson," John said, handing the photos across the desk, "you remember BJ Dupree."

Stretch stared at the mug shots and stroked his chin, uncertain and wary of the next move in John's rapidly unfolding plan. "And now what?" he asked.

"We pay a visit to his grandma." Before Stretch could voice the incredulity he felt, John added quickly, "Mary dug up her name in one of Dupree's old probation files. She used to be his legal guardian." He paused to savor Stretch's look of astonishment, then continued, "She's still in the phone book."

Under the orange rays of a picture-perfect September sunset, Adams Boulevard looked almost serene. But for the graffiti and the occasional hotheaded driver weaving dangerously in and out of traffic, the four-lane thoroughfare that crisscrossed South Central L.A. was uncommonly peaceful as John and Stretch made their way toward the campus of the University of Southern California. Only Stretch seemed ill at ease, still not completely reconciled to Mary's surprise reunion with the man whose life she had once nearly destroyed.

"I don't remember him looking this clean-cut," Stretch groused, gazing at the mug shots of BJ Dupree. "I seem to recall him with one of those militant goatees and a nasty old bald head."

"Bald head, cornrows, Afro, Jheri curl, fade, it doesn't make any difference," John replied. "The hairstyle may change; but that's BJ Dupree, and we've got to find him no matter how you feel about Mary. The least we can do is check out the lead."

Stretch sat back, thumbing the mugs and staring out the window. It was clear he was still dissatisfied, but he wasn't about to argue.

They traveled on in silence, turning south on Figueroa, then west on a small residential street lined with scrawny pepper trees and restricted parking signs pockmarked from years of target practice by local gangsters toting semiautomatics. John found a parking spot in front of a row of small wood-frame houses. Like much of the real estate on the outer edge of the huge and opulent USC campus, the homes were well into their third decade of neglect. Peeling paint, broken porch boards, and bars across every window and door gave the neighborhood the sorry look of a war zone.

John fastened a security lock onto the steering column of his Mustang and turned to Stretch. "Her name is Irene Porter," he reported. "She's seventy-five and probably hard-of-hearing, so be polite."

As it turned out, there was nothing wrong with Mrs. Porter's hearing. She was, however, half blind. The door to the Porter home was opened by her friend and personal attendant, an elderly white woman named Helen Edwards, whom the state of California paid a minimum-wage salary to cook and clean for Mrs. Porter and ensure that she did not become a danger to herself or others. Although she was unused to receiving visitors on Saturday evenings, Helen greeted John and Stretch courteously, inspected John's bar card, and escorted them into the living room. Mrs. Porter sat on the edge of an old overstuffed maroon sofa, sipping a cup of hot tea. The women had just completed an early-evening meal, and with the windows tightly closed, the cooking odors of chicken stew lingered heavily through the house.

"We've got company, Irene," Helen announced, gesturing for John and Stretch to take seats on the matching green velour-covered easy chairs across from the sofa. Except for a single floor lamp by the other end of the sofa, where Helen had placed her paperback before answering the door, the room was dark, obscuring the china bric-a-brac collecting dust on the furniture and the gallery of family photographs mounted on the walls.

"These two gentlemen have come about your grandson," Helen said, gently touching Irene on the left shoulder.

"Robert James? Where's that boy at?" For a small woman with a delicate frame, she had an unusually loud and powerful voice, as if she had spent half a lifetime reprimanding disobedient children. As she spoke, she shifted her torso sharply in the direction of her guests, squinting behind a pair of brown plastic-frame glasses with lenses so thick they could have passed for the bottoms of mayonnaise jars.

"That's what we've come about, Mrs. Porter," John told her. "We're here on a court case, and we think Robert may be an important witness. We'd like your help in finding him."

Mrs. Porter shook her head vehemently from side to side. It was unclear whether she was declining John's request or suffered from some kind of nervous tic. In any event, she said nothing.

"I don't think Mrs. Porter has seen her grandson in quite some time," Helen interjected, trying to be of assistance. She was a robust woman in her mid-sixties with a halo of neatly permed white curls, soft blue eyes, and a pink, fleshy nose in a puddle of a broad, flat face.

"Been going on four years, I expect," Mrs. Porter suddenly chimed in.

"Then maybe you can tell us a little about him," Stretch said, taking the words out of John's mouth. John nodded with approval, thankful that Stretch had elected to participate in the interview.

"Ask away," Mrs. Porter said spiritedly. "Would you like some tea?" Before they could refuse politely, Helen withdrew into the kitchen to brew another pot. With no other leads on the horizon, John and Stretch settled back for what promised to be a pleasant, if prolonged, chat.

"I understand that you were once appointed Robert's guardian," John said, hoping to steer the discussion in a legal direction. "What happened to his parents?"

Mrs. Porter shook her head again and stared into the center of the room. Then, just as before, she sprang back to life. "Robert was the firstborn of my Reginald," she said, craning her neck in John's general direction. "Reggie was a good boy, but he married bad. By the time the second baby came, little Eloise—she's now a schoolteacher over at Hoover elementary—Robert's momma was already into the drugs. Then Reggie got killed in a hit-and-run." She shifted and paused as if fighting off the pain of a long-ago incident that would never quite leave her. Despite the comical appearance of her heavy glasses and the head tic, she seemed to be an intelligent and sensitive woman.

"You mean he was shot?" John asked as Helen returned from the kitchen and refilled Mrs. Porter's teacup.

"A car accident," Helen joined in, distributing hot mugs to John and Stretch.

"It was then that Robert and his sister came to live with

me." Mrs. Porter picked up the narrative without missing a step. "Right here in this house." She pointed her right fore-finger at the floor for emphasis. "Later I became their legal guardian and raised them both through high school, with help from the county."

"That's how we first met," added Helen, who had re-turned to what was clearly her appointed spot on the end of the couch. "I was Irene's AFDC eligibility worker, so I got to know her and the two children real well. After I retired and we were both quite a bit older"—she smiled modestly—"I volunteered to become her personal attendant. It's not a high-paying job; but I have my county pension, and I live here rent free. We're the best of friends." She stopped herself before she disclosed any more personal de-tails, looking slightly embarrassed at the way she had prat-tled on.

"What kind of kid was Robert in high school?" John inquired, greatly relieved at Helen's decision to relinquish the floor.

"No good, just like his momma," Mrs. Porter answered, shaking her head yet again.

"How do you mean?" Stretch asked.

"The drugs," she replied indignantly. "First he started us-ing, always sniffing that white powder. Then he took to sell-ing." Helen reached over and placed a reassuring hand on her forearm, but Mrs. Porter was well past being calmed. "He was in and out of juvenile hall so much I took to set-ting a place at the table for his probation officer." She smiled, as if enjoying the sharpness of her own wit. "I just couldn't control the boy. If you want to know the truth, I was well rid of him when he turned eighteen."

"I'm sure it was very hard," John said sympathetically.

"The trouble was," she continued, ignoring the condo-lences, "he was such a bright child. Could have made something of his life, like his sister." She motioned impatiently with her left hand, a gesture that Helen somehow understood as an order to turn on the overhead light.

John's eyes ached for a moment as they adjusted to the light. In the brightness Mrs. Porter seemed even more diminutive than she first appeared. "Over there." She pointed, directing his attention to a large photo of a black youth in his mid-teens. He sat behind a microphone in a radio broadcast booth, the sides of his full Afro depressed by a set of headphones. He was wearing a fringed black leather vest and a button-down dress shirt with the oversize pointed collar that was all the rage at the time. Most notable of all, he had a confident smile on his face, as if he'd known he was good at what he was doing and was enjoying every minute of it.

"That was BJ the deejay." She laughed softly to herself. "Taken at a real radio station on junior careers day. The boy had a talent for electronics. He could have made something of his life." She grew silent again and suddenly seemed tired.

John waited for a moment, then decided the time had come to see if she knew anything about Dupree's storied career as a snitch. "We've also heard that your grandson used to supply information to the police," he said, trying not to sound offensive. "Is that true?"

Mrs. Porter's expression seemed to harden, as if John had touched a raw nerve. "Don't know much about that," she said.

"Oh, come on, Irene, tell them the story," Helen broke in. She had a girlish grin on her face and a slight giggle in her voice. Either she had topped her teacup off with a shot of gin or there was a whopping good yarn waiting to be told.

"You tell it," Mrs. Porter said stiffly.

Helen warmed to the opportunity to hold center stage again. "Well, this comes directly from Irene, but I don't think I'll ever forget it," she said excitedly. "On Robert's first time in the adult men's jail, there were two inmates facing murder charges for killing a wealthy Beverly Hills banker. A burglary gone awry, they said." She looked at John and Stretch to confirm their interest, then proceeded. "Anyway, Robert was in jail for drugs, and he thought he might get some kind of plea bargain if he gave the police some information. So he contacted one of the officers on the case and told him one of the men had confessed to him."

"And that's how his career as an informant got started," Stretch observed, trying to move the anecdote along.

Helen looked somewhat annoyed at the interruption. "Well, not exactly," she said. "The officer said he couldn't believe Robert unless he could prove he had actually talked with the defendant. So do you know what Robert did?" She paused again to play up the suspense. "He made friends inside the jail with one of the defendants, told him he was a jailhouse lawyer, I think that's what you call it. Well, the other man was not real bright, could hardly read, from what Robert said. Before too long he was showing Robert all the arrest reports from his case and talking about the details of the burglary. A few days later Robert spoke to the police officer again and told him something about the banker's bedroom that only a person with inside information could have known."

"What was that?" John asked.

"That the banker had a life-size oil painting hanging on his bedroom wall showing a scene from the Garden of Eden."

"And what was important about that?" Stretch inquired.

Helen smiled with embarrassment, a crimson blush coming to her cheeks. "Instead of Adam and Eve, there were two naked men in the painting—one white and one black."

"You don't happen to remember the police officer's name, do you?" John asked.

As Helen hesitated, Mrs. Porter stirred to life. "Gallagher," she proclaimed, as if emerging from a thick fog. "Big Irishman." Her fatigue was becoming more palpable by the minute, and she said no more.

"I think it's time for Mrs. Porter to get ready for bed," Helen declared, apparently feeling guilty that the conversation had exceeded Irene's endurance. "I'll walk you gentlemen to the door."

John and Stretch said their good-byes to Mrs. Porter and walked slowly from the room. "It's been very nice visiting with you both," Helen said. "I'm sorry we couldn't be of more help locating Robert, but he just doesn't come here anymore."

"I wonder," John said as he stepped outside, "if he had any close friends, a girlfriend, maybe, that you could refer us to."

Helen stopped to think. "Robert did have a young lady, once," she said, straining to recall more details. "I think her name was Grace."

"Last name?" Stretch asked.

Helen shook her head slowly. "I'm afraid I don't remember, and I'm sure Irene doesn't either. It's been so long." She smiled pleasantly and left them standing on the porch.

CHAPTER 18

It was a slow Saturday night at Swanson's Bar and Grille. With the theater crowd still caught up in the third acts at the nearby Music Center, John and Stretch had the place practically to themselves. They sat in John's corner booth, masticating their way through a pair of pastrami sandwiches, absorbed in their separate thoughts over their visit with Irene Porter. With the trial set to resume in less than thirty-six hours, the prospects of locating BJ Dupree were fast disappearing. Unless "Little Loco" returned Stretch's call with some hitherto undisclosed bombshell, John would be left with the defense attorney's proverbial last hope: trying to sell an already skeptical jury on reasonable doubt in closing argument.

Little Loco was the only member of the 65th Street Mainline Crips who had agreed to talk at any length to

Stretch in the background interviews he had been conducting off and on since the case had been referred to Superior Court. Loco was also the only member of the set who had volunteered to testify for Juan if the trial went into a penalty phase and John needed to present a case in mitigation based on Juan's socially disadvantaged upbringing.

Loco's real name was Keenan Armstrong. The oldest child of a manic-depressive mother and a father serving two consecutive life terms for felony murder, he claimed to be Juan's best friend, his "ace kool cuz," as he put it in the lingo of his set. Although he had never finished high school, Loco was both street-savvy and surprisingly good with figures, a talent that made him the gang's de facto accountant and enabled him to buy a new BMW with his drug earnings. On the all-important subject of BJ Dupree, he denied any knowledge of the informant's whereabouts, but he left a phone number with Stretch for future contact, just in case something came up. "It's the number of my lady," he had said. "It's where I be hanging when I ain't banging."

It was clearly a last resort, but it was possible that in the time since he had spoken with Loco, Dupree had been seen somewhere on the streets. Maybe Loco had heard something or could put them in touch with someone who had. With a gambler's resolve, Stretch had tried Loco's number at least three times since leaving Irene Porter's, once from John's office and twice since their arrival at Swanson's. Each time the phone was answered by the taped sweet voice of a young black woman, who announced her name, Sheila Jackson, and requested the caller to leave a message at the tone. Stretch left his and John's return numbers as well as Swanson's, but with the clock on the wall showing ten minutes to eleven, there was no way to tell if Loco had received his calls.

Linda saw John and Stretch at their corner table, her

waitress's radar telling her that it was time for refills on the Bud Lights they had been nursing. Puzzled at their silence and downcast demeanor, she walked over to ask if they wanted another round. "Not much happening around here, huh, fellas?" she said, holding her order pad in one hand and a ballpoint in the other. "At least you don't have to work. I got pulled in when the weekend girl got called away. Her sister had a baby back in Florida. What can I get you?"

"How about some company?" Stretch asked. To her surprise, he slid over and invited her to sit down.

"You know, this is the first time in all the years you guys have been coming in here that you asked me to join you," she said, squeezing in tight next to Stretch. "Something must have come up in that case of yours." Their somber expressions told her she had touched a raw nerve. She pulled out a pack of Salems from her apron and offered them a smoke.

John reached across the table and accepted a cigarette.

"Since when did you add tobacco to your list of good habits?" Stretch asked.

"First time since the Daniels case," John answered elliptically, accepting a light from Linda's Bic.

"Let's see," Stretch said, straining to remember, "1986, first-degree murder. The jury was out for four days."

"Five," John corrected.

"You guys aren't exactly the most pleasant company," Linda complained, tapping her fingernails, neatly painted a deep and shiny red, on the table. "Maybe you should take up bowling or bingo, something healthy for a change." She laughed at her own joke as she caught sight of Dennis Macguire, the night shift bartender, loading a tray of mixed drinks for a newly arrived group of theatergoers. "I think I'm about to be paged," she said, excusing herself. She blew a plume of gray smoke into the dimly lit lounge, stood up, and adjusted her apron.

She had started back to the bar when she suddenly turned around. "Oh, yeah, I nearly forgot," she said in a slightly apologetic tone, "some guy called right before you got here. Left a crazy message." She fished through her pockets and found a scrap of crumpled paper. "Here it is," she said, straining to decipher her hurried penmanship. "Little L. Said to meet him at Galaxy Liquor, in the parking lot, at eleven-thirty. Sounded like he was high and—"

They were out the door before she could finish.

John glided the Mustang out of Swanson's parking lot into the deserted downtown streets, past the Criminal Courts Building, the darkened downtown government offices, and the *Times* building, standing ever vigilant and arrogant on the corner of First and Spring. Except for an occasional passing motorist, the city remained lifeless until they approached the Union Rescue Mission. Groups of the homeless had gathered there earlier for an evening meal, and some were still milling about, discussing the prospects of finding indoor shelter. Others, resigned to another night under the stars, were busy setting up cardboard shanties on the sidewalk, counting up their day's beggings in spare change. A throng of men sharing a gallon of jug wine shouted catcalls at them as they drove by.

The sound of bottles crashing on the streets could be heard in the background as they turned west and headed for the Harbor Freeway. "Why a liquor store?" John asked, stepping on the accelerator to merge with oncoming traffic.

"It's where I interviewed him before," Stretch explained as he studied a street map under the dim glow of the light in the Mustang's glove compartment. "In South Central they're practically the only places open this time of night."

"That's comforting."

"Sixty-second and Hoover," Stretch replied. "Take the Slauson exit, and turn right." He took his eyes off the map and noticed the beads of perspiration forming on John's upper lip. "Just keep your eyes open and we'll be okay."

Galaxy Liquor was owned by Samuel and Chang Sun Kim, two cousins who had emigrated from Seoul ten years earlier. Attracted to South Central because of its depressed real estate market, they had each opened liquor stores in the area before merging them into one larger enterprise on Sixty-second Street. Like many other Korean merchants, they found their relations with the black community were fraught with mutual misunderstandings and swung between studied indifference and outright hostility. To safeguard their investment, the Kims employed two full-time security guards, who watched over the clientele like voyeurs at a peep show.

John entered the parking lot and found a space close to the entrance. He pulled out the emergency brake and shut off the lights. "What now?" He turned to Stretch.

"We wait. He knows where to find us."

A series of cars pulled in and out of the lot. A group of blue-collar workers, outfitted in grimy coveralls, emerged from the store with a bag of six-packs. A crowd of noisy young partygoers drove into the lot in a pair of late-model Hondas, radios blaring hip-hop and rap. They rolled down their windows and danced in their seats while their drivers went inside to make their purchases. As the minutes wore on, the patrons thinned out until at half past midnight the Mustang was the lone car left in the lot.

With only a half hour until closing, the only person on the street was a small boy slowly riding a bicycle up and down the block. He'd been making the same broad, lazy pattern for almost forty minutes, as though he were waiting or looking for someone. Judged by his size, no more than five feet two inches tall, he couldn't have been more than twelve years old. Finally he hopped off his bike next to a pay phone outside the liquor store. It was then that Stretch noticed the black plastic pager strapped to his belt.

"The kid's a runner," Stretch said, watching him drop a quarter in the phone. Whether it was part of the initiation ritual or the fact that they made for better cover, young boys, just like this one, were being used increasingly as lookouts. Their job was to stake out crack dens and other strategic areas in order to provide advance warning, usually by phone, of the presence of cops or rival gangs. It was the first step up on what promised for some to be a quick rise through the gang hierarchy.

Stretch got out of the Mustang and walked to the phone booth for a closer look. The kid hung up the receiver and hopped back on his bike but remained by the booth, unfazed by Stretch's looming presence. "What's your name, son?" Stretch asked.

"Tiny Jason," the kid answered quickly. Despite the lateness of the hour, he was wide-awake and clear-eyed. With a head of tightly woven cornrows and smooth, unblemished skin, he had the face of a young black angel with a Cub Scout's enthusiasm.

"You've been staking us, haven't you?"

"Ain't nothing goes down here without me knowin' it," Jason snapped back.

"Then tell me, Tiny Jason, why Little Loco's hung us up for over an hour. Don't tell me he's not coming."

"Ain't nothing like that," the boy answered. "Little L just want to be sure you didn't bring no police."

As they spoke, Loco's blue BMW wheeled into the parking lot. Four young black men in their mid-twenties alit, wearing warm-up jackets, X caps, baggy black pants, and expensive running shoes. One of their members, a tall man with an angry-looking purple-brown scar running the length of his right cheek, eyed Stretch suspiciously as he made his way back to the Mustang. Another one, short and stocky, with a blue "do-rag" underneath his cap, took up a position next to John, who was still seated behind the wheel. "My, my, my," the tall one said with a sneer, "a lawyer in the 'hood and his Oreo cookie." Both the tall banger and the stocky one had refused to speak with Stretch when he tried to interview them prior to the trial. All except Little Loco, who seemed slightly embarrassed, laughed as if they were watching a stand-up routine at the Improv.

"We didn't come here to get dissed," Stretch said, affecting the argot of his company.

"Chill, homes," Little L told his friends, taking command of the situation. "They're here to help Juan." His companions reluctantly quieted down, but the hostile looks in their eyes signaled their discomfort with the situation.

"We know the stuff about BJ Dupree is true," Stretch said, hoping to cut through the homeboy antics. "That's why I called. It's more urgent than ever that we find him."

"Shit, you might as well be lookin' for Santa Claus," the stocky gangbanger cackled. "Even his old bitch didn't know shit."

"You mean Grace?" John called from inside the Mustang.

Loco and his homies looked surprised. "How did you know?" Little L asked.

"It doesn't matter," Stretch said sharply. "Just tell us how we can find her."

"But she don't know shit," the stocky one said again. To him, the mere idea of cooperating with Juan's lawyers was only one step removed from cooperating with the LAPD. "We been there ourselves."

"Then you won't mind if we have a try," Stretch reasoned. He looked pleadingly at Little Loco, hesitated a moment, then added, "I have a map."

Located midway between South Central and the International Airport, the city of Inglewood boasted of two nationally famous landmarks: the Great Western Forum, the home court of the Los Angeles Lakers, and Hollywood Park, where Citation became horseracing's first million-dollar earner by winning the 1951 Gold Cup. Apart from that, Inglewood was a small, predominantly black incorporated municipality of approximately one hundred thousand residents plagued every bit as much as South Central by poverty, corruption, and crime.

Grace Stevens lived just where Little Loco said she did, at the end of a cul-de-sac in the small rear house on a two-house lot in one of the modest but more stable residential sections of the community. Despite the neighborhood's outward calm, the quiet of the night was broken by the concussive thumping of a police helicopter patrolling overhead. In a scene repeated on a daily basis in minority communities, the copter made a broad sweeping motion, circling a two-block area to the south, training its searchlight on the houses and stores below. The whirring of the blades touched off a chain reaction of baleful howls from the local canine population, shepherds, rottweilers, Dobermans, and mongrels alike, kept by gun-shy homeowners as a slim measure of protection in a world where reliance on the official custodians of law and order had become increasingly futile.

Grace's small house sat at the end of a narrow driveway that ran along the side of the whitewashed three-bedroom Spanish stucco house that occupied the front section of the double lot. Apart from a weak amber porch light, the front house was completely dark, its occupants having long since retired to bed. John parked the Mustang at the foot of the drive, and he and Stretch made their way cautiously down the drive, the noise of their movements drowned out by the combined cacophony of the helicopter and the dogs.

"I know it was my idea, but it's a damn fool thing to be visiting anyone this time of night," Stretch confessed as they came to the front steps of the rear house. He looked back at John with an expression of apology. "I just hope she doesn't have a pit bull."

"I don't think we have to worry about that," John said excitedly, raising his hands above his head and motioning to Stretch to do likewise. They looked up to find a young black woman in a blue bathrobe and nightgown standing at the top of the steps. In her arms she held a single-barrel pump-action shotgun, cocked and ready to fire.

"I told you motherfuckers not to come back here," she screamed. "Unless you want your balls blown off, you better get the hell away from my house." Her anger abated only slightly as she realized that the two fortyish-looking men standing before her in sports coats and ties were not the intruders she had been expecting. "Who the hell are you?" she asked, lowering the shotgun to her hip.

"Grace Stevens?" John asked politely, trying his best to sound calming. "I'm John Solomon. I'm a criminal defense lawyer appointed by the county." He lowered his arms carefully and gestured toward Stretch. "We're here about BJ Dupree."

The mention of Dupree seemed to soften her resolve, as if late-night invasions of privacy were somehow expected, if not entirely excused, where BJ was involved. She took her finger off the trigger of the shotgun but kept her eyes fixed on her visitors. "Show me some ID," she demanded.

John pulled out his wallet and displayed his California state bar card. Stretch did the same with his investigator's license. Grace inspected them briefly and, after a moment's indecision, reached for her front door. "You'd better come in before the neighbors get suspicious. Just keep it down. I don't want to wake my baby."

The interior of the one-bedroom house was sparsely furnished, but neat and clean, except for a pile of textbooks and spiral notepads scattered about a round walnut-stained wooden table that sat in the center of the combination living-dining room. The books included a late edition of *Gray's Anatomy,* a *Merck Manual,* a *Physicians' Desk Reference* for prescription medication, and several texts on nursing. Grace saw them looking at the books. "I'm studying for my LVN," she commented matter-of-factly. "I have a big exam Monday." She gestured for them to take seats at the table and waited for an explanation.

"I'm very sorry to disturb you," John said, "but we really have no choice."

She smiled ruefully, as if she understood. "So what's that lying excuse for a man done now?"

"He's a material witness in a murder case. We're trying to find him," John answered.

"You and everybody else." She sighed with resignation. Although her dark eyes were puffy with fatigue and her hair matted from sleep, she was an undeniably attractive woman in her late twenties, slim, long-legged, with a delicate chin and fine cheekbones that reminded John of Mary. "A group of Sixty-fifth Street bangers were here last week. I don't know how they got my address." She shook her head.

"Maybe BJ gave it to them," Stretch suggested. "How well did you know him?"

She stared at them for a moment, took a deep breath, and let out another soft sigh. "I'm his wife."

John and Stretch shared a look of embarrassment. "We're sorry, we didn't know," John said.

"Not as sorry as me," she responded quietly. "But we make our choices and have to live with them."

John thought about leaving, but it was clear she wanted to continue.

"Four years ago I was planning to go to nursing school. Then I met BJ." She paused, trying to contain the bitter memories. "Believe it or not, there was something special about him. He was different from the other fools around here. He wanted to do something with his life, open an electronics store or a record shop. He was really talented in that way. I knew he had a criminal record, but these days what man in this neighborhood doesn't?" She looked at them for understanding. "Anyway, he said he was going straight, and I believed him. He always seemed to know just what I wanted to hear."

"What happened?" Stretch asked.

"The usual," she replied stiffly. "We moved in together and got married. Then I told him I was pregnant. That was the beginning of the end. Two weeks later he was gone." She stared at them again and directed their attention to a group of framed photographs set on the wall above an old couch on the other side of the room. They showed a curly-haired toddler in various venues and stages of development: a birthday party in the park; an outing at the zoo; a group shot with Grace and her mother and father taken at a restaurant. "I'm almost finished with nursing school, and when I am, little Michael and I can get a proper home, where he won't have to share a bedroom with his momma."

How very much like Mary, John thought again, as Grace related the details of her story. They had the same drive, the same determination, faced many of the same social obstacles. Grace's choice in men, though, had set her back. He tried to imagine the struggles she faced as a black single mother. "Can you help us?" he asked, almost ashamed at making any request of her at all.

She paused, as if trying to decide if she could trust them. "This is confidential, right? You won't go talking to those crazies from Sixty-fifth Street?"

"Of course not," Stretch assured her.

"Three days ago he called me. He gave me some dumb excuse about wanting to see his son." Her face flushed with anger. "I told him the boy thinks his father is dead. He had the nerve to ask for money, too."

"Did he say where he was?" Stretch asked.

"He gave me a phone number. I was going to throw it away." She walked over to the coffee table in front of the couch, picked up a copy of *Newsweek,* and tore off the back cover. "I wrote the number down," she added, handing the cover to John. "Now if you don't mind, I'd like you to leave. Michael will be up by seven, demanding his Cheerios."

She escorted them to the door, calling after them as they descended the steps, "I don't know why you're actually looking for him, and I really don't care."

CHAPTER 19

"**I** really do care," Howard Ainsworth said resolutely, looking calmly and directly into the eye of the TV camera. "I care deeply about the administration of justice and *all* the people of this community. That's the fundamental reason I am running for public office."

Ainsworth's remark was delivered in the closing segment of the third and final debate among the three leading candidates in the election for district attorney. It came in response to what he considered a cheap shot from his closest rival, Richard Martinez, a public-interest lawyer and a former president of the Mexican-American Bar Association who had spent all of two years in the DA's office a decade earlier. Invoking the obligatory racial trump card of left-wing progressives, Martinez had accused Ainsworth of insensitivity toward the black and Hispanic communities, calling him the "latest in a long line of lily white cronies who care about nothing but preserving the status quo and advancing their own careers."

Martinez had entered the race not with hope of winning but for the opportunity of advancing a left-liberal agenda, "to raise consciousness and foster debate," as he put it, about racism in the justice system, police brutality, and corruption in local government. His strategy was to prevent Ainsworth from capturing more than 50 percent of the vote in the general election, thereby forcing the nonpartisan race into a two-person runoff and in the process prolonging the public debate.

Thus far the strategy was a failure. The latest *Los Angeles Times* poll showed Ainsworth holding steady with a 55 percent share of the expected vote. With the election less than two months away and a Sunday afternoon television audience looking on, Martinez had everything to gain and nothing to lose by going after Ainsworth. Much the same could be said of the sole woman on the panel, Carolyn Wyatt, a career prosecutor who had built her reputation as a hard-nosed litigator in rape and child abuse cases and had won the backing of women's and feminist groups. The problem was that Wyatt and Martinez had split the liberal-activist constituency between themselves, leaving the remainder of the electorate to Ainsworth.

Martinez and Wyatt had also spent much of the campaign fighting each other in a battle to emerge as Ainsworth's principal rival. Now that Martinez had won that distinction, he and Wyatt had joined forces to undermine the front-runner. Although they continued to run separate campaigns, they began to coordinate their press releases and appearances, emphasizing the need for a thorough housecleaning of the DA's office. Until now their efforts had done nothing to alter the outlook of the election.

Late last week, however, with Ainsworth's energies taken up by the Thomas trial, Martinez and Wyatt received a potentially important tip from a disgruntled Ainsworth supporter.

A transplanted southern Baptist named Alan Baldwin, the head of a small but militant right-to-life group and a former Ainsworth confidant, had demanded that the candidate endorse his organization's call for a state constitutional amendment that would make abortion a capital crime. Although Ainsworth's antichoice views were well known and as virulent as Baldwin's, he politely declined to make the proposal an election issue. After the election, Ainsworth told Baldwin, he'd be perfectly happy to endorse the idea.

Baldwin, however, was a true believer. At a hastily convened rally in the courtyard of the downtown commercial high-rise that housed Ainsworth's campaign office, he publicly renounced the candidate as "a heretic, a hypocrite, a false messiah, and, worst of all, a secular humanist." To Ainsworth's great relief, the demonstration generated little notice. Even the gaggle of Bible-toting prolifers who turned out to support Baldwin, bearing placards adorned with quotations from the Book of Revelation, could garner no more than a sparse two-column inch story in the *Times*. What the paper didn't report, however, was that Baldwin had concluded that it was God's will that Ainsworth be defeated. Immediately after the demonstration Baldwin placed a call to the Martinez campaign.

"The people deserve to know who they're voting for if they make Howard Ainsworth the next DA," Martinez began his final remarks of the televised debate. "It's been disclosed to me by a highly placed source that Mr. Ainsworth has diverted campaign funds to launch a private foundation he intends to form after the election to advance a broad range of militant right-wing goals. Among other things, the foundation will be used to promote a statewide ballot initiative that would make abortion a form of murder punishable by the death penalty."

"My campaign has received the same information," Wyatt chimed in as the studio audience came alive with an undercurrent of excited conversation. "If true, Mr. Ainsworth is guilty of a flagrant conflict of interest."

The TV cameras turned to Ainsworth, who did his utmost to maintain a photogenic aplomb. He was only partly successful. With only sixty seconds of airtime remaining, Martinez had pulled off what trial lawyers call a sandbag, pinning his opponent to the wall with a surprise allegation he could not rebut.

"I'd like an opportunity to reply to that scandalous allegation," Ainsworth told Jerry Arnold, the veteran bespectacled newscaster who had drawn the assignment of moderating the panel discussion. "There's no proof and no truth behind it whatsoever. If this were not such an important forum, the charge would be absolutely laughable." His voice betrayed both anxiety and anger as the red light came on over the TelePrompTer, signifying the final twenty seconds until the commercial break.

"I'm sorry"—Arnold broke in above Ainsworth's increasingly shrill complaints—"but that's all the time we have." He smiled sympathetically at Ainsworth, then turned to face the camera. "I'd like to thank the candidates for their appearances, and to our viewers in the studio and at home, remember to get out and exercise your freedom to vote."

As the credits rolled across the screen, the panelists could be seen continuing their heated exchange, with Ainsworth directing an accusing forefinger at his adversaries. An instant later the debate blinked off and was replaced by a Jeep Cherokee climbing a forty-five-degree gradient in the Arizona desert, with a craggy-faced male model wearing steel-rimmed sunglasses at the wheel.

John reached for his remote control and clicked off the TV. "So what do you make of that?"

"Just the usual political BS," Stretch answered idly from the couch. "Howard's far too smart to get caught with his pants down diverting campaign funds. He'll weather the storm and come out smelling all the sweeter for being the victim of a hatchet job."

John and Stretch had spent the better part of the day at John's apartment, taking turns pushing the redial button on John's phone, calling the number that Grace Stevens had given them. The prefix, 479, was a West Los Angeles exchange. To judge from the odd assortment of busy signals and unanswered rings they had received, they concluded that they were calling a public pay phone, one of many thousands located west of La Cienega on countless corners, inside bars, restaurants, and shopping malls, and just about everywhere else urban man has a need for instantaneous communication.

But as John found out the hard way, discovering the location of a pay phone was an enigma wrapped up tighter than a state secret. Throughout the morning and early afternoon no fewer than five operators and three flustered supervisors fed him the same bureaucratic line: Pay phones were unlisted, and only an official request from the police could force the phone company to divulge their whereabouts. One particularly snide operator suggested that John take up any complaints he might have with the business office on Monday morning. By then, of course, it would be too late. Juan Thomas might just as well make his reservations for a cell with a view at San Quentin.

John paced nervously across his living room floor, pounding his right fist into his left palm. "You're absolutely sure it's not in the reverse book?" he asked, referring to Stretch's investigator's edition of the publication that matched up known phone numbers with their corresponding addresses.

Stretch, whose thoughts had begun to return to the racquetball game he had abruptly terminated a day earlier, looked at him with irritation. "If I tell you again that phone booths aren't listed, will you believe me?" He sighed deeply and began stuffing his notes inside his briefcase.

"Try it again," John said, seeing that Stretch was preparing to leave.

Reluctantly Stretch reached over to the coffee table, pushed the redial button, and turned on the speaker. The phone began to ring, slowly, inexorably, once, twice, five times, ten times, until the repetitive monotone blended into the background noise of the apartment, barely noticeable as John continued his pacing and Stretch ambled out onto the balcony to check out the fading afternoon. They were so inured to the ringing that they were barely able to react when it suddenly ceased.

"Thank God you called," said the squeaky female voice.

John stood motionless for a moment, looking as though he had received a radio beam from another planet. "Hello, hello," he shouted toward the speakerphone. "Who is this?"

"This is Sister Sarah, and I'm so tired," the voice answered. "Can you take me to the angel?"

"Sister Sarah, where are you?"

There was an uneasy silence on the other end as Sister Sarah, formerly Sarah Rice of Denver, Colorado, paused to swallow another dose of Haldol. A fifty-year-old chronic schizophrenic who had been wandering the boulevards of West Los Angeles since her most recent hospital release, Sister Sarah would have been considered a colorful bag lady in more prosperous times. Now she was just another weary enlistee in the ever-expanding army of the homeless, invisible to all but the beleaguered outpatient staff at the county medical clinic who kept her prescription filled and occasionally gave her a few dollars for food and a cheap hotel room.

"Sister Sarah," John repeated, "where are you?"

"The Lord is my shepherd," Sarah said soothingly. "He maketh me to lie down in green pastures. I'm so tired. Can you take me to the angel?"

"First you must tell me where you are."

Sarah paused again. Reverberating over the speakerphone, John's voice was loud and commanding, the way she imagined God himself might sound on the day of judgment. "This is a phone booth," she answered, sounding suddenly coherent. "And I'm on my way to meet the angel, the angel of the tower."

"The Mormon Temple," Stretch whispered, "on Santa Monica." A West L.A. monument, the Mormon Temple was one of the largest and most imposing houses of worship the Church of Jesus Christ of Latter-day Saints had erected in California. The massive white structure was adorned with a gilded statue of the Angel Moroni that reflected the heavenly glow of the morning and evening sun from its perch atop the temple's 250-foot tower.

"The Angel Moroni, is that where you want to go?" John asked. "Tell me where you are, and I'll take you there."

"Are you the Savior?" Sarah's voice filled with excitement. "Are you coming for me?"

"In the chariot of light." John's words boomed with authority. "Just tell me where you are."

Sarah grew silent. The Haldol was beginning to take effect, bringing her slowly back into some semblance of reality. For some unexplained reason, the medication also made her terribly hungry. "Will you bring me a Big Mac?" she asked.

"And a large fries," John promised.

Sarah paused again to consider the offer. "I'm at a Shell station near Olympic and Purdue," she answered with the precision of a cab dispatcher. "Be here soon."

With John at the wheel and Stretch riding shotgun, they took off in the Mustang for the rendezvous with Sister Sarah, stopping along the way to purchase the promised feast from McDonald's. As they approached the Shell station on Olympic, they saw a middle-aged woman dressed in an old overcoat, standing inside a phone booth, chatting into the receiver.

John pulled the Mustang into the station's parking lot and ran to the booth, the McDonald's food bag, warm and pungent with the odor of onions and fries, cradled in his left hand.

The woman reacted to seeing John approach with a mixture of surprise and alarm. She quickly terminated her conversation and pushed against the folding glass door to hold it closed. "I have a canister of Mace in my handbag, mister, back off!" she screamed.

John paid her protest no mind and pressed up close against the door. "Sister Sarah, I've come for you," he said. He held up the brightly colored McDonald's bag. "Look, a Big Mac and fries. Open up."

John retreated a step back to let the woman exit and found himself staring into the aperture of a small aerosol can. The words "you fucking asshole" rang in his ears as the cloud of mist made contact with his eyes, sending him writhing to the ground in agony. He must have lain there for a good ten minutes until Stretch's face came into focus. "What the hell happened?" he cried, accepting a handkerchief and rubbing it vigorously against his bloodshot eyes.

"Looks like you picked on the wrong woman."

"You mean that wasn't Sister Sarah?"

"Sister Sarah's long gone," Stretch responded between bites on the Big Mac. "What you encountered was just another lady trying to protect herself against the dangers of the big city." He helped John to his feet. "And from my vantage point, she did a pretty good job." He smiled and dusted off John's sports coat. "At least she didn't call the police."

"What about the phone booth?"

"It's the right booth, no doubt about it."

John rubbed his temples and straightened his hair as the pain slowly subsided. "Any sign of Dupree?"

"I thought you'd never ask." Stretch slid back the glass door and tapped the steel tray below the pay phone. It was littered with obscene drawings, assorted vulgarisms and phone numbers scratched into the surface and colored over with black and blue ink. Stretch ran his big right forefinger across the literary chaos and stopped when he came to a phone number that had begun to fade but was still discernible. "Recognize it?"

"No," John answered testily. "One of your dates?"

Stretch scoffed at John's remark and dropped a quarter into the phone. He punched in a series of numbers and handed the phone to John.

John held the receiver to his ear, continuing to rub his eyes. After three rings a male voice answered. "Mustang Club, George speaking."

CHAPTER 20

The big room at the Mustang Club was as empty as a shopping mall on Super Bowl Sunday. Only the hard core were there before dark. Three washed-out–looking middle-aged men, two in sports coats and the other in a leather bomber jacket designed for a man ten years his junior, were positioned strategically about the bar, nursing a variety of mixed drinks and gazing sporadically at the ESPN highlight films of old World Series games on the club's TV.

Toward the center of the room an interracial couple sat in one of the small square tables in front of the stage made famous by Sally Sutton. The man, a young black in his mid-twenties, outfitted in an expensive tan suit over a jet black silk T-shirt, was lecturing an attractive redhead on the finer points of flesh peddling. "Always, and I mean always, baby, get your money up front. No money, no date," he declared solemnly, ostentatiously pausing to check the time on the platinum Rolex on his wrist.

John and Stretch let their eyes adjust to the dim light and walked unhurriedly across the floor. With their briefcases in hand they looked like a pair of mismatched Jehovah's Witnesses on a mission to redeem repentant sinners. Either that or a couple of IRS auditors in search of fiscal misfeasance. In any event, they were an unwelcome sight.

As they crossed the room, the curtains on a private side booth parted. The club bouncer, George Ortiz, stepped out, accompanied by two well-muscled, unsmiling men wearing the short-sleeve button-down khaki shirts with epaulets on the shoulders that are favored by third world dictators. Green and blue tattoos of serpents and naked women snaked around their exposed forearms. George looked to be in a foul mood, as though something besides keeping a lid on the club's drunks were weighing heavily on his mind. He and his crew stopped no more than a foot in front of John and Stretch. For a moment a tense silence permeated the air, like a spaghetti western before shots ring out and bodies start dropping. George eyed the visitors contemptuously. "If you're looking for Mr. Hidalgo, he ain't here," he snarled.

John and Stretch exchanged a quick look of surprise. "How did you know we were interested in him?" John asked.

"You're the lawyer in that case," Ortiz answered. "I didn't figure you came here for fun. If I'm wrong, the shows start at ten."

"No, you figured right," Stretch said, pressing his right hand against the side of his jacket to make sure his .38 was within easy reach. "Can we speak to him?"

"He's in New York," Ortiz answered quickly.

"When will he be back?" John asked.

"That depends."

"On what?" John asked again.

"On how soon we find a buyer for the club." Ortiz halted briefly to take in the surprise registering on their faces. "Depending on how things go, he may not be back at all. In the meantime, I'm in charge." He motioned to the two goons to return to the booth. "Look, we got business to do, so if you don't mind." He gestured toward the front entrance.

"Just one more thing," John said. He pulled the mug shots of BJ Dupree out of his breast pocket and showed them to Ortiz. "Ever seen this guy before?"

"Never," Ortiz said, trying to cover his surprise and irritation. He pointed toward the door again, this time with an unmistakable air of finality.

Venice Beach was quintessential Los Angeles. The grandiose dreams that spawned the district's early development contrasted sharply with its present-day ambience of freewheeling hedonism intermingled with urban decay and crime. Designed at the turn of the century by tobacco magnate Albert Kinney, the community was conceived as an American version of Venice, Italy, a graceful seaside retreat sporting an ornate amusement park, lavish bathhouses, a grand lagoon, and a labyrinth of romantic seawater canals serviced by a fleet of happy, if low-paid, gondoliers.

The vision proved short-lived, and after Kinney's death Venice merged with the city of Los Angeles. Most of the canals were filled in, and the place was slowly transformed into an offbeat urban eyesore, becoming a refuge for bohemians, beatniks, Holocaust survivors, hippies, and Rollerbladers who made the boardwalk their home, bodybuilders who pumped iron at Muscle Beach, and a never-ending contingent of vagrants and drug addicts who elevated in-your-face panhandling to an art form. Despite a recent influx of wealthy white professionals in search of real estate close to the ocean, Venice retained its sleazy and seductive image. It remained a deceptively dangerous venue, plagued by a burgeoning crack trade and volatile racial tensions between the large black and Hispanic communities that had established themselves in earlier decades and the yuppies, who were perceived as interlopers in their neighborhoods.

The tensions, which were everywhere, were always hottest in those neighborhoods where the old ghettos bordered areas undergoing new construction, architectural rehabilitation, and gentrification. Such places were often the sight of vandalism and "hot prowl" burglaries, nighttime housebreakings of occupied homes committed by gangbangers and street hoods who got their kicks terrorizing frightened residents in their pajamas, skivvies, and birthday suits.

Sally Sutton lived in an apartment house in one of the border zones off Rose Avenue on the fringes of the black neighborhood known to the locals as Oakwood. The building was a cheaply constructed two-story structure, common in the beach communities of Southern California, with an L-shape design built around a parking area striped to allocate one space for each of the eight units. The tenants were an incongruous and uncomfortable mix of surfers and college kids who took more interest in partying than studying, working singles, and a few down-at-the-heels families with children. To the families, the singles always made too much noise at night, and to the singles, the kids were a constant pain in the ass, playing in the hallways, the parking area, and the small garden outside the front entrance. One thing they all shared was the belief that they were short-termers destined to move on to bigger and better living quarters.

John and Stretch sat in the Mustang across the street,

watching the children play in the final hour of daylight before being called in for Sunday dinner.

"This is what the DMV printout shows as her current address," Stretch said, reading the computer document he had obtained from the state motor vehicles bureau. "Apartment Five." He paused to consider the odds of Sally welcoming the two of them on her doorstep, then added, "I'll let you do the talking, but go easy. I don't want to peel you off the ground again."

They exited the Mustang and crossed the street. The handle on the front door was jammed, but it gave way easily against the weight of Stretch's shoulder. Inside, a television babble of late Sunday afternoon movies and sports shows issued from the apartments, mingling with the odors of stale beer and fried food as John and Stretch climbed the stairs.

Apartment 5 was to the rear of the second floor. The Sunday *Times* was still out on the front mat, a sign that Sally either was sleeping off the escapades of Saturday night or hadn't yet returned home. John picked up the paper and rang the buzzer. A few hollow seconds went by, and he rang again. A neighbor from the next apartment poked her head into the hall, took note of their presence, and, entirely unfazed by the sight of two strange men at Sally's entrance, closed her door. Finally a voice called out from inside number 5. "All right, I'm on the phone. I'll be right there."

The expression on Sally's face as she opened the door passed through a series of rapid changes, from shock and surprise to anger and resignation. "What the hell do you guys want?" she asked.

John smiled weakly and offered her the copy of the *Times*. "Thought you might want your paper." Meant to break the ice, his feeble joke sounded lame and contrived.

Sally tightened the belt on her pink bathrobe and took the paper from him. Even without makeup, she was a beautiful woman, her green eyes large and wide, her breasts firm and inviting even behind the terry cloth. "It's about the only thing that's not nailed down around here that the neighbors won't steal." She stared at John and Stretch, waiting for some further explanation. "Well, are you going to answer my question, or did you come to gape at my cleavage?"

"We need to talk," John said, suddenly dead serious.

"About what? I've got nothing to say to you."

"Look, I don't want to argue in the hall. Can we come in?" Her body stiffened with resistance. "It'll take only a few minutes," John assured her.

She thought for a moment, then stepped aside. Inside, the apartment looked like a female version of John's place, with blouses, skirts, and panty hose taking the place of T-shirts and pants atop an old blue sofa, two easy chairs, and a chipped wooden coffee table crammed with women's magazines and ashtrays that hadn't been emptied for at least a week. John brushed aside a pair of fishnet stockings and took a seat on the sofa as Stretch eased into one of the chairs.

Sally ignored them and walked across the living room to the telephone, which was resting on top of a bookshelf half filled with tattered paperbacks. "Listen, Katie"—she spoke into the receiver to her teenage sister, who had called to announce that she, too, had outgrown Nebraska—"you should think long and hard before you leave home. L.A.'s not what it's cracked up to be in the movies. The place is full of violence and guys who think only of their cocks and their wallets." She paused to glance impatiently at John and Stretch. "Look, honey, two of those guys are here right now. I'll have to call you back. In the meantime, don't do anything stupid."

She replaced the receiver and walked over to the sofa,

running a large black plastic comb through her hair, waiting for John to explain himself.

"I'm here about BJ Dupree," he said, looking all business.

"I don't know anyone by that name," she replied quickly.

"I think you do. I think you know Dupree, I think you knew Joe Richards, and I know you knew Jim Rowinski." John sounded hostile and arrogant.

"Look, I don't have to talk to you," she said, clearly regretting her decision to let them in.

"What are you afraid of, Sally?" John asked.

"I'm not afraid of anything," she said, trying her utmost to sound convincing. "And now it's time for you to leave." She stepped back, expecting them to get up. She was startled to see they weren't at all ready to exit. "Have it your way," she said after a brief pause, grabbing a pack of Winstons on the coffee table. "I'm going to call the cops." She hurried across the room again and reached for the phone.

"Why don't you call your friend Gallagher?" John challenged her. "I'm sure he knows where BJ is."

Sally took her fingers off the telephone keypad and inhaled a deep drag from her cigarette. Then she set the receiver down and turned to face John. "What do you really want?"

"The truth." John stood and walked toward her. "The truth about Gallagher and BJ Dupree."

"The truth can get people killed," she said almost in a whisper. Her tough facade had begun to crack. Tears began to form in her eyes.

"Is that what happened to Rowinski?" The menace was still in John's voice. She turned away defensively, shielding herself from his cross-examination.

"We need to know where Dupree is." Stretch broke into the conversation. He rose to his feet, his muscular six-foot-six-inch frame filling the room. His voice, however, was tempered by a measure of kindness and understanding. "We need to know," he repeated softly.

The color rose in Sally's cheeks. She took another nervous drag and gazed out the window. When she turned again to look at them, the tears were flowing freely down her face. "He's in a flophouse near MacArthur Park, the corner of Grandview and Eighth," she said in a barely audible voice. "The penthouse suite," she added sarcastically. "Now get out."

Stretch reached inside his sports coat and pulled out a business card and pen. He scribbled his home phone number on the back of the card and handed it to Sally. "You seem like you might need a friend," he said. "Just in case."

Sally took the card and stuffed it in her bathrobe pocket as they closed the door of her apartment behind them.

Like Venice, the MacArthur Park district was a blighted swath of real estate that had seen much better days. Sandwiched between downtown and the Mid-Wilshire business corridor, the neighborhood was centered on a thirty-two-acre park of the same name. Originally known as Westlake Park, it was rechristened after the decorated general during World War II. Endowed with semitropical trees and shrubbery, a pavilion bandshell, and an artificial lake, the park was once an urban oasis, where hardworking middle-class families spent lazy Sunday afternoons piloting small pedal boats and listening to concerts in complete safety.

The passing years, however, had taken an enormous toll on the park. Rising crime had transformed it into a visual insult by day and a no-man's-land of drug deals and assaults after dark. By the late 1980s the situation had gotten so out of hand that the old boathouse had been turned into a police substation. The lake, once a soothing respite from the city's wear and tear, had become so polluted from garbage and urine that even the hardiest carp turned belly up after prolonged exposure.

The surrounding area had gone downhill every bit as radically. Squeezed by an enormous population explosion of impoverished immigrants from Mexico and Central and South America, the neighborhood suffered from a wholesale flight of white-owned businesses. The major thoroughfares that cut through the area, streets that once featured rows of fashionable shops and restaurants, had given way to cut-rate merchandise outlets, pawnshops, and a polyglot of storefronts run by Spanish-language *notarios* and self-proclaimed tax and immigration specialists of dubious integrity.

Most depressing of all was the neighborhood's housing stock. Dilapidated wood-frame boarding homes and mult-iunit apartments rivaling the worst New York tenements stretched into the distance, block after graffiti-scarred block. Owned and managed by absentee slumlords, the buildings were home to thousands of undocumented aliens and poor people, an amorphous, disenfranchised mass too frightened, too tired, and too hopeless to complain about the vermin, the lack of heat and working plumbing, and the absence of security that dogged their daily existence. In return for the silent suffering of their tenants, the slumlords offered the cold yet highly coveted consolation of anonymity and unin-terested tolerance. Whether their renters packed twelve peo-ple into a two-room unit zoned for four or were on the lam from the cops or the *migra,* the owners asked no questions as long as the monthly checks and money orders arrived on schedule.

Anonymity was exactly what BJ Dupree wanted. Al-though he had no Latin blood, he spoke passable Spanish and had no trouble blending in with the motley crew of winos and deadbeats who roamed the streets and alleys of the neighborhood like an army of lost souls. The three-story brick apartment where he had been staying since the Richards shooting was a hellhole, but it was cheap and, he told himself, merely a temporary refuge. Waiting was a way of life he had long ago mastered during his stays in prison and county jail.

It was past seven and getting dark when John and Stretch found the flophouse off Grandview Avenue. John parked the Mustang carefully around the corner, and the pair made their way cautiously to the building, avoiding direct eye contact with a group of young Latina mothers and a horde of preschool kids who had congregated on the steps outside an adjacent apartment. The row of unmarked mailboxes mounted on the wall inside Dupree's building gave no clue to the names of the occupants. Lacking a better alternative, they followed Sally's directions and took off for the top floor.

As they mounted the dimly lit stairs, they heard the familiar sounds of Spanish radio. Listening to it reminded John of his ill-fated foray into the barrios of East Los Angeles on his eviction fiasco for Irv Weinberg. Although easily several miles apart, Weinberg's building and this one had precisely the same atmosphere of dank despair. On an elemental level all slums were identical, John thought, right down to the old drunks passed out in the halls and the strains of cockroaches resistant to all but the most lethal pesticides.

Two units, numbers 7 and 8, were on the third floor. If this was the penthouse, Dupree apparently shared it with an equally fortunate slum dweller. Not knowing which door belonged to their man, they knocked on each but failed to rouse a response. They knocked again and again but heard only the sounds of *banda* music rising from the floors below. A moment of truth had finally come and yielded nothing. John heaved a sigh of disappointment and sagged against the wall, the fatigue, hunger, and futility of the day's frenzied quest finally registering on his body and mind. He closed his eyes briefly, trying to visualize the closing argument he would give without the benefit of BJ Dupree. When he opened them, he saw Stretch folding up his Swiss army knife.

"Just another trick of the trade," his partner whispered as the lock to unit 8 released. Stretch pushed open the door and motioned for John to follow.

They fumbled in the darkness until Stretch found a light switch mounted on the wall. The single hundred-watt bulb hanging from the ceiling snapped on, revealing a scene of utter chaos. An old green sofa in what passed for the living room had been overturned, the white stuffing from the slashed seat cushions scattered across the floor like discarded cotton candy. Two wooden chairs and a cheap coffee table had also been upended, the shattered remains of a ceramic table lamp lying alongside them with two broken glass ashtrays and a half dozen assorted porno magazines. The door to the living room closet was thrown open, revealing a heap of crumpled and torn clothing on the floor. Two sports jackets, still suspended on their wire hangers, had their pockets turned inside out, their linings carefully slit from top to bottom.

For a moment they warily surveyed the details of the wreckage. "Either he's a bad housekeeper or one of his friends wanted awfully bad to find something," Stretch said. Acting on instinct, he reached inside his jacket for his .38. They proceeded cautiously into the kitchen, picking their way through a minefield of saucepans, broken dishes and bottles, silverware, bags of potato chips, and beer cans that had been dumped onto the worn linoleum. Every drawer had been emptied of its contents. Even the bins in the refrigerator had been spilled onto the floor. "Whoever's been here must have known Dupree wouldn't be back," Stretch commented, pausing to kick a scattering of forks and knives from under his feet.

"Unless Dupree tore up the place himself, looking for something," John countered.

Before they could finish the debate, the sound of glass crashing in the bedroom sent them diving for cover. John took refuge on the floor, his heart pounding loudly against his chest, his face resting between a six-pack of Bud and an unopened sack of chips. Stretch crouched at his side, training his .38 in the direction of the bedroom. They stared anxiously into the darkness of the bedroom, straining to discern the slightest movement.

"Come on, motherfucker," Stretch whispered. "Come on." He rose to his feet and with his back against the wall slowly turned into the doorway to the bedroom. "Hands up," he barked, raising his revolver to the ready position.

A shrill cry issued from the bedroom, followed by the dull thump of another object falling to the floor. John had gritted his teeth, preparing for the sound of gunshots, when he saw the light come on inside the room. He struggled to his feet and hurried after Stretch to find the big man kneeling on the floor, his gun in one hand, the other tenderly stroking a black and white house cat that purred noisily under his massive palm.

"You're hungry, aren't you, boy?" Stretch said to the animal. He gave the cat a few more strokes, then stood up and turned to John with a despairing look. Lying on the bed, his face turned away toward the opposite wall, was the body of a black man. Clothed in a jogging outfit and a new pair of running shoes, he looked as if he had collapsed after a long run.

John walked slowly to the other side of the bed and stared at BJ Dupree. Blood from a walnut-sized hole in his forehead had coagulated into a network of deep red streaks across his eyes and nose. Seeping into the pillow and sheet, the blood pooled into a macabre red halo around his head. With Stretch's help, John rolled the lifeless form onto its back. The body was cold and clammy to the touch, and the large muscles of the limbs were beginning to loosen, an indication that rigor mortis was dissipating. Judging from the signs, Dupree had been dead from eighteen to twenty-four hours.

CHAPTER 21

"**T**he truth can get people killed."
Sally's words rang in John's ears. Not since he last attended
an autopsy as a deputy DA had he come eyeball to lifeless
stare with a dead body. It had been an emotionally rattling
experience back then, and it was even more so now that he
had gotten out of practice. The truth *had* gotten Dupree
killed, but what was the truth?

They drove south on La Cienega in silence, ruminating
on the unspoken question. With no more leads to follow
and the trial set to resume in less than twelve hours, Stretch
had called it quits and asked to be dropped off at home. He
lived in one of the tonier sections of Baldwin Hills, a predominantly upper-middle-class black community north of
Inglewood, in a three-thousand-square-foot ranch-style
house he bought while pulling in big bucks as a bench-

warmer with the Lakers in the mid-seventies. A relatively low mortgage rate ensured that the house would remain his even if the private eye business hit the skids.

It wasn't just the lack of leads that led Stretch to call it a night but a cute and cuddly thirty-five-year-old named Loraine whom he had met showcasing her skills at the racquetball club. Although Stretch hadn't yet lost the eye for other members of the opposite gender, Loraine had the inside track. He had given her a set of house keys and confided to John that "she just might be the one who finally gets the big man to settle down." Stretch was hoping to salvage a few hours of carnal bliss before resuming the grim rituals of the courtroom on Monday morning.

John pulled into Stretch's driveway and waited for his friend to exit. Stretch reached for the door handle, hesitated for a moment, then turned to John. "Look, I know what you're feeling," he said sympathetically.

"How the hell would you know what I'm feeling?" John snapped back.

Stretch's face registered an expression of deep concern. "Come on, man, you should go home. There's nothing left to look for."

"What about the memo?" John's voice had a tinge of desperation, like an unlucky gambler craving one last spin of the roulette wheel.

"Man, we did everything we could," Stretch said, trying to sound reassuring.

"If we did everything, then how come Dupree is dead?" John pounded his fist against the dash. "There's got to be something else."

Stretch was unable to suppress a laugh. "When you run into a dead end, it's time to turn the car around and go home," he said, pulling the door handle and climbing out of the Mustang. "We've run into a dead end, John, pure and simple."

"You can't quit on me now," John shouted as he watched his partner walk to his front door. "It's still early."

"I'll see you tomorrow," Stretch yelled back as he stepped inside. "Get some sleep."

Sleep was the last thing on John's mind as he rolled into the parking lot of the Mustang Club at a quarter to ten. Unlike the afternoon, now the lot was filled nearly to capacity with an assortment of vehicles from every corner of the globe: Jags and Beemers with personalized license plates alongside Hondas and Toyotas with smoked windows, mag-wheeled Chevys, beat-up Ford pickups, old Dodge Darts, even a handful of Volvo wagons driven by family men out on the sly for an evening of cheap thrills. A pair of young Latino attendants wielding flashlights ushered John to a parking space in the rear. They cracked a few harmless jokes about the vintage of his Mustang and left him to find his own way to the club's entrance.

For a moment John sat behind the wheel, staring blankly at the sea of cars around him. He had no reason to believe that Sally would talk to him and had nothing to threaten her with should she refuse. Still, he had no choice but to try. He reached under the front seat for the pint of J & B he'd managed to ignore since the end of the preliminary hearing. He unscrewed the cap and took a long swallow. The reassuring jolt of courage was artificial but better than none at all.

Inside, the club was even more packed than the parking lot had indicated. If this was an establishment on the verge of folding, the well-heeled throng of pleasure seekers that had come out on a Sunday night to ogle Sally and her crew of gyrating coworkers seemed intent on partying until the lights were turned out for the last time. The "girls," as Hidalgo avuncularly called the dancers, were already well into their first number as John slipped into the club's smoked-filled big room, ordered a scotch and soda, and quickly blended in with the crowd. Three dancers, outfitted in matching leopard-skin thong bikinis, were shaking and shimmying to the beat of the Stones' "Brown Sugar."

In the center of the stage, bumping rhythmically against a chrome disco pole, caressing its high-gloss lacquered finish like an oversize phallus, was the club's number two "girl," Iphigenia Jones. A stunning twenty-two-year-old black woman from nearby Hawthorne with long hair extensions plaited into dozens of beaded braids, Jeanie, as her friends called her, was a crowd pleaser and Sally's closest rival as a box-office draw. Her job was to open the first set with "Brown Sugar," a song tailor-made for her well-endowed athletic frame and unblemished chocolate complexion. It was a way to get the patrons in the mood for the revelry to follow, and it rarely failed.

John made his way to the rear of the room and took up an observation post, his back resting against a wall. The opening number came to a close, and the houselights dimmed. When they snapped on again, Sally had assumed center stage, flanked by Jeanie and a busty young Latina. The sound system clicked in with Rod Stewart's "Do You Think I'm Sexy" and the onlookers, men and women, young and old, the prosperous and those who were only able to fake prosperity with a set of gaudy clothes, roared with approval. Sally, scantily clad in an emerald green brief and halter top that offset the luster of her eyes, smiled at her public. She pranced to the music, shaking her wild mane of highlighted blond hair to the beat. The crowd began to offer up dollar bills, depositing them in the small heart-shaped containers ringing the stage.

The show continued at a fever pitch for another forty-five minutes. Rod Stewart gave way to Z.Z. Top, more Stones, some R & B, and then contemporary rap and hip-hop. Finally the lights dimmed, and the dancers made their way back to their dressing rooms. Sally, who had discarded the halter top somewhere in the middle of Jagger's "Heartbreaker," slipped into a black silk kimono as she climbed off the stage to a standing ovation from the sexually charged audience. To all outward appearances, she was a woman without a worry in the world, reveling in her open sensuality, completely at one with her work. She had long ago learned to conceal her true feelings while onstage, a technique that disguised the nervous anxiety she now felt.

Finding John seated at her dressing table quickly transformed the anxiety to anger. He had his feet propped up on the two suitcases she had brought in with her two hours earlier and a Cheshire cat's grin on his face that announced that he was able to read her mind. She stared at him for an instant, deciding whether to scream for George now or to give the intruder a chance to leave on his own power.

"You're making a nasty habit of following me around. How the hell did you get in here?" she asked.

John ignored the question and directed his gaze at the suitcases. "Going somewhere?"

"Get out of here before I have you tossed out on your ass," she hissed.

"I hope you're not planning on seeing Dupree tonight," John said.

"I told you where to find him. What more do you want?" At the mention of Dupree, her tone began to lose its bitter edge.

"Dupree is dead, Sally." The muscles in her face froze as she took in his words.

He rose to his feet and took a step toward her. "There's no place to run," he said.

"Just leave me alone and get out," she muttered in a faint voice, nervously running her fingers through her hair.

"You know too much," he said sharply.

For a split second they shared a heavy silence that confirmed John had spoken the truth.

"You have to help me," he continued. "I want you to testify tomorrow morning. They're not going to let you go."

She turned away, and he could tell that his entreaty had failed. "Ainsworth said I didn't have to stay," she answered.

"You've spoken with Ainsworth?" he asked.

She stared back at him, her expression hardening again. "It's none of your business," she snapped.

"What else did he tell you?" John pleaded.

She shook her head in a gesture of finality. "Get out. Do you hear me? Get out."

Her voice grew louder, attracting the attention of George Ortiz, who inserted his glowering presence inside the room. "Problem, Sal?" he inquired, looking menacingly at John.

"Get him out of here. Get him out now," she commanded.

George grabbed John by the lapels and threw him against the wall, sending a tray of cosmetics crashing to the floor. A right hook to the rib cage knocked the wind from his lungs and sent him doubling over in a paroxysm of pain. From there it was a quick trip through the side door to the blacktop parking lot, where he lay sprawled on the asphalt for another five minutes as the neon lights of the Mustang Club came slowly into focus. The two young Latino parking attendants knelt over him, their flashlights in his eyes. "You want us to get you to your car, man?" they asked.

John waved them off and struggled to his feet.

CHAPTER 22

John wanted nothing more than to go home and nuzzle his head in Mary's lap, to feel her gentle hands stroke his forehead. But he knew she wouldn't be there. Her father had come down with a bad case of the flu, the latest in a series of what she believed were stress-related illnesses since her mother's death last spring, and she had promised to spend the weekend caring for him. The way he saw things, as he headed east on Olympic Boulevard, he had two options: Follow Stretch's advice and head home, have a warm bath, and anesthetize himself for tomorrow's legal equivalent of a funeral or see what undisclosed secrets lurked inside Howard Ainsworth's office.

He flipped open the glove box and fished out his old district attorney's ID badge. He knew that with the ID, getting inside the office would be a piece of cake, perhaps the easiest thing he'd done all day. He had no idea what he might find there. The original Richards memo maybe or the notes of Howard's most recent conversation with Sally. He also had no idea what kind of lame excuse he would make if he got caught. All things considered, that didn't seem to matter.

It took only twenty minutes on the empty surface streets to get to the Criminal Courts Building at Broadway and Temple. Like a burglar casing an expensive home, John cruised slowly past the building and parked the Mustang a block away, in front of the deserted county law library. Hiking back on foot, his briefcase in hand, he arrived at the front entrance just after twelve. He pushed the night bell and waited as a slow-moving security guard, a man in his late fifties, shuffled over and unlocked the door. The guard was dressed in a rumpled uniform that hadn't been pressed in weeks and seemed slightly annoyed that he'd been taken away from his crossword puzzle at the front desk. John stared at the man impatiently, affecting the familiar harried image of a prosecutor with too few hours in the diurnal cycle. "Deputy DA," he said, holding up his badge. "I've got to get something from my office."

The man opened the door and allowed John to step inside. "You want me to sign the register?" John asked as he followed the guard to his night stand.

The man shrugged. "Not unless you want to." He turned back to his reading as John walked purposefully to the elevators and placed his right forefinger on the up button for the eighteenth floor.

From the outside the DA's office seemed empty and still. Simon Lasker's name, embossed in raised gold lettering on the front door, appeared dull and faded under the dim overhead lights as the elevator closed behind John. After the elections Lasker's name would give way to Ainsworth's, but little, if anything, would change in the way the office ran.

All that stood between John and the secrets of Ainsworth's files was the numeric keypad mounted on the wall that controlled the lock on the front doors. He pressed the four digits of his old PIN code—5-3-7-4—and waited for the lock to release. It didn't. He pushed the code again, and the door remained shut. His code had obviously been purged from the system. He was a fool to think it would still be valid.

Increasingly frantic and prepared to stay all night until he got lucky, John punched in a variety of random combinations. His efforts were cut short by the sound of singing, emerging from a side door down the long east corridor. Adrenaline surging through his body, he ducked for cover around the corner of the elevator bank and strained to listen.

Although the voice was strange, it was clearly that of an older black male, crooning the lazy lyrics of Fats Domino's version of "Blueberry Hill." The man had a good, if untrained, singing voice and was obviously enjoying the late-night freedom he had to exercise his vocal talents.

John poked his head from behind the elevator bank for a closer look. The singing voice belonged to a man dressed in gray coveralls, who was pushing a large janitor's cart with a trash can and set of dustpans and brooms in the direction of the service elevator at the other end of the corridor. Another man, white, mid-forties, wearing blue slacks and a button-down dress shirt, followed close on his heels. John recognized him immediately as Larry Culpepper, head of the Domestic Crimes section. Alternately ridiculed as the office nerd and praised for his unstinting efforts on behalf of battered women, Culpepper was the DA's night owl, a lifelong insomniac who was unmarried, had no social life to speak of, and practically lived in his office.

Culpepper trailed after the singing janitor like a puppy seeking affection. "Well, that just about does it for me, Mr.

Culpepper," the janitor said. "You won't tell anyone I missed the Friday shift and came tonight instead."

"Your secret's safe with me, Winston," Culpepper said reassuringly.

Winston pressed the elevator call button and stepped inside the compartment as the doors opened. Culpepper waved good night as the janitor launched into another Fats Domino imitation.

Standing no more than twenty feet away, John trained his eyes closely on the numeric keypad as Culpepper walked back to the front entrance and raised his right hand to punch in his PIN code. John could make out the first two digits, but Culpepper's palm obscured the lower row of buttons as he pressed the final numbers to release the lock.

Thinking he was alone, Culpepper broke into the refrain of "Blueberry Hill" in an exaggerated stage voice, throwing the front door open wide to make a theatrical entrance. As he disappeared inside the office, the heavy wooden door, controlled by an industrial-strength hydraulic closer, began to shut slowly. John took a few cautious steps forward, then broke into a desperate sprint. He managed to grasp the handle a split second before the door fastened.

John paused long enough for Culpepper to return to his office, then walked slowly through the reception area and the secretarial pool. The creaking of his shoes was drowned out by the sounds of all-night talk radio coming from Culpepper's direction. John slipped unnoticed past Culpepper's half-opened door and ambled down the hall and around the corner to Ainsworth's office.

Using a modified version of the trick he had seen Stretch perform at Dupree's apartment, John slid a credit card into the doorjamb. The flimsy lock gave way almost immediately. He flicked on the lights and stood motionless for a few seconds, taking in the artwork and antiques that made

Ainsworth's workplace look as if it housed a big-firm law partner rather than a civil servant. "You know, Howard," he said in a whisper, "I really hate what you've done to my office."

He walked over to the bank of three filing cabinets standing against the opposite wall and saw to his relief that they had been left unlocked. Either Ainsworth had nothing to hide or he was so confident of the security of his office that he had not even bothered to take the most elementary precautions. John pulled open the top drawer of the first cabinet and lifted out a file containing a typed multipage document entitled "Ainsworth, Howard, Closed Trial Cases."

Ainsworth had always been an exceptionally well-organized litigator, and it came as no surprise that he maintained such a master file on his old cases. Cross-indexed by the name of the defendant, the year of the complaint, and the nature of the charges, the file provided a convenient reference to well over two hundred trials that Ainsworth had conducted during his long tenure as a prosecutor. Robberies, drug busts, and homicides, the big cases and the small, were logged in one after the other, documenting the impressive string of courtroom triumphs turned in by the DA's head trial deputy.

John read quickly through the list of cases until he came to the name of Frank Garcia, the murder suspect he had been prosecuting when Ainsworth supplanted him as deputy chief. Next to Garcia's name, underscored in red ink, was the date that the jury returned its guilty verdict. A handwritten entry, also written in red, followed. "Ainsworth promoted to chief's post."

John threw the folder back with a look of disgust and resumed his clandestine tour of Ainsworth's files. The first two filing cabinets were stuffed to the brim with volumes of sample pleadings and motions that Ainsworth had developed over the years for ready use in every conceivable kind of prosecution, professional evaluations of the deputies who worked under his direct supervision, and a variety of memos, reports, and studies on the office's budget and administration. The cabinets also contained the case files on no less than three other murder trials that had been assigned to Ainsworth and were in various stages of pretrial preparation. John skimmed the materials in each drawer quickly and with a nervous glance at his watch moved on to the last cabinet.

The top drawer of the third cabinet housed the working file on the Thomas case. Fully two thirds of it were taken up by police investigation reports that had been turned over to the defense in discovery. The remainder consisted of the motions Ainsworth had filed and the handwritten outlines of the direct examinations he had conducted of the prosecution's witnesses. John marveled at the completeness of the questions. Ainsworth had done a truly professional job of presenting the People's case.

John found the outline from Sally's direct neatly stored in its own manila file. To his disappointment, there was no mention of any recent contact between Sally and the prosecution. Nor was there any sign of the Richards memo. Everything in Sally's file and all the others, for that matter, seemed in order—no surprises, no suppressed evidence, no smoking guns.

John turned from the cabinets and eyed a stack of files perched on the coffee table in front of the couch where he had encountered Mary after the prelim. It seemed like such a long time ago, the two of them pretending to be strangers, barely able to suppress the erotic attraction they shared. He shook the image from his mind and moved to the imposing black lacquered desk that dominated the center of the office like a baby grand piano. The desk first and then the files on the coffee table, he told himself. Since he had taken the reckless step of breaking into Ainsworth's office, the least he could do was explore every conceivable hiding place.

John took a seat on Ainsworth's high-backed armchair and conducted a quick inventory of the articles on the desktop, framed photos of Ainsworth and his family, an expensive Sony dictation unit, a pad of personalized memos with Ainsworth's name and title embossed in raised black script, the old leather-bound Bible resting on a small walnut-stained bookstand, an ivory-handled letter opener next to it. John reached for the letter opener, preparing to jimmy the middle drawer. But like the filing cabinets, the drawer was unlocked.

There were five drawers in all, a traditional shallow middle tray, three standard-size drawers on the right and a deep single bin on the left. John slid open the middle drawer, revealing a neatly arranged assortment of small office supplies, half a dozen pens, a cache of county-issued business cards, three fresh legal pads, a scattering of paper clips and rubber bands, and a small bottle of extra-strength Tylenol. The right-hand compartments were taken up with such equally incriminating items as Ainsworth's two-hole punch, tape dispenser, and stapler, a dozen extra legal pads, and his employee phone book, listing the office numbers of every county department and professional and managerial worker.

Expecting to find another heirloom Bible or a teddy bear earmarked as a future birthday gift for one of Ainsworth's kids, John reached for the handle of the large left-hand compartment. A bolt lock drilled into the side of the desk held it shut tight. Animated by a new sense of urgency, he worked feverishly at the lock with the letter opener, but it failed to budge. Hoping to find a spare key, he reopened the middle drawer and spread the paper clips and rubber bands with his fingers like a miner looking for a grain of gold. But there was no key and no clue as to what, if anything, lurked within the large compartment.

John closed the middle drawer and looked again at the lavish appointments of Ainsworth's office, his mind a jumble of thoughts about his past and future: how he had fallen so far from his days as chief trial deputy; how the Thomas case had given him a last shot at redemption, a shot that had now finally misfired. For some odd reason, John's eyes came to rest upon the old Bible. He had never been religious, had not even had a bar mitzvah, but there was a gold silk bookmark in the pages of the book that drew his curiosity. He picked the Bible up and held it in his hands. The marked page opened on the Book of Revelation. A passage was underlined in bright blue ink. "I am Alpha and Omega, the first and the last." Wedged tightly into the binding was a small silver key. It spilled noisily on the desktop as he spread back the pages. It fitted the bolt lock perfectly.

John released the large compartment. The manila files tucked away inside stared back at him like the answer to a prayer. He lifted them out and set them on the desktop. Five files in all, each with a cleanly typed label. They were marked, respectively, "Richards, Joseph"; "Gallagher, Thomas"; "Rowinski, James"; "Hidalgo, Jose"; and "Omega." John grabbed the Richards file first. It was almost four inches thick, with scores of photocopied papers fastened onto each side of the legal folder. John recognized most of the documents from the dead officer's LAPD personnel records that had been turned over to him before the trial. But the folder was much thicker than the official personnel file and had clearly been augmented by materials that Ainsworth had gathered. He knew the contents would have to be examined with great care, but only after he quickly scanned the rest.

He opened the file on Gallagher. It was about half the size of the dossier on Richards, consisting of a collection of LAPD investigation reports on six unrelated homicides, the oldest of which dated back more than a decade. John recalled the names of three of the arrested suspects. Two of them, according to his memory, were prosecuted by Ainsworth. Each was convicted, with one, a torturer-murderer who mutilated a mother and her two-year-old daughter before taking a knife to their throats, receiving the death penalty. All of the reports listed the chief investigating officer as "T. Gallagher."

The fact that Ainsworth and Gallagher had worked together on past cases was neither a secret nor a surprise. The way they complemented each other in court made them an imposing litigation team, the clean-cut earnest prosecutor and the police lieutenant who was all business all the time. If it was more convictions and stiffer sentences the People wanted, they were certainly getting their money's worth from that pair.

John was about to put the file aside when he noticed a photocopy of a handwritten note sandwiched behind the investigation reports. Written in Ainsworth's hand on his personal memo paper, the note was addressed to Gallagher and dated approximately three years before the Richards shooting. Below the date was a reference, in chronological order, to the six homicides from the file. Below the reference was a single terse paragraph: "In each of the above-referenced matters, you have relied on the same informant, Robert James Dupree, either as a percipient witness to certain incriminatory conversations or as a source of background information. Be advised that such reliance has become excessive and is jeopardizing the objectives of both our departments."

The memo was signed "Howard Ainsworth, Chief Trial

Deputy, Office of the District Attorney." John spotted Ainsworth's memo pad on the desk and tore off a fresh sheet. He hastily wrote down the names of the six homicides.

The Rowinski file, which he picked up next, was also jam-packed with police reports. But unlike the Gallagher folder, they centered on a single episode, a three-year-old LAPD raid on a suspected South Central crack house. Although no cocaine was found in the house, one of the occupants, a young black man named Josea Parrish, died in the raid. According to the reports, he was shot wielding a sawed-off shotgun while the cops were executing a search warrant. The name of his killer was listed as LAPD Officer James Rowinski.

John paged through the crime scene and autopsy reports until he came across a group of documents generated by the LAPD's Internal Affairs Division. The diverse threads of the story were summarized in one of the division's memos. A group of local black religious leaders had apparently organized a letter-writing campaign, alleging that the search warrant of the Parrish house had been issued without probable cause. In response to the complaints, the police department initiated an in-house investigation. After a few administrative hearings the matter was passed on to the DA's office for a determination of whether Rowinski had acted in self-defense or had committed an unjustifiable homicide.

Eventually the issue landed in Ainsworth's lap. Two junior prosecutors assigned to the case had prepared a brief recommending that Rowinski be charged with second-degree murder. As best as John could tell from a quick perusal of the paper trail of memos and forms, a criminal complaint was drafted but never filed in court. At the last minute Ainsworth pulled the plug. In a memo addressed to Simon Lasker, Ainsworth concluded that the search warrant might indeed have been issued without the required probable cause but that Rowinski had nonetheless acted in self-defense. Ainsworth recommended that the city agree to a monetary settlement with the Parrish family, who by that time had filed a wrongful-death lawsuit, in order to defuse what might otherwise grow into a public embarrassment for law enforcement.

John closed the Rowinski file and placed it on top of Gallagher's. He thought hard but had no recollection of the Parrish case. The city must have kept a tight lid on the terms of the settlement with the family. Either that or he must have been on one of his extended binges when news of the case hit the papers. In any event the file provided further proof of Rowinski's volatility and proximity to the crack trade.

Where the Gallagher and Rowinski files were thick with paper, the Hidalgo dossier contained only two thin documents. The first was the club owner's rap sheet. John checked it quickly to make sure it was the same one that had been turned over to him during discovery and was relieved to find it was.

The second document, however, was something of a puzzle, a single-page color glossy flyer announcing the unveiling of a new Cuban supper club, the Cuba Libre, on the Upper West Side of Manhattan. The flyer showed a wide-angle view of the club's interior, filled with happy, well-dressed customers seated around well-laid tables topped with white tablecloths. In the background a band dressed in fanciful mambo outfits played on a small elevated stage. The folder heralded the Cuba Libre as New York's most sophisticated late-night Latin gathering spot. The date given for the grand opening was about a year old. John could think of no reason why the folder had been stuck in Hidalgo's file, unless the Cuba Libre was owned by one of Hidalgo's old associates whom Ainsworth had contacted to dig up background information on his witness.

He laid the folder aside and turned to the Omega file, which was nearly as thin as Hidalgo's and at first glance even more puzzling. It consisted of a solitary twenty-page single-space typed document bearing the cryptic title "Secular Humanism—Personal Reflections on the Real Enemy." Beneath the title was the quotation from Revelation John had seen underlined in the old leather-bound Bible. This was followed by what seemed to be the working draft of an elaborate essay, replete with footnotes and a brief bibliography, setting forth the heartfelt private thoughts of Howard Ainsworth on religion, law, family values, and the abject state of the world, all subjects that had made Ainsworth the darling of the local religious right. John studied the document and realized that he had stumbled upon a window to the mind of his adversary, the man he blamed for his descent into professional purgatory all those years ago. Though the essay had no apparent connection to the Thomas case, the temptation to read on was irresistible. The essay read:

It is often said that California is the harbinger of things to come for America and that Los Angeles is the harbinger of things to come for California. If that is true, we are in deep and abiding trouble. We are called the City of Angels, but I see little to justify that gentle name. I see crime and corruption, avarice and greed, youth destroyed by drugs, communities torn asunder by gangs, and I see politicians and public servants unable or unwilling to tackle the root cause of these evils.

What *is* that root cause? Scholars and religious leaders have debated the question with great fervor. Not long ago it was not uncommon to place the blame on communism and the pernicious influence that perverse ideology had upon our social life and institutions. More recently the finger of blame has been directed at the decline of family values, abortion, and free sex as the overriding determinants of our collective miseries.

I believe the great danger is something different. The great danger—the overarching danger that spawns and sustains all the others—is secular humanism. Secular humanism in all its various guises and disguises. Secular humanism, with its false creed of moral relativism, with its corrupt exaltation of individual permissiveness, its unceasing questioning of law and religion, is the true culprit, the real enemy.

John shook his head in disbelief as his eyes pored over the fire and brimstone leaping from the pages. So Ainsworth's evangelical persona was no put-on. He really believed all that holier-than-thou garbage. Ainsworth may have made a good prosecutor, John thought, but he would have been a truly inspired preacher, leading the masses to salvation. John could easily visualize Ainsworth behind the pulpit, wearing a dark blue suit with a white carnation in the lapel, appealing for donations on Sunday morning TV services.

The essay moved on to a discussion of the purveyors of the false creed, the who's who of secular humanism, including such blasphemers as the ACLU, the NAACP, the B'nai B'rith, and People for the American Way. John wanted to savor it all, but time permitted only an abbreviated perusal. He skipped ahead to a section with a subheading entitled "Calvin." This portion of the text opened with a reference to the contributions that the famed sixteenth-century French theologian had made to Western civilization in general and the God-fearing entrepreneurial spirit of America in particular. Ainsworth wrote:

> The Protestant ethic places a premium on the values of hard work, thrift, individual responsibility, sobriety, and prudence. To the elect who embody these virtues shall come wealth, respect, and eternal joy. To the slothful, the spendthrifts, and, above all, the secular humanists shall come shame and eternal perdition.

Do not think that the struggle against secular humanism is of recent vintage only. It is, in truth, as old as history. Calvin, too, waged a struggle against those who sought to disparage and shun true Christian principles in favor of moral pluralism. Under Calvin's leadership the Consistory of Geneva imposed a stringent order of discipline and religious guidance. Those who ridiculed or defied the Consistory and its teachings faced stiff punishment, graded in severity to fit the harshness of the crime.

The blasphemer Jacques Gruet was beheaded for his impudence and treachery. The physician Jerome Bolsec, a former monk and Doctor of Theology, was exiled for questioning the truth of predestination. The scholar Sebastianus Castellio was not allowed to join the pastorate because of his radical notions about the Canticle of Canticles, the Song of Solomon. The Spanish unitarian Miguel Servetus, who waged a long campaign of insolent criticism against Calvin, was burned at the stake when he dared enter Geneva. When it came to heresy, Calvin was a most ardent and unashamed proponent of the death penalty.

As Calvin denounced those who would play with the Law for their own advantage, so we today must unite to condemn the civil libertarians and secular humanists among us who seek to mitigate the strict and swift application of the law against those who transgress it. Drug dealers, robbers, and rapists must be imprisoned. Abortionists must be hunted down and put out of business. They and other garden-variety murderers must be prosecuted to the full extent of the law. The death penalty must be carried out.

A final section, obviously incomplete, began with the heading "What Can Be Done?" Below it were two sentences: "As District Attorney I will be your champion. The elect shall be elected."

John stood motionless, mentally reeling from the sweep of Ainsworth's invective. So this was the real Howard Ainsworth, the zealot behind the controlled and polished public figure, a devotee of a perverse and twisted antediluvian form of Calvinism. What an uproar it would create if the essay were ever leaked to the press. He could just see the headlines. REVELATION IN THE COURTROOM. THE AYATOLLAH PROSECUTOR. GOD, MAN, AND THE NEW DISTRICT ATTORNEY.

Before John could complete the fantasy, the night bell at the front entrance sounded. Maybe the security guard had come up to check on him. Maybe another insomniac deputy prosecutor with a jury on line for Monday morning had arrived to keep Culpepper company. Whoever it was had to be avoided at all costs. John stuffed the files back in their hiding place, hurriedly placed the key inside the Bible, and slipped out the door. Taking refuge down the corridor in a dark alcove outside the women's rest room, he could hear the voices of Culpepper and Lieutenant Gallagher growing louder as they neared Ainsworth's office.

"I told you," Gallagher said as the two men paused in front of Ainsworth's door, "Ainsworth sent me to pick up some files."

"Sure thing," Culpepper said brightly, obviously intimidated by Gallagher's glowering presence. He unlocked the door and turned on the lights.

"Don't you ever go home?" Gallagher asked.

"All I need, Lieutenant, is a warm place to plug in my laptop," Culpepper answered, trying to sound hip or at least not quite as lame as he knew he appeared.

Gallagher gave Culpepper a look of incredulity and annoyance. "I think what you need, Counselor, is a warm place to plug in your dick."

Culpepper tried to take the ridicule as a form of police humor. "Need some help?" he asked meekly, hoping to tag along with the lieutenant.

"No, thanks," Gallagher replied with an air of finality. "I'll take it from here." He waited for Culpepper to leave before entering the office and closing the door behind him. It took him only ninety seconds to reemerge with a small stack of manila folders under his arm.

John waited until he heard Culpepper and Gallagher exchange good-byes outside the secretarial pool before returning to Ainsworth's office. He picked up the old Bible and turned to the Book of Revelation. The underlined passage on the Alpha and Omega stared back at him like enigmatic runes. The small silver key, however, was gone. He reached for the left side drawer and let out an audible sigh of relief as it opened freely, but the relief gave way to despair when he saw the drawer was empty.

Finding Mary asleep in his bed was a most welcome discovery after the bitter disappointment of the night. She stirred to life as he sat beside her, softly stroking her cheeks with the back of his hand. She craned her neck and kissed him on the face and mouth, once, twice, repeatedly, explaining between breaths that her father had recovered and she'd missed John terribly. He pulled her close and let the warmth of her skin, the fragrance of her hair, and the passion of her embrace overcome him. The disaster that awaited him in court receded from his mind as they fell to the sheets, their bodies moving in sweet rhythmic harmony.

CHAPTER 23

Judge Rosten's courtroom had lost none of its carnival atmosphere over the long weekend. Ainsworth and Gallagher arrived early and took their seats at the prosecution table, engaging in a businesslike conference on their strategy for dealing with the defense portion of the guilt phase.

By the time John assumed his place next to Juan Thomas, the courtroom was packed with the now-familiar assortment of reporters, lawyers, civic activists, curiosity seekers, and a rowdy collection of homies from Juan's 'hood. Whether it was a prizefight or a legal lynching, people always seemed to turn out in droves, as long as the event promised to deliver drama for the onlookers and pain for at least some of the participants.

The only person missing from the drama was Stretch. It

was nine o'clock, and there was no sign of him. He had left no message with the bailiff, and there had been no answer at either his home or his office. It wasn't like Stretch to be late, especially for a critical court appearance. Something had happened, John told himself, fighting off a mounting sense of panic, something ominous. Maybe Stretch had gotten sick, or been in a car accident, or caught a bullet in one of the city's random freeway shootings. Whatever it was, John knew he'd have to find out later.

Ainsworth stood up and walked to the defense table. He extended his hand to John in what seemed a sincere gesture of good sportsmanship as Gallagher and Juan Thomas exchanged unfriendly stares. "So what have you got for me this morning?" he asked.

"I want to talk to the judge," John replied, abruptly terminating their handshake.

"You mean you have no witnesses," Ainsworth said. He looked like a man whose private suspicions had been confirmed, calm and confident, prepared to do battle but equally ready to accept a quiet surrender without further bloodshed.

"I mean, I want to talk with the judge," John answered testily. Before he could elaborate, Rosten entered the courtroom and the bailiff began to call upon all assembled to rise and genuflect in the presence of His Honor.

"Be seated and come to order." Rosten invoked the litany. He looked unusually grumpy, even for a Monday morning. *"People versus Thomas.* The record will reflect that both counsel and all jurors are present. I also see that the investigating officer for the People is present but that the defense investigator, Mr. Johnson, is not." Rosten turned to John with the grave expression he had perfected over the years for defense attorneys with hopeless cases. "Mr. Solomon, are you ready to proceed?"

Ainsworth glanced knowingly in the direction of the defense table as John rose slowly and cleared his throat. "Uh, no, Your Honor," he stammered.

The chatter in the courtroom rose several decibels as the gallery registered its surprise and disappointment. Rosten quickly banged his gavel, and the room returned to silence.

"Before we begin, Your Honor," John said, "I'd like to request a conference in chambers."

Rosten appreciated chambers conferences about as much as sit-down dinners with his ex-wife. They were largely unnecessary and always time-consuming. There was rarely any good reason once a trial started why anything that needed to be said couldn't be uttered in open court, at a sidebar if need be. Rosten paused to consider what shenanigans the defense might be up to. The last thing he wanted was a display of histrionics in front of the media. On balance, he decided it might be best, just this one time, to hear Solomon out in private. "This had better be good, Mr. Solomon," he admonished. He rolled back the left sleeve of his black robe and glanced at his watch. "Ten minutes. I'll see counsel, with the court reporter, in my chambers. The jury will be excused."

Anticipating the usual inconsequential bellyaching that transpired at such sessions, Rosten took a seat behind his desk, the court reporter crouched in a folding chair by his side. Clutter was the motif of the judge's office. Stacks of lawbooks and transcripts lay on either side of his desktop. Bookshelves on every wall contained the last fifty years' worth of the published opinions of the California and federal appellate courts, from the United States Supreme Court on down. It was an impressive compilation of legal reports. Behind his desk hung a display of the judge's diplomas and awards, along with an assortment of photos of Rosten with prominent members of the legal profession and more informal shots of the judge with what looked like his sons and grandchildren.

"Okay, Counsel," Rosten said to John, motioning him to take a seat beside Ainsworth in the high-backed blue upholstered client chairs in front of him. "You've got ten minutes."

"I want a continuance, Your Honor," John said, steeling himself for the judicial wrath he expected to follow.

"I hope this doesn't have anything to do with the absence of your investigator," Rosten cautioned.

"No, Your Honor, it has nothing to do with that," John replied.

"A continuance is out of the question," Ainsworth chimed in before John had finished. Ainsworth knew he had John on the ropes and the judge on his side. He intended to milk the situation for all it was worth.

"I was hoping that the judge would rule on this one, Howard," John shot back sarcastically.

"Mr. Ainsworth's right," Rosten interrupted, aligning himself unequivocally with the prosecution. "You've got some nerve asking me for a continuance at this juncture, no matter what the reason." He sifted through the stack of materials to his left and pulled out a thin transcript of the pretrial hearing held earlier in the case when John first subpoenaed Joe Richards' personnel records and had asked for a brief postponement. "This is the second motion for a continuance you've made, if this transcript is accurate."

Although he had in fact forgotten the earlier request, John remained determined. He reached into his briefcase and handed Rosten a one-page document. "Maybe this will change your mind," he said.

"What's this?" Rosten asked, leaning back in his chair to examine the paper.

"The second page of an interdepartmental memorandum written by Joe Richards to the DA's office asking for help to investigate a cocaine kickback ring run by Lieutenant Gallagher out there and his deceased accomplice, Jim Rowinski." As John spoke, Rosten stared at the memo, a quizzical expression on his face. "Richards was murdered for attempting to blow the whistle. My client's been framed."

The quizzical look on Rosten's face turned into a sour scowl as he handed the memo to Ainsworth. "Mr. Ainsworth?" he inquired roughly.

Ainsworth studied the memo briefly and rudely returned it to John. "I've never seen that before in my life. I went over Richards' personnel records myself. I had his property, case files, and computer logs inventoried. There's been no mention of any such memo," he protested, looking straight at Rosten. "I'd also point out, Your Honor, that this document isn't an original. For all we know, it could have been typed last night." He turned toward John and shook his head in disgust. "I've seen some pretty desperate tactics in my time, but this one smacks of duplicity."

Rosten's back stiffened, and he took another quick glance at his watch. "Would you care to tell us how this document came into your possession, Mr. Solomon?" he asked dryly.

"I'm afraid I can't reveal that," John said. "But I can assure the court that the defense hasn't fabricated it." Even though he had told the truth, he knew his explanation sounded unconvincing.

It was clear Rosten had heard enough. "Mr. Solomon," he lectured, "I don't know where this document came from, and at this particular point in time I don't really care. What I do know is that this is a trial and we're not going to disrupt it over a bunch of wild speculation and possible chicanery. We're going to march back out there and finish this case whether you like it or not. That's what you're being paid for." He paused briefly, took a deep breath, and added in a soft but chiding tone, "A man with your recent record should be very happy to get a trial like this."

It was a low blow, and John reacted instantly, without thinking of the consequences. "This isn't a trial, Judge," he said. "It's a public execution."

No judge, least of all Joseph Rosten, would take kindly to such insubordination. But where some might content themselves with a warning for first-time offenders, Rosten believed in swift and decisive action. "Counsel, I've had it up to here with you," he said, lifting a clenched fist to the level of his chin. "When your client's trial is over, yours is going to begin—for contempt of court."

Back in the courtroom the spectators greeted the return of the judge and counsel with respectful silence. Rosten summoned the jury and once again called the morning session to order. Before he proceeded further, his gaze settled briefly on Simon Lasker, the DA himself, who had entered the court and commandeered a front-row seat during the recess. The two men seemed to share a silent acknowledgment about the importance of their respective positions in the legal community. "Mr. Solomon," Rosten said, returning to the business at hand, "are we ready to proceed?"

John rose and fastened the middle button of his jacket, like the attorneys on *LA Law*. "Yes, Your Honor, *we* are ready," he replied sarcastically. "The defense calls Lieutenant Thomas Gallagher."

Though surprised and visibly annoyed at being made a defense witness, Gallagher strode to the witness stand with the cowboy confidence that was his trademark and was calmly resworn by the clerk.

"Proceed, Mr. Solomon," Rosten said, warming to the sight of the ritual dance of the desperate defense lawyer.

John walked to the lectern and briefly scanned the notes he had taken on a yellow legal pad during Gallagher's direct examination. They were of no use. His only hope was to hammer away at Gallagher's involvement in the kickback scheme. He knew that in doing so, he ran the risk of touching off another firefight with Rosten, but he was already headed for a contempt hearing and had long since abandoned the principle of self-preservation that normally restrained even the most zealous advocates.

"Lieutenant Gallagher," he asked, "how long have you been a member of the Los Angeles Police Department?"

"Fifteen years," the steely-eyed witness answered.

"With that kind of seniority, you must know what an interdepartmental memo is."

Before Gallagher could respond, Ainsworth jumped to his feet to register a relevance objection.

To John's surprise, Rosten rejected the complaint. "Overruled," he declared, directing a hard gaze at the witness. "Get on with it."

"Well, Lieutenant?" John prompted.

"It's a written communication from a member of the police department or sheriff's office to the district attorney." Gallagher had no difficulty answering and did not look the least bit uncomfortable.

John lifted the Richards memo from the top of the legal pad and, with Rosten signaling his grudging approval, walked to the witness stand. "I'd like you to take a look at this document, Lieutenant," he said, leaning in close to the witness.

Gallagher perused the document quickly and handed it back to John. He looked prepared for any questions that might be thrown at him.

"You recognize it, don't you?" John asked.

"I'm afraid I don't, Counselor." Gallagher took his eyes off John just long enough to look reassuringly at Ainsworth.

John took a few steps back and surveyed the muted expressions on the faces of the jury. He knew that unless Gallagher admitted to recognizing the memo, he would never be able to authenticate it under the rules of evidence and would never be able to have it read into the record. He turned again to Gallagher. "Do you recognize the name of Joe Richards that appears at the bottom of the document?"

"I'm sure everybody in this courtroom recognizes that name," Gallagher replied condescendingly. "He's the victim in this case." Several spectators chuckled audibly at Gallagher's comeback.

John pretended to ignore the laughter and pressed on. "Richards was a good cop, an *honest* cop, wasn't he?"

"Yes," Gallagher answered with a straight face. "I considered him a friend."

"But not everyone in the police department felt that way, did they?" John took a step closer to Gallagher. "Jim Rowinski, for example."

"Rowinski was a different story," Gallagher conceded, showing the first signs of discomfort.

"Rowinski was your friend, too, wasn't he?"

"Yes." That made two admissions in a row. Gallagher began to shift in his seat.

"How did you feel when your friend Jim Rowinski shot down and killed a young black man named Josea Parrish in a drug raid three years ago?"

The question brought Ainsworth to his feet again. "Objection, Your Honor, irrelevant, inflammatory, and prejudicial." His voice had just the right mix of dignity and insistence one would expect from an experienced prosecutor.

"I agree." Rosten ruled without hesitation. "Move on, Mr. Solomon. You know better than that."

John took another half step toward the witness, a maneuver designed to invade his comfort zone. "How did you feel when your friend Jim Rowinski sent Joe Richards to the hospital with two broken ribs?"

"Objection," said Ainsworth authoritatively.

"Sustained," Rosten ruled reflexively. "Do try to pose some relevant inquiries for us, Mr. Solomon."

Undaunted by Rosten's chastising, John waved the memo in front of Gallagher like a toreador shaking a red flag before a bull. "How did you feel when your friend Joe Richards sent this memo to the DA, naming you, Rowinski, and a street informant named BJ Dupree at the center of a cocaine kickback ring? It pissed you off, didn't it?"

Gallagher's ruddy complexion turned beet red with barely suppressed anger as John's question lingered in the air. In one stroke John had managed to rattle his witness and reveal the gist of the memo. It mattered little that Gallagher was spared the embarrassment of answering after Rosten upheld yet another objection by Ainsworth. The damage was done. Gallagher was pissed off, flustered, and ready to display his ugly and violent nature to the jury.

"Lieutenant Gallagher," John persisted, still clutching the memo in his hand, "the document I'm holding is a photocopy. What happened to the original?"

"What original?" Gallagher sneered, blowing his cool but unable to contain himself. All he could think of was getting his hands on Solomon.

John leaned on the railing of the witness stand, affecting the casual posture of a man discussing gardening with a neighbor across a backyard fence. His calm demeanor only served to enrage Gallagher further. "The original that you removed from the district attorney's files last night."

It was impossible to tell who sprang to his feet first, Gallagher or Ainsworth.

"How the hell do you know where I was last night, Counselor?" Gallagher bellowed, forcing John to step back defensively.

"Your Honor," Ainsworth shouted, "this is contemptible. This whole line of questioning is hopelessly irrelevant and inflammatory." The mounting noise level in the courtroom accentuated the urgency of his protest.

It was moments like these that made being a judge one of life's biggest pains in the ass, Rosten thought quickly as he gazed upon the rows of spectators chatting away as if they were watching a Dodger game. He reached for his gavel again and brought it down sharply three times. "Sit down, gentlemen," he ordered. Rosten rapped the gavel down hard once more and pointed it at John. "Mr. Solomon, unless you're prepared to produce the original memorandum and unless you come up with a witness to authenticate it, I'm ordering you to move on to another subject." He paused for a moment and took a hard swallow. "This is the last such ruling I intend to make."

John knew that he had pushed Rosten to the breaking point. There was no merit in pushing further. He walked slowly back to the lectern and began to flip through his notes, then readied himself for another assault. "You know the police informant BJ Dupree, don't you, Lieutenant Gallagher?" he asked.

"What difference does it make if I do?" Gallagher had resumed his seat but had not given up on the fantasy of snapping John's spine like a dry twig.

"Come on, Lieutenant, you were his juice man, isn't that what you call it? You were the one he turned to when he wanted to trade phony information to get out of jail."

"You're doing the talking," Gallagher answered stiffly.

John returned to the defense table and reached into his briefcase for the notes he had taken from Gallagher's file in Ainsworth's office. "According to my research, Lieutenant," he said, glancing quickly at the case names he had scribbled on Ainsworth's memo pad, "Dupree has testified for the prosecution in at least a half dozen cases in which you were the investigating officer. Isn't that true?"

"It might be."

"It might be?" John looked over at the jury. For the first time since opening statements, several members smiled at him. They were faint Mona Lisa grins, but it was clear that he had touched a responsive chord. Encouraged, he returned to Gallagher. "Would you like me to read the names of the cases, Lieutenant?"

"A lot of officers used Dupree," Gallagher said grudgingly. "He got results. That's all I care about."

John paused to let Gallagher's remarks register. Here was a police officer who was all but admitting that he cared only about convictions and was totally unconcerned with the truth. The basic goal of cross-examination is to destroy the credibility of the witness by revealing contradictions and inconsistencies in his testimony, by exposing his bias and prejudice, or by simply provoking him into alienating the jury to such a degree that nothing he says will be believed. John had to incite Gallagher only one more time into doing or saying something outrageous and his credibility would go down the toilet so far it would take a Roto-Rooter to rescue it.

John found the avenue of attack easily. "By the way, Lieutenant Gallagher," he said in a tone of feigned innocence, "where is BJ Dupree today?"

"How should I know?" Gallagher answered hostilely.

John dropped his notes and strolled over to the rear of the jury box, forcing Gallagher to face the jury. "Because you know he was shot through the head yesterday. He was shot because he knew about the cocaine kickback ring. He was shot because he knew that Juan Thomas was set up and framed for the murder of Joe Richards. He was shot because you knew he could no longer be trusted. Because of that, he had to be eliminated, just like Joe Richards."

John's staccatolike interrogation brought Gallagher off his seat again. "That's the biggest crock of shit I've ever heard," he bellowed, pounding his fist so hard against the wooden railing of the witness stand that it shook violently. For a moment it seemed he was ready to bolt the stand and take off after John. The courtroom came alive with alarm as two burly bailiffs rose and warned Gallagher to remain calm.

One of Juan Thomas' homies, a kid in his late teens who had sat quietly in the gallery through the morning, suddenly rose to his feet amid the commotion. "Ain't no white man can judge you, Juan," he yelled. "White men can't judge." The kid stood and flashed a gang hand signal as the noise in the courtroom rose to a new level of confusion.

Shouting above the din, Rosten ordered the young man escorted from the courtroom. Rosten was well aware of the growing spate of violence in courtrooms across California and the country. Irate witnesses, spectators, and defendants had even shot and killed people. Although the spectators had been screened for weapons, Rosten was determined to prevent a free-for-all from erupting in his domain. "I'll have order in this courtroom or I'll have *everyone* cleared from it," he declared, his right hand clutching the gavel. Fortunately the young man accepted his expulsion without resistance, and the tumult slowly subsided.

"Lieutenant Gallagher," Rosten continued angrily after the bailiffs returned to the courtroom, "no matter how provoked you become, you are never, ever to display that kind of behavior in my courtroom. Do you understand?"

"Yes, sir," Gallagher answered like a contrite schoolboy.

"Your Honor." Ainsworth spoke up, gambling that Rosten was even more vexed by John's cross-examination tactics than Gallagher's lack of self-control. "The People move that the testimony of Lieutenant Gallagher be stricken."

"On what grounds?" John demanded, daring Ainsworth to articulate an objection that could support such a wide-ranging sanction.

"Counsel has devoted his entire examination to the frivolous theory that this witness is responsible for the murder of Joe Richards," Ainsworth answered. "It is a theory entirely without foundation, designed solely to prejudice the People's case."

Rosten rubbed his forehead with his left hand and hesitated, pondering how the state supreme court might rule on his handling of Ainsworth's motion. In the end he yielded to his gut instincts. "The jury shall be instructed to disregard the entire examination of Lieutenant Gallagher." He turned to the witness. "Lieutenant, you may step down." As Gallagher made his way back to the counsel table, Rosten cast a hard look at John. "Mr. Solomon, do you have anything further for us?" he asked.

John returned the hostility in Rosten's stare. He stood at the defense table, leafing through his papers but said nothing. The seconds peeled away, and Rosten declared again, "Mr. Solomon, we're waiting for an answer. Be good enough to give it to us this morning."

John remained mute. Just three words—"the defense rests"—and the reporters would have their story, Ainsworth would have his victory, and Juan Thomas would be only a penalty trial away from the gas chamber. John felt the eyes of all assembled focused on him: the bailiffs, the jury, the spectators, Ainsworth, Gallagher, Rosten, Juan Thomas. Only he could deliver the official pronouncement of surrender, and everyone was waiting for him to do just that.

John glanced at Juan Thomas and then turned his eyes to the floor, his thoughts racing wildly. He had come a long way from that day Stretch found him drowning in his Bud Light at Swanson's. He had even managed to convince himself that his client was innocent and that the case was winnable. If only he had dug up more dirt on Gallagher. If only he had found the original Richards memo before Gallagher had shown up and taken it. If only he had been a better lawyer. He knew the doubts and second-guessing would haunt him.

Another undercurrent of restlessness rippled through the courtroom, bringing John's recriminations to an end. Rosten snapped his gavel, trying to rein in the excitement before it once again got out of hand. The noise abated, but as John looked up, he was no longer the center of attention. Every person with two functioning eyes had turned his head to the rear, trying to get a glimpse of Sally Sutton and Stretch Johnson as they entered the courtroom together and took seats in the spectator section.

Dressed in a long sleeve white blouse buttoned at the wrists and a pair of faded blue jeans, Sally looked like someone who wanted to be comfortable for a long bus ride out of town but had undergone a sudden change of heart. Everyone, from Rosten and Ainsworth on down, was staring at her, out of curiosity, shock, anticipation, or thinly veiled lust. She ignored them all and trained her gaze solely upon John. It was an anxious and fearful look, as if she were staring at the headstone of her own grave.

John shifted his gaze from Sally to Stretch. The wry smile on Stretch's lips needed no translation. The big man hadn't overslept, nor had his car been rear-ended. He'd been tending to business and had come through again.

"Your Honor," John said, breaking the hush that had settled in, "the defense calls Sally Sutton as its next witness."

CHAPTER 24

Ainsworth rose to his feet like a man who had spotted a small explosive. "Request a sidebar, Your Honor," he shouted with a mocking sidelong glance at John.

Rosten beckoned the adversaries forward, and the three men huddled together at the bench, with the court reporter crowding in behind them, preparing to transcribe the barbs. "All right," Rosten announced in a low voice, "let's hear it."

Ainsworth looked squarely at Rosten as though appealing to a member of some sacred inner circle for a special dispensation. "This witness has already been excused, Your Honor," he said earnestly.

"Since when does that stop me from calling her back?" John rejoined abruptly.

"You know that she has nothing to add," Ainsworth snapped back.

"Let's put her in the box and see," John said.

Rosten raised his right hand to put an end to the bickering. When he spoke, he sounded tired and tested. "As much as I fear this may simply be another fishing expedition, I have to agree with counsel's due process right to present a defense. But I'm warning you, Mr. Solomon. This better go somewhere or I'll excuse the witness and you'd better be ready for closing argument." He gave the lawyers an exasperated look, letting them know that he was losing patience with both of them. "Now let's finish this up."

Her face drawn and taut, Sally took the stand. She held her hands in her lap, nervously rubbing her thumbs together, waiting for John to hammer away at her earlier testimony. John would have preferred to ease into his examination, to throw her a few easy questions about her background that might help to ease the tension. But Ainsworth had already covered the name, rank, and serial number inquiries in Sally's previous turn at bat, and John knew that Rosten would not permit him any unnecessary leeway with the witness. He had no choice but to go straight after her, even if it meant exposing her role in the framing of Juan Thomas.

"Ms. Sutton," he said in a grave voice, "you know what it means to commit perjury, don't you?"

The question brought an immediate objection from Ainsworth. "The witness doesn't need a lecture on ethics from the defense," he shouted.

"I quite agree," Rosten responded quickly, sustaining the protest.

Unfazed by the setback, John plowed ahead. "You testified earlier that Joe Richards was looking for someone. You know who that person was, don't you?"

For the first time since reentering the courtroom Sally

glanced at Ainsworth. She hesitated, as if rethinking the wisdom of her return. "Yeah, like I said," she answered sharply, "a young black guy."

"You already gave us a description," John reminded her sternly. "I want his name."

Ainsworth slammed his hand on the defense table and shouted out another objection. "Calls for speculation, Your Honor. The witness can't possibly know what Officer Richards was thinking."

"Sustained," Rosten droned from the bench. "Move along, Mr. Solomon."

John stepped from the counsel table to the rear of the jury box and waited briefly for the sting of Rosten's latest denial to abate. He folded his arms in front of his chest and gazed at Sally like an impatient parent waiting for one of his kids to own up to the truth. "Ms. Sutton," he said, "who is BJ Dupree?"

From out of the corner of his eye John could see Gallagher beginning to squirm in his seat. Sally, too, was visibly uncomfortable at the prospect of answering the question. She looked at the ceiling and then down at her hands, realizing there was no escape. "Just another loser who hung out at the Mustang Club," she answered in a virtual whisper.

"And you knew him, didn't you?"

"In a way," she replied evasively.

"In a way?" John unfolded his arms, his tone becoming incredulous. "Come on, you knew him better than that. You knew he was an informant and a bagman for the cops, didn't you?"

"No foundation," Ainsworth protested. "Calls for hearsay."

"Sustained," Rosten ruled again, cutting off yet another avenue of attack.

"Well, here's something that isn't hearsay," John doggedly persisted. "Your lover Jim Rowinski was a cop, wasn't he?"

"Yes," Sally answered, uncertain where John's questions were taking her.

"And you, Dupree, and Rowinski were all at the Mustang Club together on the night Richards was killed, weren't you?" John took a few paces toward Sally and waited for her response. "I don't have to remind you that you're under oath, do I?"

"Look, I'm here, aren't I?" she replied. "I called your investigator this morning and told him I *wanted* to testify."

"Then answer the question," John said. "You were all at the club together that night, weren't you?"

"Yes," she said softly.

"And what was Dupree doing there?"

Sally delivered her answer before Ainsworth could rise to register another objection. "He was there to meet Jim. They met at the club a lot."

Having failed to head off Sally's answer, Ainsworth moved to strike her remarks from the record, expecting another instantaneous ruling in his favor.

This time the ruling came neither quickly nor easily. Joseph Rosten was not one accustomed to changing his mind once he had it made up. In this case he had long ago concluded that the defendant was guilty and that all of John's maneuvers were nothing more than the typical smoke and mirrors thrown up by defense lawyers who must do something to justify their stipends. Now Rosten was no longer sure. It was an uncomfortable and unaccustomed feeling, but the defense was clearly on to something.

Rosten reminded himself that he, unlike the prosecution, had no personal interest in securing a conviction just for the sake of taking another gangbanger off the streets. No, his personal interest was to protect his own reputation. If the prosecution's case was destined to go down in flames, he wanted to make sure his chances for an appellate court appointment didn't go down with it because of one too many knee-jerk rulings. "Your motion is denied, Mr. Ainsworth," he said sharply. "I will permit the witness to answer."

John let out a deep sigh and glanced over at Ainsworth. An anxious expression had settled over the prosecutor's face. John took comfort from his adversary's distress and walked to the witness stand, his confidence growing with each step. "Dupree came to the club to make payoffs, didn't he?" he asked Sally.

"Yes." Her answer was given clearly and without the slightest hesitation. "BJ used to call Jimmy from a pay phone not far from the club to arrange things. Sometimes BJ brought the money directly to the club, and sometimes he brought it to my apartment. He gave the money to Jimmy, and Jimmy handled things from there."

"And Richards found out about it, didn't he?"

"Yes."

Gallagher looked quickly at Ainsworth, expecting an objection, but Ainsworth continued to stare ahead in silence as though paralyzed by the unexpected turn of events.

"And that's why Richards and Jim got in a fight late last year, isn't it?" John asked, capitalizing on Ainsworth's lapse.

"Jimmy had a nasty temper, especially when he was on coke," Sally answered. She seemed genuinely relieved to be unburdening herself.

"Dupree was the man Richards was chasing, wasn't he?" John asked in a commanding tone he had not displayed in a courtroom in over four years.

"Objection," Ainsworth protested mildly, without bothering to stand. "Calls for a conclusion."

"Yes, it does," Rosten observed dryly, "and I'm dying to hear it. Overruled."

"Yes," Sally answered again. "They knew Richards would be at the club. They set him up."

"And Dupree was hired to do the job, wasn't he?"

Another halfhearted objection was denied, and Rosten gently instructed Sally to answer.

"Yes," came the response.

"And you know who hired him, don't you?" John asked, looking back at Gallagher.

It was the question the entire courtroom was waiting for, and it packed just enough wallop to stir Ainsworth out of his torpor. "Objection," he called out desperately, rising from his chair. "Lieutenant Gallagher is not on trial here."

"Nobody has said that he is," Rosten answered. The anger in his voice sent Ainsworth slumping back into his seat. Rosten turned to John and nodded. "Proceed."

John stepped away from Sally and positioned himself at the midline of the jury box. "Who had Joe Richards killed?" he asked calmly.

Sally avoided John's eyes and looked over at the prosecution table. She took a hard swallow and seemed to catch her breath. "He did," she said, pointing an accusing finger directly at Ainsworth. "And then he had Jim killed, too." She reached into her handbag and retrieved a mini audio-cassette. "It's all right here, on tape. A conversation between Dupree and Howard Ainsworth." She held the cassette aloft in her right palm, displaying it like a mascara kit at a cosmetics counter. "I took it from BJ's apartment the night before he was killed."

John walked slowly back to Sally and took the tape from her. He handed it to Rosten's clerk and asked that it be marked for identification, rehearsing in his mind the questions he would have to ask in order to have the tape played for the jury.

As he waited for the clerk to perform her ministerial duties, he turned and gazed at Ainsworth. Their eyes met in a form of silent but intimate communication. For an instant it seemed as though he and Ainsworth had the courtroom all to themselves.

"It's what you were after when you shot Dupree and tore up his apartment, isn't it, Howard?" John asked in a voice loud enough for all to hear.

Ainsworth stared back at John with the hollow expression of the damned. Although he was still outfitted in his Brooks Brothers finery, the arrogance and pride that once accompanied the expensive suits were completely gone. He folded his hands in prayer and pressed them against his forehead. "Father, forgive me," he uttered softly.

The rest of Ainsworth's remarks were drowned out by the noise that erupted from every corner. Gasps, cries of surprise, racial epithets were shouted and exchanged. A minor scuffle broke out between a group of off-duty cops and a handful of Juan Thomas' homies. Powerless to restore the peace by verbal command, Rosten hastily excused the jury and ordered the bailiffs to clear the courtroom. Through the bedlam, the judge's voice could be heard declaring the proceedings a mistrial.

CHAPTER 25

The message on John's office answering machine sounded at first as if nothing had changed. Except for the disjointed background chatter of other inmates waiting to take their turns on the phone, it seemed for an instant that Howard Ainsworth was back in his corner office on the eighteenth floor of the Criminal Courts Building, still preaching his unique gospel of law and order.

John took a quick glance at his desk calendar just to make certain that three weeks had actually gone by since Stretch had escorted Sally Sutton into court and that the Thomas case was really over. Stretch hadn't known what Sally was going to say that morning, only that she wanted to tell the truth. It was Sally's truth that had proved Ainsworth's undoing.

Reassured that he had not tumbled into some unseen

time warp, John took a sip of his morning coffee, reversed the tape, and pressed the play button a second time. "This is Howard Ainsworth." The message began smoothly and confidently. "I realize this call may take you by surprise, and I truly hope that all is well with you. I'm calling because we have to speak about a matter of grave and mutual concern." A few seconds of silence followed. When Ainsworth spoke again, it was in a voice quavering with unaccustomed emotion. "My salvation and perhaps your own are at stake," he struggled to say. "Things that were said and done a long time ago have led us to our present stations." He paused again and took a slow breath. "You know where to find me. I know you'll come."

John rewound the tape again and played the message over and over, each time more intrigued than the last at both the obtuse content and the sudden shift in tone. Ainsworth, the fallen giant, was requesting—no, begging—an audience with his archnemesis. How poignant and pathetic he sounded. In the span of a fortnight the chief trial deputy had gone from the next district attorney to a jumpsuited resident of the men's central jail. The county grand jury had taken all of three days to return an indictment against him for three counts of murder for his role in the shooting deaths of Dupree, Richards, and Rowinski. Because of the obvious conflict of interest involving the DA's office, prosecution of the case had been turned over to the state attorney general. The AG was seeking the death penalty on a "multiple murder" special circumstance.

Ainsworth's demise was the biggest scandal to rock the DA's office in memory, and John stood squarely in the middle of it. In a city noted for manufacturing disposable celebrities, John became an overnight conversation piece. The papers called him "the man who brought the prosecution to its knees." He was invited onto radio talk shows and the eleven o'clock TV news. There were even a couple of mid-level Hollywood producers who had broached the subject of putting together a movie deal on his courtroom triumph.

The producers, two thirtyish Perrier-sipping schmoozers from Beverly Hills, somehow found their way into Rosten's courtroom the day after the judge had declared a mistrial. The proceeding they witnessed was brief but powerful. Although Ainsworth had yet to be formally charged, the handwriting was already on the wall. Seeking to protect his public image and prevent his future job prospects from going down with his chief trial deputy, Simon Lasker had hastily calendared a motion to dismiss the Thomas prosecution officially.

In a humbling presentation Lasker begged the court's forgiveness for the expense and embarrassment of placing the life of an innocent young man in jeopardy. "Bringing this case to trial was a grievous and unfortunate error on the part of my office and the police department," he told the judge.

"A prejudicial error from start to finish," Rosten replied, invoking the legal term used to describe a miscarriage of justice. He then proceeded to announce the dismissal order.

Juan Thomas sat through the hearing wearing a grin only slightly smaller than the Grand Canyon. After it was all over, he gave John and Stretch hugs, told them they were one straight-up combo, and walked out of the jaws of death in the company of Little Loco and his posse of homies.

It was a dramatic moment, the kind that big-time reputations are built on. The producers talked up a storm about doing a movie of the week for one of the networks, possibly even a feature. They forecast a six-figure package for the rights to John's story. In the end it turned out to be so much Hollywood hype. For ten days running, John's phone calls had gone unreturned.

Most attorneys would have continued to pursue the Hollywood angle until they received a definite and unambiguous no, were served with a restraining order, or otherwise dropped from exhaustion. After money and power there was nothing lawyers as a species craved more than publicity, not even sex.

Although John was by no means averse to seeing his name in headlines, he liked to think he was above the shameless self-promotion of other attorneys. Maybe he was, and then again maybe he really wasn't cut out for life as a public figure. Whatever the reason, he felt a sense of relief that the producers had moved on to other things. Soon the hoopla surrounding his role in the Thomas case would die down, and he'd be able to rebuild his practice and restore a semblance of normality to his life. It had been a long time, far too long, since he had led anything that might have passed for a normal life.

His thoughts drifted to Mary. Would she remain a part of his world? He hoped so, but the answer was far from certain. They seemed to bring out the best in each other, and the sexual attraction between them had lost none of its heat. But they were two different and very independent people, and they still had a difficult past to overcome if they were to make things work.

Ainsworth's call was a rude reminder that it was never easy to leave the past behind. Like it or not, fate had joined John and Ainsworth at the hip like a pair of antagonistic Siamese twins. He had no idea what Ainsworth wanted, possibly to tell him he would be subpoenaed as a witness at his upcoming trial, perhaps to reveal some long-held secret about John's firing from the DA's office, perhaps just to rant one last time about man, God, and the law. Ainsworth's call lent no clue. Whatever it was, John knew that he had to find out.

He double-checked his appointment book. Two suppression motions on a pair of routine robberies in the morning and a late-afternoon interview with a partner at a downtown firm who was looking for a "seasoned litigator." John wasn't especially interested in joining a big firm, but he wanted to hear what the man had to say. If his visit with Ainsworth ran past three, he could always call and reschedule.

No matter how much the rest of the local landscape changed, the county jail stayed the same. Riots could torch whole sections of the city, earthquakes could reduce entire blocks to rubble, immigration could transform English into a second language. The county jail remained an island of stability, housing the area's outlaws and malefactors behind its austere cement and steel exterior. Its impassive immutability was matched only by cemeteries and ancient monuments.

The inmate log had Ainsworth's name listed in the "Protective Custody" module, the area of the jail reserved for wayward law enforcement officials, snitches, and others who had to be segregated from the mainstream population for their own protection. John filled out a visitor's slip and passed through the X-ray screen and the sliding steel door that opened onto the interview room. It wasn't quite two o'clock, and the big room was only half filled with lawyers conducting client interviews. In another two or three hours, when the afternoon sessions at the courthouse let out, it would be standing room only.

John found a seat in the same Plexiglas interview booth where Juan Thomas had left his fingerprints on his neck only months earlier. He unfolded the copy of the *Times* he had been carrying around since Ainsworth's phone call had caused him to rearrange his day. His eyes turned to the front-page story on the DA's race, the latest installment in a continuing series of articles chronicling the chaotic free-for-all that had developed with Ainsworth out of the running. With less than a month left in the contest, the latest polls showed the race as a three-way dead heat.

Pulling even with Richard Martinez and Carol Wyatt was Bob Ferguson, one of the good ol' boys from the bowels of the DA's office whose candidacy had been resurrected by Ainsworth's sudden fall from grace. While Martinez and Wyatt were calling more stridently than ever for a thorough housecleaning of the prosecutor's office, Ferguson advocated a return to business as usual, and the quicker the better. He was Ainsworth without the panache or the stain of a murder indictment, and large segments of the public seemed to find him appealing. As no candidate appeared capable of garnering more than 50 percent of the vote, a runoff election between the two top vote getters was anticipated for January. In the meantime, the office continued to limp along under Simon Lasker's morally bankrupt leadership.

John had barely finished the story when he heard the duty officer shout Ainsworth's name from the reception desk where the inmates summoned for interviews checked in before being allowed to meet with their visitors. John raised his hand to let the officer see his location and settled back to watch Ainsworth, escorted toward him by a uniformed deputy, a clean-shaven baby-faced white kid no more than twenty-two years old on his first assignment since graduating from the sheriff's academy. When they arrived at the interview booth, the deputy uncuffed Ainsworth's hands and guided him into the seat across from John. "Just raise your hand when you're through," the deputy told John in an exaggerated deadpan before walking off. If Hollywood ever needed another Jack Webb, the kid was ready to audition.

John stared at Ainsworth for a moment, absorbed by the

total transformation of the man before him. It had to be one of the all-time ironies that Ainsworth was now housed on a no-bail hold in the same section of the jail that BJ Dupree, the man he had killed, once called home. Dupree the master snitch, Ainsworth the master prosecutor, each had made his mark playing mind games with the justice system, and each had paid dearly for it. The pressure had already taken a heavy toll on Ainsworth. The suntanned good looks had been replaced by a gray jailhouse pallor; the once self-assured countenance had given way to a worried, stoop-shouldered posture. The piercing eyes now seemed vague and disoriented. The man who in his late forties had looked ten years younger than his age now seemed ten years older.

"Well, Howard, you were right," John said finally. "I'm here. What now?"

Ainsworth smiled childishly and shook his head like a little boy trying hard to keep a secret. " 'The song of songs, which is Solomon's,' " he answered, laughing softly to himself.

Ainsworth's response and the faraway look on his face took John aback. He didn't know whether to feel anger, curiosity, or compassion. "I'm not sure I understand the reference," he said, hoping to engage Ainsworth on the cryptic level he had chosen.

"It's a reference to one of the most controversial books of the Old Testament," Ainsworth explained. "The Song of Solomon." He placed both his hands palms down on the small table that separated him from John, and his expression became serious. "It's your song, the song of a man possessing all the wonders and joys of the earth."

John felt a touch of irritation at what he considered Ainsworth's deliberate evasiveness. "Is that why you asked me here, to tell me that I have a special kinship with one of the stories from the Bible?"

Ainsworth folded his hands into his lap and closed his eyes, as if appealing to some superior power. " 'I am Alpha and Omega,' " he muttered half under his breath. " 'The first and the last.' " When he opened his eyes again, he seemed suddenly clearheaded and alert, as if the old rational lawyer within him had somehow been awakened. He gazed at John for an instant. "Don't tell me you've never heard the quotation before. Revelation, chapter one, verse eleven?"

"I'm not sure I have," John said, doing a poor job at concealing his discomfort.

"You know, John," Ainsworth said in a tone that sounded something like a lecture, "my lawyer has advised me to plead insanity. I refused, of course. It's amazing what you defense attorneys are willing to try. Even if they could find a doctor willing to fabricate a diagnosis, I'm certain that no jury would believe a man like me was insane." He paused to give his next comment added force. "There's one other thing I know for certain. Would you like me to tell you?" He didn't wait for John's response. "I know you broke into my office the night before the trial ended."

"That's an outrageous accusation," John countered, striving to sound suitably aggrieved.

For the first time since he sat down, Ainsworth looked the part of a prosecutor. "The list of cases you referred to in court, the ones in which Gallagher used the services of BJ Dupree," he said accusingly. "You were reading off one of my personal memo papers. How could you have discovered that list and written the cases down on my stationery unless you had searched through my files?"

John thought for a moment about denying the charge but reconsidered. Ainsworth may have been crazier than a shithouse rat, but he was still a dangerously cunning adversary. There was no point in ticking him off unnecessarily. "Why bring that up now?" John asked.

Ainsworth closed his eyes again, and a look of intense concentration passed across his face. "Do you believe in predestination?"

"How do you mean?" John asked, unsure whether Ainsworth had abruptly changed the subject.

"You and I, we're linked together." Ainsworth smiled, almost warmly, as if to underscore the unseen bond between them. "You had the position of chief trial deputy, and I coveted it."

"So you plotted against me with Simon."

"And I prevailed. Because I was *meant* to prevail."

"And what about the Thomas case? Were you meant to prevail on that, too?"

Ainsworth grinned and shook his head again, the image of a man rocked by an equal measure of shock and regret over the disaster he had made of his life. "I certainly thought so, and I thought that you, once more, were destined to help me. But I was wrong, tragically wrong. You were protected by your Song of Solomon. *You* were meant to prevail. All of this"—he gestured with outstretched arms at the four corners of the interview room—"was predestined."

John folded up his newspaper, stood up, and prepared to leave. He was no expert on insanity defenses, but he had always believed that the sickest defendants were the ones who protested the loudest that they were perfectly sane. The way Ainsworth was lapsing in and out of lucidity was either a terrific acting job or the symptom of a profound mental disorder. Exactly when and why Ainsworth had crossed the line into full-blown psychosis was a question that would no doubt be debated by his doctors for years to come. For his part, however, John felt that he had heard enough about predestination and the Book of Revelation.

"Take care, Howard," he said, extending his right hand.

Ainsworth accepted John's handshake eagerly but looked wounded and surprised at the imminent departure of his visitor. "I asked you here so I could tell you why I became a murderer. Please don't leave until I've finished." He gazed searchingly at John. "Don't tell me you don't want to know."

John was in truth dying to know, but he was deeply concerned about receiving any information from Ainsworth that could either make him a potential trial witness or interfere with the relationship between Ainsworth and his attorney. The last thing he needed was to become the guardian of Ainsworth's macabre secrets. "Shouldn't you discuss that with your lawyer?" he asked.

"John, I've already given the attorney general a full confession," Ainsworth said in his most sincere lawyer's voice. "You need not worry about getting into any hot water. Besides, I've been advised to enter an insanity plea, remember?"

"All right," John replied, uneasily resuming his seat to listen.

As he spoke, Ainsworth's demeanor was all business, almost, as at the outset of his phone call, as if nothing had changed. "Three years ago, well after you lost your position in the office, I was asked to study a homicide referral from LAPD Internal Affairs for the possible prosecution of Jim Rowinski. The matter concerned the shooting of Josea Parrish, the case you referred to in court in your cross of Gallagher."

Ainsworth waited for a look of recognition from John and then continued. "I began investigating Rowinski, examining his personnel file, and looking into the facts of the case. What I discovered was that Rowinski had a drug problem. Cocaine addiction. He had received treatment for it, but he continued to show strange and inexcusable outbursts of temper, which arguably accounted for his quick trigger in the Parrish case. Anyway, when I called Rowinski into my office one afternoon to ask him some questions, he arrived without his lawyer and told me he wanted to talk. I listened, as any good prosecutor would.

"Although he never admitted his guilt for shooting the Parrish boy, he said he had come to make a proposition. He offered me half the net proceeds from a cocaine kickback ring he had become involved in, a ring centered on the street gang your client Juan Thomas belongs to."

"And you took the deal?" John asked incredulously.

"My first reaction," Ainsworth answered earnestly, "was to arrest him on the spot. The man had an incredible nerve. I picked up the phone and was about to call for assistance when suddenly I put the receiver down. I thought, Who was this Josea Parrish anyway? Just another street hoodlum who would never amount to anything worthwhile. Then I looked at Rowinski and realized that for all his weaknesses, we were on the same side in a solemn life-and-death struggle waged every day on the streets of this city against the Josea Parrishes of this world. I declined his offer, but a few days later, after much prayer and contemplation, I called him back to my office. I told him I'd accept his offer and decline to prosecute on one condition: that he give up his drug habit and never let my identity be known to anyone involved in the ring."

"So what went wrong?"

Ainsworth smiled wistfully as if remembering better days. "For a long time nothing went wrong. I was the chief deputy prosecutor, and I had a safe-deposit box filled with two hundred and fifty thousand dollars. I was finally receiving the earthly rewards that I was destined to have, that I deserved. I had ambitions to establish a legal foundation for the protection of Christian values. I was the favorite to succeed Simon as the next DA. With any luck, I might someday become state attorney general, even governor of California. The money enabled me to act the part of a man destined for greatness. It all seemed such a small transgression for the good that I could do in the world."

Ainsworth paused again, and the wistful smile became a mask of sadness. "Then it all came tumbling down. Rowinski returned to his drugs. He told Dupree and Hidalgo about me. He bragged about his buddy the chief prosecutor. My involvement became so open that Hidalgo even approached me to suggest I launder my money through some nightclub in New York. Before long Joe Richards became suspicious. The rest of the story is rather obvious, I'm afraid. One by one they had to be eliminated. I had no choice. I was a prisoner of destiny, as are we all."

John sat silent for a good minute, letting the details of Ainsworth's story register. He thought again about leaving but felt compelled to ask one final question. "What about the tape, Howard?"

Another sly grin passed across Ainsworth's face. "The tape was the most brilliant trial tactic I've ever seen. I always knew you were good, but I never realized just how good. The tape was the reason I confessed."

"What was on the tape, Howard?"

Ainsworth slumped forward, placed his head in his hands, and began sobbing softly. The rational lawyer was gone, replaced by the jail inmate whose attorney wanted him declared a basket case. " 'And I looked, and behold a pale horse,' " Ainsworth whispered, " 'and his name that sat on him was Death, and Hell followed with him.' " He began to rock slowly back and forth in his seat, repeating the verse from the Book of Revelation. It was clear that the question would go unanswered.

John summoned the young deputy to lead Ainsworth

away and watched as his old rival disappeared inside the jail. As he pulled his Mustang out of the dank underground parking lot ten minutes later, John felt only pity for the man he once had despised.

CHAPTER 26

By the time John found a parking space in the public lot down the street from the Criminal Courts Building it was already four o'clock. He had blown his interview with the downtown firm without even bothering to phone. Whatever chances he had for a job offer had undoubtedly gone up in smoke, but he didn't care. All he could think of was whether Simon Lasker would still be in his office and, if he were, whether he could push his way in to see him.

A quick elevator ride to the eighteenth floor deposited John in the outer foyer of the DA's office. It must have been his lucky half hour because Gloria was staffing the reception desk, filling in for one of the regulars who had taken off early or called in sick. She gave him one of her typically broad smiles and waved him inside. "Back again so soon?"

she said as she met him at the doorway and gave him a maternal embrace. "Business or pleasure?"

"I'm here to see Simon, Glo," John replied in a somber tone, breaking away from her bear hug. "Is he still in?"

"Unless some lynch mob has carried him away, he's probably still in his office," she answered wryly. "But I think he's in a meeting. If you'd like, I can buzz him."

"I'll save you the trouble," he answered, and took off through the office suite, leaving Glo somewhat stunned at her desk. Any other receptionist would have phoned security immediately. John knew Glo would bite her tongue and dream up some excuse about how the phone lines had jammed or she thought John had a bona fide appointment if she were ever called to account for his unannounced visit. Glo was more adept at manufacturing explanations than most trial attorneys he knew.

John entered the hallway where the lawyers' offices were located and rounded the corner. Even from the top of the corridor he could see that the door to Lasker's office was half open, a sure sign that the boss was indeed still at home. He walked quickly down the hall and pushed open the door without knocking. Lasker and a tall brown-haired man dressed in a conservative blue pinstripe suit seated in front of the DA turned their heads to the door, looking slightly startled.

"John, what brings you here?" Lasker said, trying not to seem overly alarmed. He had his jacket off and the sleeves of his white button-down dress shirt rolled halfway up his forearms. Although slightly fatigued as he approached the end of another day full of meetings with disgruntled deputies and irritating phone calls from reporters, not a strand of his silver gray fringe was out of place.

"We have to talk, Simon," John replied sharply as he

walked resolutely to the edge of Lasker's desk within arm's reach of the other man.

"Perhaps I should come back later," the brown-haired man said, trying to sound accommodating. A lean WASPish-looking type in his mid-forties with close-set eyes and pale pink lips as thin as ribbons, he was a dead ringer for a prosecutor.

"John," Lasker said, gesturing toward the man, "I'd like you to meet Bob Ferguson. I'm not sure if you two ever got to know each other when you worked here."

Ferguson extended his hand to John. "Pleased to meet you. I think I spent most of my time in Van Nuys when you were the chief."

"Bob and I were just having a strategy session about his campaign," Lasker explained. Seeing that John was in no mood to be put off, he added, "But I'm sure we can pick up where we left off if you don't plan on being very long."

Ferguson smiled obligingly and excused himself, shutting the door behind him as he made his exit.

Lasker motioned to John to take the chair vacated by Ferguson. "So what's so urgent that you couldn't schedule a regular appointment?" he asked impatiently.

John looked at Lasker with a combination of contempt and wonder. "How do you do it, Simon?" he inquired.

"How do I do what?"

"How do you always manage to find a way to cover your own ass?"

Lasker thought for moment, debating whether to order John to leave or endure his insults long enough to find out if he had anything important to say. "If you mean Ferguson," Lasker said in a halfhearted attempt at friendly humor, "I think you're looking at the next district attorney of Los Angeles." He paused to take in the consternation on John's face before continuing in an uneasy manner. "I know we were meeting on county time, but as the retiring DA I have a right to brief my apparent successor."

"It's not Ferguson that I was thinking of, Simon," John replied angrily. "I don't care who you support or when you conduct your bull sessions."

"Then what?" Lasker asked with a shrug of his narrow shoulders.

"How is it that at a time when your chief deputy is on trial for murder, you're not even threatened with an ethics investigation?"

Lasker gazed at John and smiled. Although the last thing he wanted was a major confrontation, he realized that no amount of verbal tap dancing was going to avoid one. "As you said, I always find a way to cover my ass. It's an art form you never mastered, I'm afraid. Now, if what you came here to tell me is that I ought to be paying some kind of price for Howard Ainsworth's crimes, you've delivered your message, and you can leave."

His eyes burning with barely concealed rage, John looked deeply at Lasker. "I'm not leaving until you tell me what was on the tape."

"What tape?" Lasker asked incredulously.

"The tape between Ainsworth and Dupree, the one that Sally Sutton brought to court."

Lasker knitted his brow and chose his answer carefully, like a politician measuring his responses at a difficult press conference. "The tape was turned over to the attorney general's office by Judge Rosten himself when we declared a conflict before the grand jury. How the hell should I know what's on it? You know that grand jury records are kept secret prior to trial. Besides, Sally Sutton was your witness." He studied John closely. "You mean, you really don't know what was on the tape?"

"No. But I'm sure you do, grand jury secrecy notwith-standing," John said.

"I'm afraid that's just not so," Lasker replied conde-scendingly.

"That's not what Ainsworth told me," John snapped back. The lie sounded convincing. He watched as Lasker's complexion turned a lush beet red. "And it's not what I'll tell the *Times* if you don't answer my question."

Lasker stopped to weigh the odds that John was bluffing, then stood up at his desk and motioned with his right hand toward the door. "Lock it," he said.

John stepped back to fasten the bolt lock while Lasker walked over to one of the black filing cabinets lining the wall to his left. He slid open the top drawer, looked inside, and within seconds pulled out a black-and-white mini-cassette. "I had to make sure there was nothing on it about me."

"How did you get it?" John asked, resuming his seat.

"A friend, or perhaps I should say a political ally," Lasker replied evasively. "Does it matter, or do you want to listen?" He popped the tape into the high-tech Dictaphone mounted on his desk and placed his long right forefinger on the play button.

At first the background noise made the dialogue difficult to decipher, but it quickly became clear that a conversation was unfolding in a busy coffee shop.

BJ Dupree's was the first voice to be heard. "Look here," he said in an agitated tone. "I called you so we could talk."

"So let's talk," Ainsworth answered, trying to sound ami-able and reassuring. "I'll buy, you talk, and I'll listen."

A waitress came up and took their orders. Ainsworth or-dered a bowl of clam chowder and a side salad; Dupree a burger and fries. After the waitress left, Dupree resumed the conversation, still angry and insistent. "You think I'm some kind of punk."

"Now why do you say that?" Ainsworth asked.

"You think I'm gonna lay low for the rest of my life? Well, I'm not going away."

"Maybe it would be a good idea if you did go away for a while. Just a little while," Ainsworth suggested.

Dupree found the idea extremely disagreeable. "Listen here, Mr. Prosecutor," he said, raising his voice, "you owe me. I pulled two hits for you. The Camaro was nice, but it's not enough. I want the rest of my money, and I want it now. You understand, motherfucker?"

"I think you should settle down," Ainsworth said soothingly.

But Dupree was in no mood to be calmed. "I don't think you heard me, Mr. Juice Man. I killed Richards and Rowinksi, two sworn LAPD officers, on your orders. You owe me." There was the sound of an angry fist pounding on the table, and the tape went dead.

John looked at Lasker in confusion while the cassette reeled forward in silence. "Where's the rest?" he asked after a few heavy seconds had passed.

"That's all there is," Lasker said with a sadistic grin.

"That's why Ainsworth confessed? I'm afraid I don't get it."

"The way I heard it," Lasker explained, "he confessed to two investigators from the state attorney general's office before the tape was even played for him. It was what he thought was on the tape that prompted him to talk. He had no idea the cassette jammed before he said anything incriminating." Lasker fished a chocolate mint out of his middle drawer and propped his feet up on his desk in a relaxed after-hours pose. If he felt the least bit compromised by his former relationship with Ainsworth, he was a master at masking his emotions. "I don't know if the son of a bitch was overcome by a religious urge to spill his guts or whether he was crazy all along. But if he had only kept his mouth shut, he'd be redecorating this office right now. He would have been one terrific shit-kicking DA."

"Howard Ainsworth would have been the worst thing that ever happened to this office, Simon," John said in disgust.

Lasker placed his feet back on the floor and swung around on his swivel chair to face John squarely. "You know what your problem is, John?" he asked rhetorically. "You're too much of a moralist. You always were and always will be."

"And your problem, Simon, is that you've abandoned every principle you ever believed in."

"Every principle but the first principle," Lasker corrected him. "The principle of self-preservation. You really ought to try it sometime." He smiled and helped himself to another mint. "I'll be joining the MacMillan firm next January in case you'd like a lesson or two."

Lasker's announcement hit John like a shot to the solar plexus. MacMillan Standard was the second-largest and highest-paying private law firm in the city, its downtown headquarters occupying the top six floors of a new smoked-glass-and-steel high-rise. It had been rumored that it was courting Lasker for a senior partner post before the Ainsworth scandal broke, but John had assumed that any offer would have been quickly withdrawn in light of what had happened. The fact that it had not been withdrawn was a tribute to Lasker's political savvy and the mercenary ethos of the legal community. Even a district attorney steeped in controversy was perceived as a valuable asset to a firm that coveted as many inside connections as it could get to the upper echelons of local government.

John had to admire Lasker's resilience if nothing else. "No, thanks, Simon," he said sarcastically, "you've taught me far too much already."

The two men stood, realizing that their encounter had outlived its usefulness. Lasker extended his hand across the desk. John shook it reluctantly, unable to take it for anything other than the hollow gesture it was. "Say hello to that girl of yours," Lasker said in parting as John began to step away.

"You mean Mary?" John asked, wheeling around to face Lasker again.

"Unless you've gotten another girl in the last week," Lasker said. "She was here to announce her resignation as DA liaison. Too bad. She's a smart cookie. I must say I was kind of surprised to see you two back together."

John suppressed the urge to grab Lasker by the shirt collar and shake the smug expression off his face. "Maybe you don't know people as well as you think you do, Simon," he said instead as he reached for the door. "Life's full of surprises."

CHAPTER 27

Why hadn't Mary told him she had been to see Simon? The question stuck like a thorn in John's mind as he inched his way into the stream of rush-hour traffic on the Santa Monica Freeway. The Monday afternoon commute was always deadly, but today was especially bad. An overhead electronic sign just past downtown announced that the freeway was backed up all the way to the west side. A chorus of enraged motorists blared their horns, shouted obscenities, and waved their fists as they jockeyed for position in the slowly moving line of cars. There was nothing like gridlock on the freeway to bring out the baser instincts in one's fellow citizens.

Trapped for the duration in his Mustang, John turned up the radio but was unable to escape his thoughts of Mary. It was probably just an oversight, he tried to convince himself of her encounter with Lasker, something she merely had forgotten to mention. They both had been extremely busy the last weeks, John with the continuing salvo of media inquiries on the Thomas case and Mary with the evening college classes she needed to complete to get her undergrad degree and apply for law school. He tried to convince himself that the only logical answer, given the circumstances, was that she had forgotten.

The problem was that after his sessions with Ainsworth and Lasker, logic was no longer one of John's strong suits. The exhaust fumes seeping inside the Mustang from the overheated cars around him only made him more vexed as he crept along the jammed roadway, his eyes tracking the sun as it slowly disappeared through the smog into the Pacific. Each time he tried to think of something else, the image of that smirking grin on Lasker's face flashed in his mind. Had Mary gone to see Simon only to tender her resignation or was there more to it, something she was afraid or even ashamed to tell him? Just the thought of her being polite to Lasker made him wish that he had gone ahead and taken a poke at the old fart. The questions continued to gnaw at him for another forty-five minutes until he came to Mary's exit.

John parked the Mustang in a hurry and walked quickly to Mary's front porch. He rang the doorbell and waited. It was odd, he thought, that she had never given him a set of keys. He had long ago insisted that she take the keys to his apartment. She had used them on many occasions to let herself in and surprise him with a late-night meal or an unscheduled session between the sheets. Mary's home was her sanctuary, and while he was always welcome, she had yet to offer to share it with him.

Mary answered the door dressed in a red blouse and

black slacks. She looked tired from a full day's work, but she smiled warmly and gave him a tender kiss on the lips. "I didn't expect to see you tonight," she said, stepping back to let him inside. "I have to be at my class in a half hour. It's not easy being a cop by day and a student by night. I need to get to class on time."

"I'm sorry if I caught you by surprise," he said apologetically.

"No, it's okay," she reassured him. "I was just finishing some coffee in the kitchen. Want a cup?"

She led him back and poured him a mug of dark European roast. One of the things Mary appreciated most in life was good coffee. He took a seat at her kitchen table and savored the pungent aroma, feeling slightly embarrassed at how he had gotten so worked up in the car. "I've had a really rough day," he said, taking his first sip of the rich brew.

"You want to talk about it?" she asked.

"I've been to see Ainsworth and Lasker." He appeared shell-shocked from the experience.

She looked at him but said nothing, by her silence encouraging him to continue.

"Lasker told me you went to see him," he said gravely.

"Is that what's bothering you?" She gently placed her hand on top of his and smiled comfortingly.

But John was in no mood to be comforted, at least not until he displayed the full measure of his annoyance. He moved her hand away, and the smile on her face disappeared. "Why didn't you tell me?"

"Because I didn't think it was a big deal," she said indignantly. "I was there for only ten minutes."

"He spoke of you quite warmly." The sarcasm in his voice was evident.

"And what's so bad about that?"

"Simon Lasker is a whore. He'd indict his own mother

if he thought it would advance his career. How can you stand him?"

She stood up abruptly and walked to the far side of the kitchen, distancing herself as much as possible from John while remaining in the same room. She hadn't planned on beginning her evening with a verbal brawl, but she wasn't about to back down either, even if John had been through a rough day. "I know who Simon Lasker is," she said icily, "and I know who I am."

"And what exactly does that mean?"

"Simon may be everything you say, but he has a lot of influence. It never hurts to be friendly with a person like that." She gave him a beseeching look. "I thought he might be able to help me with a letter of recommendation for law school."

"So there was more to your visit than a simple resignation."

Her arms lifted and fell in a gesture of exasperation. "John, it's how people like me get ahead in the world. You've got to learn to play the game."

He gazed into his coffee cup and realized that he had begun to sound like a possessive husband. "I'm sorry," he said. "Maybe I was out of line."

"That's all right." She walked over to the sink and began to rinse the unwashed glasses and cups that had accumulated on the countertop. "So what's with Ainsworth?" she asked idly, trying to change the subject. "I hear he's gone off the deep end."

"Off the deep end with a pair of cement shoes." John shook his head in disbelief and began to recount the details of Ainsworth's confession and Lasker's playing of the tape.

Mary listened intently but impassively, like a police officer long used to hearing tales of morbid criminality. "You know it's amazing how clear things seem when you look back on them," she said when John finished, "but I don't think anyone had Ainsworth figured until Sally came up with the tape. What's going to happen to her? She's facing perjury charges, isn't she?"

"My guess is that she'll get probation and county jail time in exchange for her testimony against Ainsworth," John answered, gulping down the rest of his coffee before it got cold. "I can't see the AG asking for a state prison term."

"And Hidalgo, I take it, is still on the lam."

"Probably in Central America by now, if he has any brains."

"So now you know it all," she remarked calmly, placing the last of the cups and plates in the dish rack. "All the pieces fit together."

John studied her as she meticulously squeezed the last drops of soapy water from the sponge she had been using and neatly replaced the dish towel in its rack above the sink.

"I'm not so sure that they do, at least not entirely," he said.

"Of course they do." She seemed annoyed at his expression of doubt, and she did nothing to disguise how she felt. "What else is there?"

He fell silent as if canvassing his mind for an elusive thought. A few seconds passed, and he stood up, looking suddenly uneasy. "Everything fits together but Gallagher and Richards' memo," he answered finally.

Mary glanced nervously at her watch, her eyes avoiding John as he stood no more than five feet away. "It's time for me to go," she said.

"What about the memo, Mary?" he asked again, taking a step closer. "There was no trace of it in Ainsworth's office."

"Maybe he threw it away," she suggested quickly. "Maybe you didn't look in the right places." She straightened her blouse as she spoke. "I've got to go. The class won't wait for me."

"Don't you think Ainsworth would have mentioned the memo? He told me everything else."

"It's hard to know how a crazy person thinks, John." She walked into the living room as he followed after her.

"I don't think Ainsworth ever got the memo," he said as she neared the front door, opened the coat closet, and reached for her jacket. "I think he was genuinely shocked when I produced it in court."

"Look, I'm going to be late. We can talk about this later." She tried to walk past him, but he blocked her path.

They stood no more than a foot apart, joined in a momentary test of wills. "I don't think there ever was a memo," John said harshly.

"That's nonsense. I found it in Richards' things," she insisted, her anger mounting at what had plainly turned into an interrogation.

He stepped back and diverted his eyes to the floor. A sick and sour sensation came to his stomach. "You wrote the memo, Mary," he said softly. "I'm sure of it."

His words hung in the air. He wanted to retract them almost as soon as he had uttered them, but that was impossible. For a few seconds they just looked at each other, locked in a piercing stare.

"Just tell me that you did it for me," he said finally, reaching out his hand for her.

She smiled derisively as she slipped into her jacket and grabbed for her briefcase, ignoring his offered embrace. He looked at her, searching for some small sign of contrition but saw only contempt.

"I did it for me," she snapped back, "the day Gallagher threatened me."

She opened the front door, and he followed her onto the

porch. "It wasn't the first time he put his hands on me, but I swore it would be the last. I'm not ashamed of what I did." She walked angrily to the driveway and threw her case into the passenger side of her car.

John stood on the edge of the drive, unwilling to give up the fight. "You manipulated me. Doesn't that matter?"

"Your case was nothing until you found the memo. You were ready to go home and give up," she shouted as she rounded the car and reached for the driver's door. "You should be thanking me for what I did. You won, didn't you?" She slipped into the driver's seat, closed the door, and rolled up the window.

He pressed up against the car and watched as she started the ignition. "The law isn't only about winning and losing, at least not to me," he shouted above the motor. "You nearly placed the life of an innocent man in jeopardy, Mary."

She rolled the window down and paused just long enough to give him another hateful glare. "If Gallagher isn't guilty of taking kickbacks, he's sure to be guilty of something else. Trust me. I've seen the man in action."

"That's what Ainsworth said about Juan Thomas."

"Well, that's one thing he probably got right," she shouted back. "Think about it." She put the car in reverse and pulled out of the drive, leaving him standing in her yard as she drove away.

John remained on Mary's lawn for another fifteen minutes, half dazed and half hoping that she would return to continue the fight. He tried to comprehend the massive fissure that had suddenly opened in his life, his mind a jumble of anger and confusion. How had he been so wrong about Mary? They had been so close, but then again they had failed before. He should have seen it coming, he told himself. Her hatred for Gallagher was so obvious; the memo was so convenient. Only a man desperate to turn his career around could have failed to notice. In the end, when the truth came out, he and Mary were reduced to two warring strangers. In the end he was left pretty much where he had started, with a license to practice law and little else.

As night set in and the lights of the neighborhood came on, he realized that except for the argument inside his own head, the battle with Mary was over. He took a final look at her house and walked slowly back to his Mustang. Despite the autumn chill in the air, he let the top down, got in, and gunned the engine. A moment later he was back on the freeway, stepping on the gas and heading for his apartment. An eclectic medley of Otis Redding, Sam Cooke, Buddy Holly, and Jackson Browne came over the oldies station on his AM radio. Everyone, it seemed, suffered from the same problems of love gone wrong. At least he wasn't unique. The songs of misspent passion played on as the Mustang accelerated past eighty and the wind sent his hair dancing crazily across his face. In another twenty minutes he was home.

Except for Earl Warren, his dark apartment was lifeless. The ravenous cat waited in ambush just inside the front door, demanding to be fed in total disdain of the unhappy turn John's life had taken. John knelt down and gave Earl a few tender strokes behind the ears, then picked him up and cradled him like a newborn.

"Just you and me again, buddy," he whispered as he walked into the kitchen. After some aimless rummaging, he located a can of fancy albacore, opened it, and scooped half of its contents into the cat's bowl. He hastily assembled a sandwich with the remainder and stepped out onto his balcony, leaving Earl behind, purring with the ecstasy of a full stomach.

The smog had lifted and the stars had come out, transforming the view of the city into one of those picture-perfect panoramas you see in TV movies. Somewhere out there, he thought as he wolfed down the tuna, there had to be people who saw their relationships as something more than a means for professional advancement or personal revenge. He just wasn't meant to be one of them. He thought about going back to the kitchen to fish out a bottle of J & B for a long night of soul-searching and self-pity but decided against it. He had lost Mary, but the idea of drowning his sorrows just wasn't appealing. He needed a clear head if he stood any chance of figuring out what to do with the rest of his life.

He sank into the old Adirondack chair and closed his eyes. Maybe what he needed was a long vacation. Maybe he'd rent a Jeep and drive through Mexico or sail off for Alaska to climb mountains. Maybe he'd take off for England and look up the friends he'd made there more than two decades earlier, when he spent his junior year in college studying in London. Maybe he'd quit the law once and for all. The idea caused him to open his eyes as if stirring from a dream. He ran his left hand through his hair and with his right reached nervously for the old basketball he had left one weekend wedged between the chair and the railing.

He picked up the ball and twirled it in his hands as he continued to contemplate his future. There were no easy answers, at least not out here on the balcony. The ball, on the other hand, offered at least the promise of a physical release, and the local playground, a mere three blocks away, was a lot closer than Mexico, Alaska, or England. If he hustled, he could get in a good hour's workout before the lights were turned off. He hurried into his bedroom, slipped on a pair of Nikes and sweats, and dribbled his way out the front door.

* * *

It was nearly nine o'clock when John pushed open the chain-link gate to the recreation center and stepped onto the basketball court. He had hoped to find some players for a possible pickup game, but except for a young couple finishing up a tennis match on a nearby court and a teenager perfecting a routine of daredevil skateboard tricks in the parking lot, the playground was deserted. Lacking a better alternative, he launched into a one-man shooting drill, dribbling as fast as he could from one end of the court to the other, executing a variety of underhand scoops, reverse lay-ins, and pull-up jumpers. At first his shots fell short or clanged off the back of the rim, but slowly, as the sweat began to pour off his face and his breathing became labored with fatigue, the shots began to fall, one after the other in seemingly unending succession.

There was something about the rotation on a basketball as it left your fingertips and the way the ball snapped the cords of the net before falling to the blacktop that did wonders for peace of mind, he thought, as he swished another soft ten-footer. When you were in your rhythm, the ball had a special texture, the basket seemed at least a foot wider than it actually was, and no matter where you launched your shot from, you felt you couldn't miss. You felt that as long as you kept on shooting and hitting, you could outwit even the fiercest personal demons and keep your life under control.

He knew that it was here, right here in this small neighborhood playground, that he would decide whether he'd stay in L.A. or pack a knapsack and head out for parts unknown. He imagined himself going one-on-one again with Stretch in another best-of-ten showdown to determine the issue. If he won, the first order of business would be to get his passport renewed. If he lost, he'd resign himself to trying any new case of Stretch's choosing.

As the shorter and decidedly more out-of-shape player, John claimed first outs to start the contest. He took the ball at the top of the key and stared determinedly at Stretch, the way that Magic used to face down Bird in big games. He pumped once, twice, then threw a nasty fake to his right that left Stretch grabbing for his jockstrap as he strolled to the basket for an easy deuce. He followed the drive in rapid succession with a high archer from just inside the three-point line and a twisting left-handed layup along the baseline. He had Stretch huffing and puffing and feeling every one of his forty-five years when his next shot caromed off the side of the rim and skittered into the corner.

It was only then that John noticed he had attracted a one-person audience. The kid with the skateboard had entered the court, intrigued by John's exuberant pantomime. He hustled after the rebound and fired the ball back to John without saying a word. He was a short kid, about five feet three, no more than fourteen, with curly brown hair tucked beneath a Dodger cap that he wore backward on his head. He looked thin and wiry, but his body was well concealed behind a pair of baggy plaid shorts that hung down almost to his ankles and one of those loose-fitting red and black Stüssy shirts that were all the rage with teenagers.

John looked at the kid and determined instinctively that he wanted attention. "You want to shoot a few buckets?" he asked.

"Sure," the kid called back. He left his skateboard at the edge of the court and ran over to the free-throw stripe. John flipped him the ball, and the kid lofted a jumper that skimmed the front of the rim before dropping through the hoop. His form was straight and clean, a sure sign that he had done more with his time at the playground than hang ten on a skateboard.

"What's your name?" John asked as the kid glided to the basket for an overhand layup.

"Max," the kid answered shyly, feeding the ball back to John for a jumper that failed to draw iron.

"Max, that was my father's name," John remarked with surprise. "Glad to meet you, Max. I'm John Solomon." He shook the kid's hand, and they exchanged easy smiles. In addition to having a nice jump shot, he was blessed with a likable, if low-key, personality.

"I've seen you around," Max said.

"Really?"

"Me and my mom moved into the first floor of your apartment building about three weeks ago."

John thought for a moment as he watched Max fire up a turnaround jumper. He had been so busy it hadn't completely registered that a new family had moved into the building. He couldn't say that he had ever noticed Max before, but he did seem to recall passing a cute brunette in a pair of tight jeans collecting her *L.A. Times* one morning.

"Was that your mother I saw reading the newspaper outside apartment one-A?"

"Yeah, that's my mom," the kid answered nonchalantly. "She's always reading something."

"What about your dad?"

The kid's happy expression turned serious, and John knew right away he had opened a wound. "We're divorced," the kid said, "two years ago."

"I'm sorry," John said. "I didn't mean to pry."

"That's okay," Max told him as they continued to trade baskets. "What kind of game were you playing just now?" he asked. "It looked pretty serious."

John felt slightly embarrassed at the sight he must have presented. "It's a little game I play whenever I have to make a big decision."

"But who's Stretch?" the kid persisted.

"You heard me say 'Stretch'?" He hadn't realized that his "in-your-face" epithets had been audible. Now that was really embarrassing. "He's a friend of mine who used to play for the Lakers."

"Really? That's great. Can I meet him?" The kid took another jumper, then suddenly looked contrite, as though he expected to be turned down. "I mean, if it's not too much trouble or anything."

"I'm sure it can be arranged," John said. "Stretch never met a hoops fan he didn't like."

"So what was the game you were playing?" Max continued. The kid had potential as a cross-examiner.

"Well," John replied, realizing that he'd have to divulge his adolescent secret, "it's like this. I pretend to play Stretch. If I win, I get to do whatever I want." The uncomprehending look on Max's face told him his explanation was wanting. "It's a wishing game. If I win, my wishes come true; if I lose, they don't. It's just pretend."

"So what was it you were wishing for?"

John took a few dribbles and went in for a layup, trying to decide how candid he should be. "That I'll quit my day job and go mountain climbing in Alaska." He took a couple of quick hook shots close to the basket, then flipped the ball back to Max. "Does that sound like a pretty good wish?"

"I guess that depends on what your day job is," Max said thoughtfully.

"I'm a lawyer." As John spoke, he noticed Max's body stiffen, as though he had just received discomforting news. "What's the matter, are you one of those people who don't like lawyers?"

"I like 'em all right," Max said softly. "They just charge too much money."

"There's no doubt about that," John said loudly. "Divorce lawyers especially."

"Criminal lawyers, too," the kid said dismissively as he fired up his first brick of the evening. It was clear he was preoccupied by something.

"Is your mom in trouble?" John asked.

"No, not my mom."

"Your dad?"

Max turned away and took another jump shot. "Me," he said, looking back at John with a worried expression. "I got arrested for breaking into another kid's home. Burglary."

"That's pretty serious stuff," John said with surprise. He had the kid figured for a loner but never as a troublemaker. He gathered up the basketball, bringing an abrupt end to the shootaround. "You want to talk about it?"

Max hesitated, debating whether he could trust this middle-aged man who played weird games to decide his future. "If you want to know if I'm guilty, I didn't do it," he said, his chest heaving with emotion. "But I know who did."

"And the trouble is, you can't snitch on them," John observed adroitly.

"Yeah, how did you know?"

"Oh, I've handled a few cases like that in my time."

"My mom's been looking all over town for a lawyer she can afford," the kid explained, his face flushed with emotion. "My dad hasn't sent any child support for six months, but mom still makes too much money for the public whatchamacallit, the public—"

"The public defender."

"Yeah, the public defender."

"When does your case go to court, Max?" John asked.

"Day after tomorrow. Mom says she's going to ask the judge for more time to find someone to defend me."

John paused to look around the deserted playground as

Max's words sank in. The chopping sound of a police helicopter on nightly patrol grew louder as it approached the
area. No matter where you were in this city, you were only
a heartbeat away from some aspect of the justice system.
The system was like a giant voracious octopus, enveloping
everyone and everything within the sweep of its enormous
tentacles. He knew that for him there was no escape. He
could either let the octopus swallow him up or fight back
and win its respect. "It's getting late, Max," he said finally.
"We'd better get going. It's a school night, isn't it?"

Max frowned with disappointment at the prospect of
heading home. "My mom knows where I am," he said,
voicing a mild protest. "You go on if you need to get back."

"No deal," John said. "Your mom and I have a lot to
talk about, and I'm going to need you to introduce us." He
took Max's arm and began to lead him toward the gate of
the rec center.

"About what?" the kid inquired nervously.

"About your new lawyer," John answered bluntly.

"You mean you?" The kid's face lit up like a Christmas
tree. "But I thought you were going mountain climbing. I
mean, the game with Stretch, it looked like you won."

"I'll let you in on a little secret, Max," John said as they
walked onto the street. "Stretch always wins." He tugged at
Max's Dodger cap, spinning it around and pulling the bill
over the kid's eyes. "Besides, I'd never make it in Alaska.
I'm afraid of heights."

They took turns dribbling the ball the rest of the three-
block trip home. The kid would make a very appealing witness, John thought, as he began to run through the checklist
that every good lawyer instinctively inventories on the eve
of a new trial.

A NOTE ON THE TEXT

The typeface used in this book is a version of Sabon, originally designed in the 1960s by Jan Tschichold (1902–1974) at the behest of a consortium of manufacturers of metal type. As one who began as an outspoken design revolutionary—calling for the elimination of serifs, scorning revivals of historic typefaces—Tschichold seemed an odd choice, but he met the challenge brilliantly: The typeface was to be based on the fonts of the sixteenth-century French typefounder Claude Garamond but five percent narrower; it had to be identical for three different processes, working around the quirks of each, such as linotype's inability to "kern" (allow one character into the space of another, the way the top of a lowercase *f* overhangs other letters). Aside from Sabon, named for a sixteenth-century French punchcutter to avoid problems of attribution to Garamond, Tschichold is best remembered as the designer of the Penguin paperbacks of the late 1940s.